Collection

Other Red Fox Story Collections

Three in One Animal Stories
Spooky Stories
Cool School Stories
More Cool School Stories
Adventure Stories
Biggles Story Collection
Three in One Pony Stories
King Arthur Stories
Completely Wild Stories
Three in One Ballet Stories
U.N.C.L.E. Stories
Mrs Pepperpot Stories
Professor Branestawm Stories

Snotty Bumstead

Collection

by

Hunter Davies

Illustrated by Paul Thomas

RED FOX

A Red Fox Book

Published by Random House Children's Books
20 Vauxhall Bridge Road, London SW1V 2SA

A division of The Random House Group Ltd
London Melbourne Sydney Auckland
Johannesburg and agencies throughout the world

1 3 5 7 9 10 8 6 4 2

Snotty Bumstead first published in Great Britain by
The Bodley Head Children's Books 1991
Snotty Bumstead Rent-A-Mum first published in Great Britain by
The Bodley Head Children's Books 1993
Snotty Bumstead The Hostage published in Great Britain by
The Bodley Head Children's Books 1995
Red Fox edition 2000

Printed and bound in Norway by
AIT Trondheim AS

Papers used by Random House Group Ltd are natural,
recyclable products made from wood grown in sustainable forests.
The manufacturing processes conform to the
environmental regulations of the country of origins.

The Random House Group Limited Reg. No. 954009
www.randomhouse.co.uk
ISBN 0 09 941142 3

CONTENTS

1. Snotty Bumstead   7

2. Snotty Bumstead and the Rent-a-Mum   163

3. Snotty Bumstead The Hostage   287

SNOTTY BUMSTEAD

For Christopher Forster,
for him to read when he grows up.

I

Nottingham Bumstead is coming home from school. Shuffle shuffle, shilly shally, wearily drearily, not far to go now and he'll be home, another boring day over.

He has put on his coming-home-from-school face, a worn-out, scowling sort of face. He usually tries to keep it like that till he gets home, so his mother will say, "Oh, poor Nottingham, another hard day! Here's something nice for you."

He sees a stone in the gutter, just right for kicking, so he lets fly and it zings across the road, chipping the paintwork on a newly painted door.

"That counts as *in*," exclaims Nottingham Bumstead, giving a victory wave to a non-existent crowd. His face lights up. A smirky smile creeps over his countenance.

"I saw that," says a voice behind him.

It's Mrs Cheatham. She lives next door to Nottingham and has elected herself the street's resident Nosy Parker. Nottingham expects that soon she will become Camden Town's champion Nosy Parker. After that, she'll probably represent London in the World Nosy Parker Finals.

"So you're not blind, you old bat," says Nottingham. To himself. Not out loud. His mother is always telling him that Mrs Cheatham is a kind person at heart, and he must not be rude to her. She does organize the Neighbourhood Watch scheme, so we *should* all be grateful to her.

"Can you see what you did to that door?" asks Mrs Cheatham.

"What door?" says Nottingham. He has now assumed his half-witted stare, his mouth hanging open, looking up at the sky, as if there might be a low-flying door about to land.

"I saw you kick that stone."

"Kick?" mumbles Nottingham, looking down at his feet as if they have nothing to do with him.

"Don't be stupid," says Mrs Cheatham.

The half-witted look must not be overdone. It is meant to repel adults, especially nosy adults, to make them give up asking silly questions, but it mustn't alarm them into thinking that he has gone round the bend.

"Oh, the stone, oh yeh, the stone," says Nottingham. "I was just moving it away, in case someone fell over it."

"Well, you should be more careful."

"Hmm," says Nottingham, deciding it is now time for his blank look.

This is his new school look, perfected only this week and designed to give nothing away. Last term, which was his first at St Andrew's, a Comprehensive of some fourteen hundred pupils, he did try to be reasonably bright and eager, as he had been at his Primary, but the size of the new school has set him back a bit.

Now, he has decided instead to lie low. Henceforth, he will be a spy, an undercover agent, whom the teachers don't know, and will *never* get to know. This means affecting a blank stare, a bland expression, particularly when anything is happening in class.

"Is there something wrong with your eyes, Nottingham?" asks Mrs Cheatham.

"Hmm," says Nottingham.

"Perhaps you need glasses."

"I prefer drinks out of a can," says Nottingham.

He didn't mean to make a joke. It just came out.

Mrs Cheatham stares at him, wondering what he's talking about.

"Are you on your way home?"

Nottingham groans. She obviously intends to walk down the street with him. How embarrassing. He could say he's left home and is now living on the pavement, as many people do in Camden Town. Or he could say he's actually on his way *to* school, putting in a few hours' overtime, because he loves school so much.

"I'm waiting for someone," he says at last.

"Who?"

What a cheek! Now that is rude. *He* would never ask such a personal question.

"Just someone."

He looks at his watch, swinging his sports bag aimlessly, just missing Mrs Cheatham's legs.

"Hiya, Snotty," shouts a kid from his class, riding a bike down the other side of the street.

"That's who I'm waiting to see," says Nottingham. "Byee."

His expression is now normal, quite smiley really, open and cheerful, at the same time cocky and cheeky, which is how he usually is with his friends. This is his Snotty face, reserved for when he is Snotty.

"Hi," he says, catching up with the kid on the bike.

"Hi, Snotty," says the kid, not slowing down.

"See you," says Snotty.

Not a long conversation, as conversations go, but it *has* served its purpose. He looks back and sees that Mrs Cheatham has disappeared. He can now finish his journey home and complete his transformation from Nottingham Bumstead, as he is always known at school, into Snotty.

At school, it is only his name that stands out. He is otherwise middle of the class, middle of the road, middle of the rowdies, middle of the goodies, middling bright, middling dim, middling popular, middling boring, middling scruffy, middling weedy, middling small. Well, perhaps just below middling weedy. And just below middling small. All right, Nottingham Bumstead is weedy and small.

This is something of an irritation. By the end of Primary school, he felt quite tall, at least inside. Now at St Andrew's there be giants, all over the place, not just in the Sixth Form, but in his own year, in his own class.

"Those kids should have a dope test," he often thinks to himself. "I bet some of them have been on steroids."

Last week a PE teacher, whom he had already dismissed as a thicko, macho, wally, called him out to ask what he presumed was going to be a civilized question.

"Why are you such a weed, Nottingham Bumstead?"

Typical! Certain teachers are always like that. And it didn't stop there. Other people seemed to notice his size. His enemies teased him if he missed a goal in the playground, or was last in the dinner queue, or late into class.

That was when he decided to go underground at school, to keep his *real* personality a secret. Only at home, or with his real friends, would he be Snotty from now on.

The nickname Snotty started early on at Primary school, when his clothes always looked untidy, his hair scruffy, his body unwashed and, yes, his nose did run. Not a hundred metres' run. More a marathon, a long drawn-out drip that never seemed to drop.

One of those inevitable cleverdicks had called out to him one day, "Come here, you snotty kid". And that was it. His enemies latched on to it. The name stuck.

Snotty didn't mind. He smiled, accepted it, took it in his stride, and very soon the name became meaningless. Snotty meant Snotty, nothing else.

It's like a new teacher arriving when everyone sniggers because she's called Mrs Smellie. There are lots of people called Smellie. Look them up in the London telephone directory. There are six altogether. Very quickly, these funny names are forgotten; only the people they stand for come to mind.

One reason Snotty doesn't care is that he hates being called Nottingham – anything is better than that.

"It was where your father proposed to me, darling," his mother once told him. "Oh, it was *so* romantic . . ." Snotty did not want to know any more. It all sounded revolting.

"Liverpool, I might not have minded, or Manchester, but imagine being named after boring old Nottingham, with their boring old team. Forget it."

Neither of his parents came from Nottingham. It just happened to be where they met at university. Snotty has now forgotten the details. It was a long time ago. Many things have changed since then. His mother is now in the film world, or trying to be, though he's not quite sure what she does. His father is elsewhere. "Round the bend," according to Snotty's mother.

At St Andrew's, when new people first asked, he said Snotty was a derivative of Nottingham. Notty, Snotty, gerrit? Naturally, he did not go into the snot bag bit, the runny-nose kid he once was.

What Snotty does object to is being called Snotty Bum Bum. This, too, goes back to Primary school days, and anyone daring to use it now will get thumped. Verbally, of course. He's not quite big enough to take on people physically, though his sports bag does come in handy, if swung the right way.

Snotty does have some enemies, from his own and other schools; the sort of people who may try to trip him up, lunge at him from a doorway, or shout some really objectionable comment, like "Spurs are Rubbish".

"That's the worst thing about living in North London," he says to himself, as he sets off again. "There are Arsenal supporters everywhere."

Snotty's home is quite near Camden High Street: not

on the main road, with its shops and stalls and street markets and scruffy bits, but just behind, in the middle of a row of terraced houses. Some are smartly painted, some peeling and rotting, but they are all considered desirable, being large and spacious, mostly with four floors, counting the basement.

When Snotty reaches his own house, his weedy, scruffy, insignificant figure can be seen shambling up the steps of a rather handsome house.

He gives the dark green front door a nasty kick, imperiously, as if expecting a uniformed butler to open it. This is *supposed* to bring his mother to the door at once, saving him the bother of getting out his own key. After a hard day at school, he is naturally exhausted.

Today there is no reaction, no noise from inside. Snotty lifts the flap of the letter box, glares inside, then lets out a sequence of moans and groans.

"Oh, come on, you silly woman," moans Snotty. "Stop messing around. I've had a long day."

Snotty loves his mother. He knows she has had problems of her own, especially since his dad left. Whoever he was. Whatever he did. Snotty has no memory of him.

In recent years, Snotty likes to think that he has become his mother's friend. Even her Best Friend.

"She does have a few faults, though. Such as being house-proud," thinks Snotty, giving the letter box a rattle, just in case she is busy cleaning.

"All those precious knick-knacks, that pinewood rubbish, rotten paintings, silly Indian carpets. She thinks it looks so arty. Just boring. Oh hurry up, please!"

He rattles the letter box again, then stops to listen, just in case Mrs Cheatham next door has heard him. He doesn't want her coming out, interfering, sticking in her nose. Then he remembers Mrs Cheatham always watches television at this time of day.

"Mum, come on, what are you doing in there?"

Still no answer. What can she be playing at?

"I bet she's washing her stupid plants," thinks Snotty. "She'll have them in the sink, and she'll be fussing over them, cooing and clucking like an old hen. They get far more attention than I do.

"I know. She must be upstairs, hoovering. That's why she can't hear. Once she's finished, it'll be a strip search, before I even get inside the door. It's easier to go through London Airport than cross our front hall."

Snotty's mother is not worried about security but about Snotty's filthy clothes. In winter, she checks his Doc Marten boots for mud and other nasty substances.

In summer his sweaty, tatty trainers are inspected. Very often they have to come straight off and he must put on his slippers, which he *hates*. Then he has to wash his filthy hands and filthy face before sitting down at the table.

It is strange, in a way, that his mother should be so house-proud when in most other areas she is very liberal. She allows Snotty a lot of freedom, doesn't force him to say exactly where he is going, or to give a minute-by-minute description of his intended movements. She trusts him to be sensible, to make his own decisions. She is not very strict on punctuality, being not very punctual herself. She often acts on whims and can be quite eccentric in behaviour, playing jokes, enjoying fun and games. And never, never does she ask him if he has done his homework.

"Mum?" he shouts again through the letter box. "Let me in, you silly old woman!"

Snotty listens. Perhaps he shouldn't have said that. Perhaps he should be more polite and start taking his trainers off now, before she tells him to. Perhaps he should speak nicely and properly and be ready to wash his hands.

"Hello, Mother!" He coughs, swallows hard, then puts on his sweetest face. "It's me. Your very own Nottingham. Hi. I'm home. Darling Mummy. Yes, it's your little one."

Still no reply. He lets the flap drop, waits, then lifts it again, hoping the scene may have changed and she will be there, standing behind the door, playing one of her silly tricks, all smiles and giggles.

"Mum, what's for tea? I'm starving."

She is usually waiting for him. She works from home these days, with only occasional overnight trips away.

About a month ago she went to Wigan, wherever that is, on a shoot, whatever that means. It was some BBC natural history documentary, so she told him on her return.

Snotty feels in his pocket for his key, but it isn't there. "What *am* I going to do? That telly programme will have started."

Snotty gives the door a final kick.

"Now, where does she keep that spare key? Should be in one of these stupid plant pots . . ."

Snotty pulls up a geranium by the roots, one of his mother's favourite plants, lovingly watered every day. Nothing. He throws the plant down the steps. Then in a temper he kicks the plant pot itself.

The pot crashes into the basement well beneath. Luckily, it misses Mrs Cheatham's side. In its place, among

some weedy worms and bits of soil, lies the key.

Snotty opens the door and goes in, still muttering to himself.

Everything looks normal, neat and tidy, warm and cosy, bright and welcoming. On the hall shelf is a note.

Snotty grabs it with one hand, squeezing it into a scruffy bit of paper. In the large open-plan dining-room kitchen he throws his sports bag on the floor. Then he reads the note.

Dear Snotty

I have gone away for a bit. Special project. Very hush hush. The silly fridge is full, the silly bills paid. Some silly cash in usual place. Help yourself, take what you want, look after your silly self, I hope I won't be long. I know I'm leaving the house in your wonderfully caring hands! Will ring as soon as I can and explain all, but I'm fine, just fine, don't worry. Must dash. The plane is leaving. Have fun. I know you will. Love   Mum

---

Snotty lets the paper drop on the floor. He slowly opens the fridge and gets out the only can of Coke, his ration for the day, his treat to welcome him home. Then he reads the note again.

"The bills are paid," thinks Snotty as he goes upstairs to his room. "What does that mean? Very strange. I wonder why she's done that? It's as if she's gone away for a long, long time . . ."

2

Snotty wakes up early on Saturday morning, sighs and breathes in deeply. Not to inhale the fresh and fragrant North London air – lovely though it is – but to savour the aroma of dawn-kissed bacon and eggs, followed by freshly picked croissants and newly ground coffee. This is their Saturday morning ritual, has been for yonkers. The fry-up is for Snotty, to build up his strength, and the croissants are his mother's treat. During the week, there's never a proper breakfast: Snotty fends for himself if he wants anything before he goes to school.

Then he remembers. His mother has still not come home. It is now two nights since he found that note, the longest he has *ever* been on his own.

But the strange thing is, the time has passed quite quickly. Going to school yesterday was easy. After school, he went straight to the fridge and stuffed his tummy, then straight to the telly and stuffed his mind. Life, basically, has gone on much as before, except that the fridge is now almost empty.

"I'll have to do some shopping," moans Snotty, turning over in bed. "What a drag."

Snotty can do the shopping, but he hates it. When his mother sends him to buy things she always gives him a list. How will he manage without it? Shutting his eyes, he pretends to go back to sleep, which is silly, because he is alone in the house.

Suddenly, there is a loud banging on the front door.

"Mrs Cheatham, I bet. Come to check up on me. Trust her. Well, I'm not answering."

He puts a pillow over his ears, but then he has another thought.

"Mum! She'll have forgotten her key. She's always doing that."

Snotty rushes to his bedroom window and looks down on the front doorstep. He can see a bald head. It can't be his mother. Whoever it is, is wearing uniform. She doesn't wear uniform either.

"Oh, it's only the postman. Well, I'm not going down. Let him knock. Nobody ever writes to *me*."

He can hear the postman forcing the post through the letter box. They have a box his mother specially installed, big enough to take books and scripts. Snotty waits till the postman has gone, then he slowly goes downstairs.

"Boring, boring, boring," mutters Snotty, kicking over the letters and packages with his bare feet. He should have put his slippers on, but if his mother is not around, who is to know, who is to care, who is to fuss?

Snotty goes into the kitchen and opens the fridge door. Empty, empty. How can he have eaten so much in just two days? He looks in the deepfreeze section at the top and pulls out some frozen packets of liver – yuck, who would ever eat *that* – and some kidneys – horrible, he'd rather starve than touch *them*. Just to make sure they are what he thinks they are, he scrapes off the ice and frost with a scrubbing brush from under the kitchen sink.

"She'd go mad if she could see me," thinks Snotty. The scrubbing brush is not very clean; it is gunged up with hairs and dirt, some of which attach themselves to the kidneys and the liver.

"I never want to see them again," says Snotty, putting the packets into the very back of the deepfreeze tray. "So they'll probably stay there for ever. Bye bye, liver. Farewell, kidneys."

He slams the door shut; then he remembers what he was looking for.

"Oh, no," he yells, opening the door again.

Snotty removes a thin, flat packet. It looks like frozen strips of lasagne – at least, that's what his mother maintains burglars will think. In North London, she says, you get a trendy class of burglar – designer burglars – so you must take suitable precautions.

Snotty puts the packet under the hot-water tap, letting it slowly de-frost. Out of the packet he pulls ten ten-pound notes, still part frozen. One falls on the floor like a rather heavy playing card.

His mother keeps small change in her purse, and that is on the hall shelf. She's also left her Midland Bank cash-card and her Barclaycard, but she's taken her cheque book. The credit and cash cards will be useful, *if* Snotty can remember how to use them. But the small change in the purse was very small, just a couple of pounds, and he spent that last night on biscuits.

Now he needs cash to buy proper supplies. It was lucky he remembered his mother's secret hiding-place. The ten-pound notes are for emergencies, whenever she needs "silly cash", as she calls it, in a hurry.

Snotty gets dressed, finds a shopping bag, and sets off

24

round the corner to Mr Patel's. He much prefers this shop to the big supermarket. He doesn't have so far to carry things home, and his mother is well known to Mr Patel because she goes there all the time.

"Oh, my hands are killing me," moans Snotty, his fingers sticking to the icy notes. "I should have worn gloves."

He puts the money at the bottom of his carrier bag, where it joins the mess of old bills, credit card slips and out-of-date shopping lists.

"Now, first things first," thinks Snotty, seizing a trolley.

He heads straight for the sweets counter, where he selects three bars of Kit Kat, three Double Decker, three Mars bars and three others that he picks at random, with his eyes closed. He likes to spread his favours around,

so one company does not become *too* rich. He sees there is a special offer on Penguin, twelve for the price of ten, so he takes them.

"Mum will be pleased. I must have saved her quite a bit already."

Hob-nobs are on special offer as well, so he gets some of them. Then he takes some bars of Fruit & Nut, for emergencies.

Next he moves on to crisps, going for the bigger, giant bags that are the most economical. He gets three, one plain, one salt-and-vinegar, and a new line, hamburger flavour. Snotty likes to help manufacturers by trying out their new products. He knows what a lot of work is put into new lines, and he likes to encourage this. He's always telling his mother this, every time he sees something new and exciting advertised on television, but she usually ignores him.

"Right, that should be enough food for the weekend. Now what about drinks?"

This is easy. Snotty only drinks Coke. His mother rations it, because she says it is bad for his teeth, but now he can buy as much as he likes, as much as he can drink.

"Let me see, one before breakfast, one with breakfast, one after breakfast, mid-morning break, pre-lunch, lunch, after lunch, oh, I'll need about eight a day. Let's say twenty for the weekend. That should be enough."

He pushes the trolley to the counter where a boy called Kevin is on the till. He is in the Sixth Form at Snotty's school, but he lives locally and works in the shop every Saturday.

"Hi, Snotty," he says. "Is it your birthday?"

"What?" says Snotty, carefully. He doesn't like Sixth Formers knowing his business, any more than teachers.

26

"I didn't notice it listed in *The Times* this morning. Keeping it a secret, are you?"

"No, it's not my birthday," grunts Snotty.

"So what sort of party is it?" says Kevin, putting all the sweets and biscuits through the till. "Can I come?"

"No, it's human beings only," says Snotty.

"Good one, Snot!" Kevin is trying to be friendly, but he's a bit *too* friendly, thinks Snotty, and anyway he hates being called Snot.

"Tell you what," says Kevin, "how about taking another four cans? I'm sure you can manage that, even with your little tum."

"My mum said twenty," says Snotty, pretending to look at a list. "So that's all, thanks."

"I was only asking, 'cos we're doing discounts on crates of twenty-four. That will save, let me see, ten per cent of . . ."

Kevin gets his calculator out. The price for twenty-four works out at almost the same as for twenty, so Snotty agrees to take the extra.

"Thanks, Kevin. My mum will be pleased."

"It's my pleasure; we are here to serve. How is she, anyway?"

"Fine, thank you," says Snotty quickly, wishing he had never mentioned her. "How much does this lot come to?"

Snotty pulls his money out of the carrier bag. The notes are soggy and limp. He tries to separate them, but this is difficult because they are stuck together.

"You're into laundering money now, are you, Snot?" says Kevin. "I always thought you were an international crook. Small-time, of course. Gerrit? Small-time . . ."

Kevin leans over the counter and pokes a fat finger at Snotty's thin and weedy chest.

That's someone else for the hit list when the revolution comes, thinks Snotty. He manages not to show pain or fury and concentrates on separating the notes.

"I can't take those," says Kevin. "They'll muck up the till. Haven't you any others? You know, dry ones, the ones you made last week."

Snotty looks alarmed. He is not sure if this is one of Kevin's jokes or not. His trolley is full to overflowing and he doesn't want to have to put everything back on the shelves. Behind him several people are becoming restless.

"They do look dodgy to me," says Kevin. "Very dodgy. I'd better check. The police have given us a list of numbers to look out for . . ."

From under the counter he brings out a little black book. Snotty looks towards the door, wondering if he should make a dash for it.

"Only kidding," says Kevin, seeing Snotty's face. "B for Bumstead, here we are. I'll put it on our little list. Your mum can pay at the end of the month, like she always does."

"Oh, thanks," says Snotty.

"You can use that trolley, but make sure you return it. Or I really will have the police on you. Next, please."

Back home, Snotty opens a can of Coke and a packet of crisps. Then he takes them upstairs to the sitting room, his mother's best room, where he is not supposed to eat crisps, or wear trainers. He flops onto the best sofa, feeling very pleased with himself.

"Shopping is easy peasy. Dunno why she always moans about it. No problem. I've got enough food and drink for the weekend, and I've still got the hundred pounds. She's bound to be back by the end of the month, and she'll pay the bill by cheque. Or perhaps I can . . . I wonder if she left any loose cheques."

He goes downstairs to the hall where he left his mother's purse. There's no sign of any cheques, but beside the purse he notices a little booklet from Barclaycard, full of glossy adverts for all the things you can buy with their credit card.

He takes it back upstairs to read, along with another Coke, and another packet of crisps.

"Now, do I want the luxury holiday of a lifetime in the Caribbean? Looks good, nice pictures. Oh no, useless. I'd never get back for school on Monday. Forget it.

"Chateau-bottled wine delivered to my very door? Yuck. I hate wine.

"Transform your garden with this Special Shrub offer. How boring.

"Hmm, a Conservatory. Mum's always wanted one of those. Should I put a deposit on one, as a surprise? No, no, I couldn't play football in the back garden any more.

"Hey, this is more like it. The latest video recorder. Long play, two heads, still and frame advance, TV monitor function, sixty minutes timer memory back-up. I wonder what all that means? Well, only one way to find out. We do need a new one. Ours is ancient, really ancient."

Snotty reads all the details carefully, how to order, all the guarantees, and is most impressed.

" 'Free home approval! Can be returned within a month, if not satisfied! Convenient, direct to your home delivery! Ring at once, twenty-four hour service, no fuss payment with your Barclaycard.'

"I never realized shopping was so easy. If she doesn't like it, she can always send it back . . ."

Snotty picks up the phone and dials the number. He has his mother's card in front of him.

He clears his throat. Perhaps he'll use a woman's

voice, just in case of complications. Snotty prides himself on being a master of voices, as well as faces.

"Now I'd better not laugh if they call me Mrs Bumstead. I hope they don't ask too many questions . . ."

A recorded message answers him, telling him to give the details, and his Barclaycard number, after the bleep.

"Well, that was easy," says Snotty. He opens the packet of Penguins, just to try them out, and flicks through the rest of the catalogue.

"Now what else can I buy? I mean, what other essentials do I require to keep me going? After all, she did say 'Have fun' . . ."

3

Snotty is in the bathroom playing snooker with Sluke, his best friend.

Sluke is a tall boy with spectacles, silly hair and a gormless expression, one he has worked on for many years. He has assumed the camouflage of a buffoon to disguise his deep, caring, sensitive and poetic nature – something that Snotty, as his best friend, knows about. And usually ridicules.

Sluke is wearing his school tie and shirt, which he always does. According to Snotty he's the only boy in London, in fact in the whole of the universe, mad enough to wear his uniform *outside* school.

"What happens if your mum wants a bath?" asks Sluke.

"She won't," says Snotty, taking his shot, aiming at the pink, but missing completely.

"On form, I see," says Sluke, slyly.

"You can go home now, if you like," retorts Snotty.

"That was an observation, not a criticism," says Sluke.

"If I want a commentary, I'll hire David Coleman," says Snotty, suddenly turning round and poking Sluke with his cue.

"That hurt."

"Serves you right, you great nelly. You shouldn't get in the way," says Snotty.

"You should look before you leap around with your cue."

"Will you stop wittering on," says Snotty. "Do something useful! Turn that tap off. I can hear it dripping."

Sluke bends down, leaning under the table to locate the dripping bath tap. As he does so, Snotty smartly places the pink in the hole.

"Right, that's another six to me," says Snotty, marking the score on the bathroom wall with a large piece of red chalk.

One wall of the bathroom is covered in snooker scores, completely obliterating the *very* expensive William Morris wallpaper that his mother herself put up.

Snotty's mother was also responsible for finding and renovating the ever-so-artistic Victorian bath, complete with legs. Until last week, it stood in splendid isolation in the middle of the bathroom. Then Snotty decided it would make a perfect base for his snooker top.

"Still my go," says Snotty, looking round for an easy red. There are only two left, both obscured.

"I haven't missed my turn, have I?" says Sluke, straightening up, stretching his long limbs, blinking at the scores, trying to work out the hieroglyphics. Snotty's handwriting has never been good, but it is even more difficult to read because he has written over old scores that have been only half rubbed out.

"I thought I told you to stop that water," says Snotty. "I can still hear it. What a dum dum you are. Turn the tap really tight this time. Use that spanner."

Sluke bends down again, turning the tap so hard he hears a slight click, like a bone fracturing.

Snotty quickly picks up both reds, moves them into much easier positions, and carries on playing. Now that he is on a winning streak – if only a winning streak at cheating – there is little to stop him.

"I've done it well hard this time, Snotty," says Sluke. "Using all my best strength."

"That's the only reason I have you round here." Snotty smiles, then he narrows his eyes, trying to look tough. "Out of my way, peasant. Now you're in my light."

"What if *you* want a bath?" asks Sluke.

"A what?" asks Snotty, giving a shudder. "A *bath*?" Snotty makes it sound as if Sluke is offering him the choice of hanging or the guillotine.

"I bet you haven't had one for a week! You pong . . ."

Sluke moves away as he says this, knowing that Snotty

is likely to poke him with his snooker cue again, somewhere nasty this time.

"Dead right, man," says Snotty. "A whole week without a bath. It's my ambition in life never to have another. Never again."

"Oh, yeh," said Sluke. "I bet your mum won't let you."

"I've always hated baths," says Snotty, ignoring Sluke's comment. "Complete waste of time. Complete waste of water. All that taking your stupid clothes off, getting into the stupid bath, which is a really stupid shape, I dunno who invented the stupid thing, then you have to get out and put on your stupid clothes again. Who needs it."

"You do, by the smell . . ." says Sluke, making a dash for the door.

Snotty pretends to lunge at him, but instead he puts the black in a very easy spot, perfect for finishing off the game.

"Right, I've won," shouts Snotty. "Champion, champion, champion!"

Snotty does a little victory dance round the bathroom, turning a few cartwheels, waving to the crowd, clenching his fist, punching the air, pulling faces for the TV cameras.

"I think I'll keep the score next time," says Sluke, quietly. "Then I might have a better chance . . ."

"Are you incinerating . . ."

"No, I'm not on fire," says Sluke, smiling.

In class, Sluke is near the top in everything, including English, though his best subject is science. He's especially good at anything to do with computers and electronics.

"You mean insinuating," says Sluke.

"Don't tell me what I mean, beanpole," says Snotty. "If you are referring that I've been cheating . . ."

"Inferring," says Sluke.

"Just because you're losing," says Snotty. He is now all smiles, forgetting he was supposed to be hard, chanting out the football refrain: "*Just because you're losing losing!*"

Snotty then flops on the bathroom floor, exhausted by his efforts, but very pleased with himself.

"Close your eyes, Sluke," he says, and puts his hand under the snooker table. From the bath he produces two cans of Coke.

"Here you are, mate," says Snotty.

"Thanks," says Sluke.

"I cheated in that game, you know," says Snotty.

"I saw you," says Sluke. "And I cheated in the first game."

"How?"

"Every time you bent down to play a shot, I leaned over you and rubbed out a few scores."

"You rotten lot," says Snotty. "Just 'cos you're tall. It *is* my house. I'm supposed to be the one who always wins."

"You're so lucky, Snotty," says Sluke, slurping his drink.

"Am I?" asks Snotty, quietly.

"Yeh, this big house. It's always been great coming here. And now you've got this amazing bathroom. It's incredible. I've never seen a bath with a snooker table on top before."

"Well, you've hardly travelled, have you?" Snotty smiles.

"No, really. Your mum spoils you."

"Does she?" says Snotty, standing up. "We'll see. Right, final game. No cheating this time . . ."

★

"Shall we put the table away, now?" asks Sluke.

"Why?" asks Snotty.

"Your mum."

"What about her?"

"Well, I mean, when she wants a bath," mumbles Sluke, not quite knowing how to phrase his questions, aware that Snotty hates any sort of personal cross-examination.

"It'll be a bit dark under there," continues Sluke. "She'll keep banging her head, and she won't be very pleased if snooker balls keep falling on her bonce, will she. She'll want a proper bath . . ."

"I've told you. She won't."

"Where is she anyway, Snotty? I don't think I've seen her for about, I dunno, must be a week. Fact my mum was only saying how was she and that. Strange, really."

"No, it's not. You ain't seen her, 'cos you ain't seen her."

"Come again?"

"Nobody's seen her, not round here," says Snotty, quietly. "She's gone off somewhere, really important, just for a while. And don't you say anything about it. Right?"

"'Course not, Snotty."

"I'm in charge here, see. This is my house, OK? If

you wanna stay my friend, you keep dead quiet about what happens here. Understood?"

Snotty stands very still, assuming his most serious face, glaring straight at Sluke.

This is quite hard to do. Eyeball to eyeball contact is not easy when one person is a good twelve inches higher than the other, but Sluke gets the Message.

Snotty turns away abruptly and starts to walk down the stairs.

"Shall I close the bathroom door, Snotty?" asks Sluke.

"What?"

"The bathroom door . . ."

"It is no longer a bathroom, you half-wit," says Snotty. "Haven't you noticed? That snooker table stays there permanently."

"What a good idea," says Sluke, following Snotty down the stairs.

"We can play there all day and every day," says Snotty. "All night, if I want to. I can do anything I like, see."

"Sounds great."

"And you can play with me, if you're good."

"Thanks, Snot."

"This is only the beginning," says Snotty. "There are several other little improvements I want to make. I'll probably need your help with some of them."

"Fine, count on me, man."

"Just watch what you say from now on," says Snotty, stopping at the bottom of the stairs. "OK?"

Snotty gives Sluke his best glare, then his face changes and he looks nervous and apprehensive. Sluke puts an arm round his shoulder.

"I was worried at first," says Snotty, softly. "When I found she'd gone."

"Who wouldn't be?" says Sluke.

"For the first couple of days I was really sick."

"Yeh, I would have been. Sick as a parrot."

"Then I decided I'd got to be positive," says Snotty quietly. "Make the most of it. Get something out of it. Do all the things I've always wanted to do. Do the things *everyone* has always wanted to do!"

Snotty's voice has grown louder. He now looks pleased again, quite excited even.

Sluke nods his head vigorously. He doesn't know what's going on, or what has happened, but at last, after a whole week of mystery, when he has puzzled long and hard about the apparent absence of Snotty's mother, he has been honoured with Snotty's secret.

"Hey," says Sluke, smiling. "I'm really looking forward to this. Whatever it is . . ."

4

It's one week later and the Arsenal-Spurs match has reached a climax. Two goals each, and all to play for. The players are going wild, screaming and shouting, straining every muscle to get the winner.

Representing Spurs is the one and only Snotty, ace striker, midfield dynamo and lethal defender. Alongside him is the Incredible Sluke.

Perhaps not quite alongside him. Sluke is standing at the back of the pitch, protecting the chalk marks on the front window shutters. They are closed, as they have been for a lot of the last two weeks.

Sluke is goalie. All other positions and responsibilities, from free kicks to penalties, are taken by Snotty. He also happens to be referee and both linesmen. Well, it is his pitch.

It's a perfect indoor pitch stretching right across the ground floor of Snotty's house, but it does have one or two unusual features and unique rules. Snotty devised them all and he is the final arbiter, should anyone be unwise enough to argue with him.

The walls, floors, ceilings and the remaining bits of furniture are all considered part of the field of play. There are no throw-ins or corners or offsides. No wonder the game is proceeding at such an exciting, non-stop pace.

Snotty could, if he wanted to, use the pitch for five-a-side; there is enough space now that most of the furniture has been moved out. But Snotty prefers to keep it intimate and exclusive, hand-picking his all-star players. Tonight, and every night, it's a two-a-side competition.

Arsenal is represented by Jessie and Bessie, two very good players, twin girls from the same school as Sluke and Snotty.

They are all in the same class at school. When it comes to football, however, the girls are probably a shade higher on the quality scale.

For a start, Jessie and Bessie are better built, solid and athletic, unlike either Snotty or Sluke. They also play fair, never cheat, never kick people after the ball has gone, never appeal for non-existent penalties or argue with the referee – even when it's Snotty. Perhaps if they did, they might now be winning, on goals disallowed, not just on merit.

"That counts as in," exclaims Snotty, finishing off a solo run, taking a rebound off the living-room door, a free kick after a floor-board allegedly tripped him up, then finishing with a lucky header after the ball bounces off the top of the fridge, banging it against the back of the kitchen door.

"You said the sink unit was the goal," protests Jessie.

"And I thought you said the cooker was the goal post?" adds Bessie.

"I said *everything* at your end is your goal," says Snotty. "I changed the rules at half-time. Don't you listen? You got cloff ears, or somefink? Anyway, there ain't no cooker. So we won. Champions!"

Snotty is being street-wise today, putting on a Cockney accent. Bessie and Jessie watch him carefully, amused, but they wonder whether he is covering up for something.

Snotty rushes down the pitch, still yelling, then he slides to his knees along the polished floor, allowing himself to be cuddled and congratulated by Sluke.

Together they go on a victory parade, right round the entire pitch, across the kitchen end (or the North Bank as it's sometimes called), along the Shelf (taking care to avoid the door into the hall), until they reach the Kop where they throw kisses to the crowd. Then they fall down, laughing, convulsed by their own jokes.

"Thanks for the game anyway," say Bessie and Jessie in unison, holding out their hands, magnanimous in defeat.

"We enjoyed it," says Jessie, shaking their hands.

"Great match, great pitch," says Bessie.

"Yes, I have to thank my mum for that," says Snotty, going to the fridge.

Jessie and Bessie exchange looks. Are they going to hear more about Snotty's mother?

They were let in on the secret just one week ago. But all they know is what Sluke knows: that she has gone away for a while, destination unknown, purpose not explained.

Snotty has told them that no one else must know. The world at large must believe that Snotty's mother is still at home as usual. Otherwise, their *un*usual way of life, which all four of them have come to love over the last two weeks, will come to a sudden and probably sad end.

Jessie looks worried. She does tend to see things too clearly at times, imagining problems before they arise, and is not sure she wants to know the whole story, just in case she can see obstacles the others can't. But she is very good at coping when things do go wrong.

Bessie is always much more optimistic, thinking the best of everyone, willing to accept situations as they are. She can see that Snotty is enjoying himself, and his new life, so all is well.

"Yeh," says Snotty, finishing a can of Coke in almost one gulp. "I'm grateful to my mum . . ."

"You mean, er," begins Jessie, "for going away . . . ?"

"I mean for opening up this ground floor, you wally," says Snotty. "She made it into one big room, didn't she? Then she got rid of the fitted carpet and sanded the boards."

"You mean she wanted you to turn it into a football pitch?" insists Jessie, still worried.

"Don't be potty," says Snotty. "It was full of all her junk, wasn't it? Boring antiques and Persian rugs and soppy plants and stupid sofas and yucky oil paintings."

"Where are they?" asks Bessie, looking around.

"In the basement," says Snotty. "Sluke dragged them all down there. He's stronger than me, but not so clever. If you hadn't let in those two goals, you div, we would have really hammered them . . ."

"Whatchamean? Was your fault. You *did* say in the first half that the cooker was the goal, so I was trying to find it, weren't I, when she dribbled past me . . ."

"The cooker's gone," says Snotty. "That was a trick. Don't you listen to nuffink? I gave it to a bloke with a barrow who came round collecting scrap metal. He took the iron as well. Don't need that either. Who needs to wash clothes, never mind iron them?"

"I think you do," says Jessie. "There is a bit of a . . .
you know . . . smell in here."

"Watch it," says Snotty. "That's honest sweat you
can smell."

"But don't you want a bath?" asks Jessie. "Or a
shower?"

"Nope. The bathroom's being used properly for
once."

"What about the shower?" asks Bessie.

"That's full of comics, and don't any of yous touch them."

"Yeh, one of your best ideas," says Sluke. "Wish I could do that in our place. My mum makes me throw out all my old comics. She says they make the flat look untidy."

"Anyway, that stupid cooker was in the way," says Snotty, handing round more Cokes. The fridge is completely filled with cans of all sorts, mainly fizzy drinks. There is no food at all, no normal provisions. Not even milk. Snotty has always hated milk.

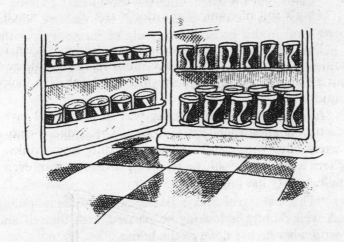

"The kitchen looks great, don't you think?" says Snotty. "Now all that junk's gone. Everything's in a dead straight line. Makes for perfect goals."

The kitchen unit has been boarded up, to stop any doors or drawers flying open when a ball hits them. The sink has also been covered over, so people can now stand on it to retrieve the ball.

Everything else in the kitchen has been removed. Only the fridge is still on the ground floor. Snotty judged it the only useful domestic appliance. This has been placed at the half-way line, opposite the door into the hall, in a little alcove.

Snotty, when alone, has practised hard working out the best angles from which to aim the ball at the fridge.

"Don't you miss cooked things?" asks Jessie. "You really can't do much cooking here . . ."

"You're not looking for a job, are you?" says Sluke. "I thought you were going to be a football manager?"

"I am," says Jessie. "And, anyway, I hate cooking."

"You're in the right place then," says Snotty. "Cooking is off in this house. So is going to Sainsbury's or the market. None of that stuff. There's no making lists, queuing up, cooking the rotten stuff, laying the table."

"And best of all," says Sluke, "no one has to wash up."

"You *are* lucky!" says Bessie.

"Yous are all lucky," says Snotty, beaming. "Being my friends!"

"That's true," says Sluke.

"Creep," says Snotty.

"That's also true," says Jessie, but now she is smiling as well. Snotty is looking so pleased with himself and with what he has done to the house.

"I've got a bit more to do yet," says Snotty, waving his hands about in a proprietorial manner. "And it's gonna be really brilliant, mega brilliant. And as you are my friends, I want you all to share in it."

"Do we cheer or clap or what?" asks Jessie, cheekily.

"Neither," says Snotty. "Just play. First to five goals . . ."

"All right then," says Snotty. "It's decision time. I can either take yous all to Marine Ices, or we can get something from McDonald's. That's the choice. I don't take my custom anywhere else."

For the last two weeks, Snotty has survived on pizzas and ice-cream from Marine Ices, or chips and hamburgers from McDonald's, though not necessarily in that order. He now enjoys the diet he always wanted, but was never allowed before.

"Chips," says Sluke.

"Right, you can go and get them," says Snotty.

"Oh, but I'm knackered," says Sluke.

"Dunno why, you did nothing in that game," says Snotty.

"That's 'cos you're so brilliant, Snotty. Anyone on your side is bound to win . . ."

"OK then, the losers will have to go and get the nosh."

"Oh, no," say Jessie and Bessie together, but they get up from the floor where they have been recovering their breath.

"Er, what about the money?" asks Bessie.

"Close your eyes, everyone," says Snotty. "No cheating."

Snotty tramps noisily to the kitchen end of the football stadium, then creeps back to the shuttered front window. There he carefully edges up a floorboard and pulls out his mother's purse. He removes a ten-pound note and puts back the purse.

"Big Macs and French Fries each," says Snotty. "But no milk shakes today, folks. Money doesn't grow on trees you know. Right, open your eyes now. Here's the cash and don't be long!"

"Shall we get the bus?"

"Certainly not," says Snotty. "You two should keep in training, if you want to beat us next time . . ."

"Good thinking," says Jessie.

"And don't forget," says Snotty. "When you come back, pretend to give my mum a wave. And if you see any nosy parkers around, shout something to her."

"What shall we shout?" asks Bessie, looking puzzled.

"I dunno," says Snotty. "Use your intelligence."

"Just say, 'Hello, Mrs Bumstead'," says Sluke. " 'Can Nottingham come out to play?' "

The girls rush out of the front door, then head down the street in the direction of McDonald's.

"This is the life," says Sluke, going upstairs, following Snotty.

They both go to the front window of what was, till two weeks ago, Snotty's mother's posh drawing-room. In the window, sitting at a desk, is a figure dressed in Snotty's mother's clothes.

It is a stone bust, taken from the back garden, with a column underneath.

Snotty moves it so that only the profile can be seen from outside.

"What a brilliant idea!" says Sluke. "That's really amazing."

"Yes, I was quite pleased with it," says Snotty.

"Pity she can't talk," says Sluke. "Then you'd have everything."

"Who says she can't?"

"Come on," says Sluke. "You're winding me up."

"She never stops talking," says Snotty. "Mind you, it's the same old stuff. Over and over again."

"Like all mums, you mean," says Sluke.

"No, she's a bit wittier and livelier than your run-of-the-mill, common-or-garden mum."

"Well, she would be," says Sluke, sarcastically. "Being your mum."

"I can see you don't believe me, clever clogs."

"Not really, Snotty," says Sluke.

"Right, close your stupid eyes, and listen carefully . . ."

Snotty goes to the phone. There is an answering machine attached to it. He sets it to play.

Sluke listens, his eyes closed. He can't understand what is happening until he opens his eyes and realizes what it is. Then he bursts out laughing.

"Hi, it's Zoe Bumstead here. Many apologies. I've got the usual panics and dramas and catastrophes and some sort of dreaded lurgy, so I'm sorry I just can't make it to the phone at the moment! If you want Nottingham, he should be in from school soon. Unless he's late. You know how he loves school! I hope he won't be kept in, well not for too long! If you have any messages, speak slowly. Here is a silly old bleep . . . Byee."

5

While Snotty and Sluke wait for the girls to return with their sumptuous post-match repast, they play Space Invaders.

Snotty has installed three machines that are lined up along the walls of what was the posh drawing-room, all whizzing and pinging and singing away.

Snotty's "mother" appears to watch them playing quite happily, without ever complaining or interfering.

When Snotty and Sluke tire of the Space Invaders, they move next door into her bedroom where there are computer games, electronic toys, remote-controlled cars and toy trains racing along miniature tracks.

Snotty has thought it all out very logically. He is very pleased with his rearrangement of the whole house.

GROUND FLOOR. This is mainly for FOOTBALL, but can also be used as a venue for other physical activities.

FIRST FLOOR. This is for GAMES, some mental, some just pushing and pulling, holding and twisting, waiting and watching, and now and again kicking, if they don't work. SNOOKER is played on this floor as well as assorted electronic games.

TOP FLOOR. This is completely different. It is for listening – in other words, MUSIC.

Music happens to come in many forms, so Snotty has

had to reshape the top-floor rooms a little, to get in all the jukeboxes, the wiring and amps for his stereos, the CD players, the electric guitar which he occasionally practises on and the mail-order drum kit which he is still trying to put together.

"It's really great, your house," says Sluke.

"My mum did tell me to have fun," says Snotty.

"Wish I had fun in our house," says Sluke. "The only larf I get is when the old man opens the post and thinks he's won a Time Share or a Car of his Choice."

"I thought of buying a car," says Snotty, "on my mum's credit card, but there's one problem."

"What's that, Snot?"

"I can't drive."

"How do you know she's got enough money?"

"She's got loads o' money and I must be saving her a fortune, not using the gas cooker. She'll be well pleased with me, when she comes home . . ."

Snotty pauses, looking at Sluke. He was about to add, "If she ever comes home", then he thought better of it.

Sluke blinks, showing no expression, knowing what was in Snotty's mind.

"The trouble is cash," says Snotty. "She left about a hundred pounds in the deepfreeze, but that's almost gone. Pizzas aren't cheap, you know."

"How did you buy all this stuff then, you know, video games, stereos and that?"

"Most of them are rented, using her credit card numbers."

"What if she goes mad when she gets back and sees all this stuff?"

"Easy peasy," says Snotty. "If she doesn't like them, she can send them back."

"You are lucky," says Sluke. "Wish I had a house like this, wish I could live like this."

"Stick around," says Snotty.

"But don't you er, you know, miss your mum, you know, doing things for you. They do have their uses, mums . . ."

"I have people to do things for me," says Snotty, loftily. "Hark, I think I hear two of the staff now."

There is a rhythmic series of knocks on the front door, then three taps on the front window, the secret signs that tell Snotty friends have arrived. It is Jessie and Bessie, returning with the chips and hamburgers.

*

"I've discovered something," says Snotty, sitting on the sink top, stuffing himself with chips, surveying the ground floor of his kingdom with pride and satisfaction.

"Your bum's wet," says Sluke.

"Oh no," moans Snotty, jumping down. "I thought I felt something funny."

"Sorry about that," says Bessie. "It's where I emptied the ice cubes."

"What else have you discovered, Snotty?" asks Jessie, sweetly.

"Do tell," says Bessie.

"If you two are going to take the micky . . ." says Snotty.

"We're listening, oh great one," says Jessie.

"I've discovered that you don't actually need cash in this day and age," says Snotty.

"The Queen's the only person who really does without cash," says Jessie.

"And pop stars," says Bessie. "They get everything free."

"OK for big things," says Sluke, "using your mum's credit cards. But you'll need cash for little things, like getting into the cinema."

"Who needs the cinema? I've got three tellys, no, four, just rented a new one for the toilet, plus two video recorders and my own video library. It used to be my mum's bed, a stupid four-poster she bought herself. Brilliant for stacking videos."

"Bus fares then," says Jessie.

"Don't be mad! I don't go on buses, not any more. I can walk to school, and if I need a taxi, well, then I can take a taxi."

"Oh yeh," says Bessie.

"On my mum's account. She has it through her firm. Got you there."

"What about school dinners?"

"You potty? Not eaten them for centuries. Load o' rubbish. Not even fit for teachers. I go to Fred's Caff, don't I."

"Ah," says Sluke. "There could be a problem there. Fred won't give credit. I saw a Sixth Former trying it last week. Cash only."

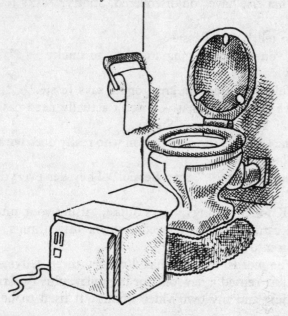

"So I'll give up Fred's, if I run out of cash. Mum always ran up bills at the local shop. I can get all my food there, if I want to. I'll manage. No problem. Everything is under control."

Snotty beams while Sluke, Jessie and Bessie look at each other, wondering, worrying. There must be a flaw somewhere in this new fantasy life Snotty has created inside his own house, but they hope not. They like coming to Snotty's house and want nothing to go wrong, nothing to change.

"Right, some more work to do, you guys," announces Snotty.

"Oh, no," says Sluke. "Can't we just have another game of football?"

"Later," says Snotty. "I have a new game in mind. I'm fed up walking downstairs in the morning. I want to do it in style and have fun."

"What's wrong with your bannisters?" says Sluke. "I've seen you using them before, till your mother stopped you."

"Useless," says Snotty. "You can't slide all the way down. You have to get off at every floor. That's really boring. And there's a few bits missing now. Not my fault. Those stupid men who brought in the jukeboxes. They got stuck. I dunno. Workmen these days are so clumsy . . ."

"You could jump out of your window with a parachute," says Jessie.

"Or how about a lift?" suggests Bessie.

"Good thinking," says Snotty. "But I've got a much better idea. Sluke, get that spanner you were using the other day in the bathroom. Then find the saw, hammers and nails.

"Jessie and Bessie, you two follow me. This is an equal opportunities household. I need yous for some heavy work."

Snotty goes down to the basement, followed by the girls. The basement is very crowded, full of furniture and carpets and pictures that Snotty has had moved from the other floors.

"Your mother will go mad," says Jessie. "Look at all this dust."

"Are you just going to leave it here?" asks Bessie.

"I dunno. I might get Sotheby's on the blower and sell the lot."

"You wouldn't dare."

"If I run out of dosh, I might have to. Who knows."

They fight their way through the furniture and into the storeroom. There they find several sheets of hardboard, left over from one of Snotty's mother's projects.

"Grab those sheets of hardboard," commands Snotty bossily. "Then carry them upstairs to the hall."

"What are you going to do?" asks Jessie.

"Watch," says Snotty.

"Tell you what, I'll watch," says Jessie.

"Look," says Snotty. "I'm only trying to help, widen your horizons, give you a proper role in life. Anyway, I have weak arms. My mum said, 'Snotty, be careful you never strain your little arms'."

The girls push him out of the way, smiling, but it's quite hard pushing against someone who has a weak chest. Snotty pretends to be knocked flat, panting for breath, while he watches them carry the hardboard upstairs.

"Right, Sluke, I want all the hardboard cut up into strips, about two feet wide," says Snotty. "Just big enough to take the average-sized bottom of the average-sized twelve-year-old . . ."

When the sheets have been cut to size, Snotty gets the three of them to start fitting and fixing, hammering and nailing, shiny side up, all the way down the stairs, from the top to the bottom.

He walks up and down the stairs like a foreman, keeping an eye on their work. Jessie and Bessie are doing a particularly good job, but Sluke proves a bit slap-dash.

"I don't want to have to make you do it again, Sluke," says Snotty, standing over Sluke and using his best teacher's voice.

"Up your bum," says Sluke, putting all his strength into the banging and hammering.

"Right, that's a detention for you," says Snotty.

Sluke stops, looking up, listening.

"What's that noise? Listen. It's someone next door. I think I can hear someone shouting for you, Snotty."

"It's probably Mrs Cheatham. Your fault, Sluke, making so much noise." Sluke gives one more bang, to finish off the last sheet.

"Right, that's enough, gang," says Snotty. "You've done rather well, for amateurs. I'm quite pleased, considering how useless some of you are, mentioning no names, Sluke . . ."

Snotty starts to go downstairs, but falls over, unable to lift his right foot.

Sluke has nailed his right trainer to the floor.

"You idiot," yells Snotty.

"Your fault, wearing trainers too big for you."

"Just as well, or you would have gone right through my foot."

"Look, stop messing around, you two," says Jessie, taking a pair of pliers to release Snotty.

Snotty is very pleased with the finished result. The stairs are still walkable, if you are not too big, too broad or too fat. But one half has been turned into a slide, and more than just an ordinary slide. Snotty has created a helter-skelter that twists and turns all the way down the house.

"Bags me have first go," says Sluke.

"Me! Me!" says Bessie. "I did the hardest work."

"Yes, women and workers first," says Jessie.

"Hard luck, peasants," says Snotty, bounding up the stairs. "I thought of it. And it *is* my house. You lot stay here. I shall expect a big cheer when I make the inaugural Slide of the Century . . ."

"Perhaps we should christen it," says Bessie.

"Yeh, a bottle of champagne on his head when he comes down," says Sluke.

"A bottle of shampoo, you mean," says Jessie.

"I heard that," shouts Snotty from somewhere above. "Right, here I go! Bombs away . . ."

An hour later they are all resting on the football pitch, working their way through the last of the drinks from the fridge.

Snotty is especially tired. His first go lasted almost half an hour before he finally agreed to let anyone else have a turn.

"I think I've torn my trousers," says Sluke. "Look!"

"You must have caught yourself on a nail," says Bessie.

"My mother will go mad," says Sluke. "These are my school pair. It's all your fault, Snotty."

"Blame the workers, not me. You lot put the nails in."

"I think it's really great," says Bessie. "The slide is your best invention so far, Snotty."

"I like the football pitch best," says Sluke.

"It's just the whole house that's so brilliant," says Jessie. "All houses should be like this."

"Thanks, fans," smirks Snotty. "Just takes brains, flair and a bit of organizational skill."

"And an empty house," says Jessie.

"I wonder how long you'll get away with it," says Bessie.

"Whatchamean?" demands Snotty. "Everything's under control. Don't you worry. More drinks? There's one left for each of us. Plus two for me of course . . ."

They drink their fill. Then they lie down exhausted, full of fizzy drink and happy memories, plus a few small splinters in a few small bottoms.

"What's that drip?" says Jessie at last.

"He's called Sluke," says Snotty. "The long drip that never dropped."

"Ha ha," says Sluke, getting up.

"I can hear it," says Bessie. "Sounds like water somewhere."

"Ouch!" screams Sluke. "Look at the ceiling. There's water coming through."

Snotty thinks it is some sort of joke, so he just smiles. Slowly he looks up at the ceiling, unconcerned, determined not to be caught.

"I'm getting wet!" exclaims Sluke. "What the hell's happening?"

Snotty now sees that something is definitely wrong, but he is still determined to be cool and unfazed, not like those boring house-proud people who worry about little things, dusty marks, dirty feet or fingerprints.

"Oh yeh," says Snotty. "I forgot to tell you. I took your advice. I do need a wash sometimes, like after I've been sliding or played football. So I installed this new shower thing. Clever, huh?"

Snotty stands under the drip, letting it splash on his head. Soon all his clothes and his trainers are wet, and a pool is forming at his feet, seeping across the football pitch.

"Don't be silly, Snotty," yells Bessie. "What are you going to do?"

"I think hair dryers, that's the next thing: a row of hair dryers, fixed to the ceiling to come on when . . ."

Snotty's next words are drowned. Literally. The drips have turned into a torrent, bringing down a large piece of the ceiling on Snotty's head.

"Snotty, *do* something!" shouts Bessie. "The house is falling down!"

6

The top of the snooker table is floating gently back and forth across the bathroom floor, the balls changing sides in unison, clinking eerily, like applause in an empty stadium.

"It's your stupid fault," shouts Snotty, splashing his way into the bathroom.

The Victorian bath is full and water is pouring onto the carpet. The floor is already about three inches deep in water.

"Whatchamean? Don't blame me," says Sluke behind him.

"I told you to tighten that tap, not break the stupid thing. What am I going to do now?"

"Well, you were thinking of having an indoor swimming pool, Snotty. You said that was your next ambition . . ."

"Don't be such an idiot," shouts Snotty. He wades across the bathroom floor and tries to turn the broken tap but water goes on rushing out of it.

"What are you standing there for with that stupid look on your face?" yells Snotty. "You caused all this."

Sluke tries to turn the tap, putting his hand over Snotty's, which makes Snotty cry out in pain. Snotty tries to pull his hand away and they both end up on the floor, wet through.

Snotty stops yelling. "This is terrible."

He splashes to the bathroom door, half walking, half sliding down the stairs. Trickles of water are already running down the hardboard slide.

"Heh, we could make a Slide 'N Splash on the stairs," says Sluke, pensively. "You know, those water chutes they have. They're really great. This could be the Black Run . . ."

"Will you just belt up," shouts Snotty, his bad temper returning. "You're really annoying me, you are."

"I dunno," says Sluke, half to himself. "It's all right when things are going well, dead cool, dead in command, aren't we, Snotty? But when things go wrong, it's panic panic panic . . ."

On the ground floor Jessie is on her hands and knees trying to prise open the boarded-up sink unit. Bessie is beside her, handing over a knife and fork.

"If you want to get out of here, Jess," says Sluke, "try the front door. Much easier . . ."

"Keep out of the way, Sluke," says Bessie. "While you two idiots have been playing silly games, Jessie is the only one who is doing something positive."

"Oh, yeh," says Snotty.

"I think our house is the same as yours," mutters Jessie, her mouth full of nails which she is taking out of the boards. The last nail comes out and the door swings open.

"Ah, yes, there it is. What a lot of junk in here!"

Jessie half crawls inside the sink unit. She looks for the main stopcock that controls the water coming into the house, and turns it off. After a few minutes the rush of water from the ceiling begins to slow down. As Sluke watches it, his mouth half open, another large piece of

plaster falls, hitting him on the head.

"When you've finished eating the ceiling," says Snotty, "perhaps you can start drinking the bathroom floor."

"Oh, it's all jokes now," says Sluke, giving Snotty a push.

"Stand back, both of you," says Jessie.

She waits until the final drip has dropped, then she nods her head.

"Right, we've done it," says Jessie.

"Thanks, Jess," says Snotty, very contrite.

"Next thing is to clear up," says Jessie. "Bessie, you go with those two and start mopping up in the bathroom.

Use towels and sheets. Open the windows, put the heat on, things will soon dry out."

"All right, Jess," says Bessie.

"Hey, it's an enormous hole," says Sluke. "Look, you can see daylight through it, right into the bathroom."

"Hmm, you'll have to get that mended," says Jess.

"I don't care," announces Snotty.

"And you'll have to have that broken tap seen to."

"That's not necessary either," says Snotty. "Or is it?"

He is suddenly deferring to Jessie for a change. She is clearly the expert on practical matters.

"You'll have no water in the whole house otherwise," says Jessie. "I've turned it off at the mains. If we turn it on, the flood will start again."

"Well, I don't have baths," says Snotty. "I don't drink water. I don't see that water's really important . . ."

"The toilet," says Jessie. "It won't flush for a start. So don't be silly. You've got to have water. Your mother will want the water and the bath working when she comes home, won't she?"

Snotty does not reply.

"Right then," continues Jessie. "While you clear up, I'll get a plumber."

She goes to the notice board on the kitchen wall, where Snotty's mother has pinned up lots of notices and important telephone numbers. They are a bit hard to read, as Snotty's indoor football scores cover most of the board, as well as the wall.

"Thanks, Jessie," says Snotty, going with Sluke to clear up the bathroom. "Actually, you and Bessie won the football match," adds Snotty. "I shouldn't have disallowed your goals."

"That's all right, Snot," says Jessie. "We understand."

75

The "Round the Bend" Emergency Plumber ("No Job Too Big or Too Wet") is in the bathroom. He is standing on the soggy carpet, staring at the Victorian bath, still full of water. The floor is no longer flooded, but everything is very damp and squelchy.

The Plumber has a large beer belly that droops under an England World Cup T-shirt, long greasy hair and fat arms covered with tattoos. On his head he wears a baseball cap, back to front.

He doesn't look at all like a plumber, so Jessie thinks, or capable of any job, big or wet, but then she is not quite sure what plumbers should look like. She rang five numbers. He was the only one who would come.

"You've had some right cowboys in here," says the Plumber, standing back, shaking his head, pursing his lips.

"Excuse me?" says Jessie.

"Diabolical," continues the Plumber, sighing.

Jessie has been detailed to do the talking, as she always appears sensible.

She can also put on a rather posh voice, which helps to lend authority, not to be confused with her normal voice, the one she uses at school and with her friends.

Snotty is good at voices as well, but they work best on the phone, when he is disembodied. Once people see him, they can never take him seriously. As for Sluke, the very sight of him makes most people laugh.

"Cowboys," continues the Plumber. "They've been playing games in here, I see."

"Snooker, I think," says Jessie. "That's the only game my friend, I mean my brother, plays in here."

"Snooker?" asks the Plumber.

"He plays with his dad," puts in Sluke from the doorway where he is crouching with Snotty and Bessie, none of whom is meant to interrupt Jessie in her negotiations with the Plumber.

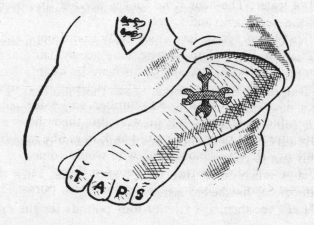

"Where is your dad then?" asks the Plumber.

"At work," says Snotty. "He's in the Police Force."

"And very high up," says Sluke.

"Yes, he is very tall," adds Bessie.

The Plumber smiles. He is not really listening to them. He has just seen how the pipes have been connected up under the bath.

He gives another heavy sigh and an exaggerated shudder that makes his tattoos shake like jellies. Then he leans over and pulls the plug out of the bath.

"Oh, no," says Snotty. "Was that all that was wrong? So it was your stupid fault, Sluke. Didn't you see the plug was in?"

"Not my fault. I didn't touch it."

"My mother always leaves the plug in," says Bessie. "She worries about spiders and creepy things. Very silly, really, I'm always telling her . . ."

Jessie glares at Bessie and the other two, motioning them to shut up and let her do the talking.

"No, that wouldn't have made much difference," says the Plumber. "Your tap's a gonner, ain't it?"

"Perhaps it just needs a new washer," says Jessie helpfully.

"No chance. Look. Finished. You need a completely new tap. And it's gonna costya."

"Oh, no," moans Snotty.

"But you're in luck, folks," says the Plumber. "I've got a new one in the van. Not cheap though. None of your rubbish. Not like this load of old junk."

He gives a kick at the pipes before going downstairs to his van to collect the new part.

"How much do we owe you?" asks Jessie, when the Plumber has finished at last.

"Let's see then. It's twenty-four pounds for the call-out, twenty pounds an hour, then the materials. Let's call it eighty pounds, love."

"Come on, Snotty," says Jessie.

"Here's the number of my mother's Barclaycard," says Snotty, holding out a damp scrap of paper. "Just charge your bill to her account."

"This is no good to me," says the Plumber. "Cash only."

"What?"

"Dosh, ackers, smackeroos, oncers," says the Plumber.

"But we don't actually have cash, at the moment, I mean my mother hasn't got any. She has it of course, in the bank, but not in the house . . ."

"Then she'll have to go to the bank, won't she?"

"Hmm, not sure she can," stutters Jessie. "You see she's got a bad back, and she's very busy . . ."

"That's her problem," says the Plumber, packing up his tools.

"But what can we do?" asks Jessie.

"I've got another job nearby," says the Plumber, glancing at his watch. His arms are very big. He looks very annoyed.

"It shouldn't take me long," he continues, narrowing his eyes. "I'll be back in two hours. For the cash. Or else. Understand? You just tell her to have the money ready . . ."

The Plumber slams out of the front door.

"Now what are we going to do?" says Sluke.

"How can anyone get hold of eighty pounds in two hours?" asks Bessie.

"I dunno," says Snotty. "Rob a bank, I suppose . . ."

7

Snotty is standing outside the Midland Bank at Camden Town. He is holding the hand of a tall, thin figure in a very long coat with a floppy hat pulled well down.

They have walked past the front door of the bank several times, trying to look casual. Snotty is decidedly nervous. It is hard to tell whether his companion is a man or a woman.

"Look, there's no need to hold my rotten hand," mutters Sluke, pushing Snotty away. "Someone from school might see us."

Sluke is wearing an old coat and hat of Snotty's mother's. The idea is for him to look like an adult, so that any bank official will be reassured.

"Have you got it?" whispers Snotty.

"Yeh, don't panic," says Sluke. "It's in my pocket."

"Perhaps I should carry it."

"No, I'll do the business," says Sluke. "Just you keep an eye on Jess and Bess."

Bessie and Jessie are standing on the opposite corner of the crossroads, beside the flower stall, pretending to examine some plants, but ready to signal to Snotty and Sluke should they see a policeman.

"I think we'd better wait till there's no one around," says Snotty.

"Good thinking," says Sluke.

They wait for a while, then walk determinedly towards the front door of the bank once again – but they carry straight on, past the bank, when they see a group of people coming out. They turn round, but now more people are coming, so they keep on walking, up and down . . .

"This could be more complicated than we thought," says Snotty. "And more dangerous."

"No, there's no danger," says Sluke. "I just stick it in, then I get the money, and wow! we're off, man. Come on, let's do it now. I'm tired of waiting. Let's sock it to them."

"Look, stop messing around," says Snotty. "You're supposed to be a woman, not a tough guy."

"Sorry," says Sluke, in a high-pitched voice. "I mean sorry, petal."

Snotty told Sluke, many years ago, that when his mother was being affectionate she called him "petal", just as a joke. He now regrets this.

"I think it's all clear," says Sluke. "Come on, we'll have a go."

"All right then," says Snotty, looking across the road. Jess and Bess are watching, but there's no warning signal.

Sluke and Snotty march up to the Midland self-service cash-dispensing machine in the wall of the Midland Bank, trying to look as if they do this every day. They join the queue behind a large man, who blocks their view of the machine. Both shuffle about nervously until it's their turn. Then Sluke puts his hand in his pocket and takes out Snotty's mother's bank card. Casually, he tries to slide it in. It hits a wall of glass, and falls to the ground.

"You idiot, haven't you done this before?" snarls

Snotty.

"Never, have you?"

"I've seen my mum do it," says Snotty. "That doesn't happen to her."

There is a whirring sound, the cover folds back, and a message lights up, instructing the next customer to insert his card.

"See, it's dead easy," says Sluke. "I was just pretending I didn't know what to do."

There is more whirring noise and some sort of message starts flashing on the screen.

"You fool," says Sluke. "This isn't the Midland Bank after all. It's a video game. You've brought us to the amusement arcade."

"No, this is the place," says Snotty. "It's the one my mum uses."

They stare at the message. Snotty wishes he had brought Jessie. Sluke may be an electronics wizard, but Jessie is good at understanding instructions. Snotty can't

understand how to play a new card game, or even switch on the gas cooker unless someone explains it to him slowly.

The message disappears, the screen goes blank. Snotty groans.

"Don't panic," says Sluke. "We'll try again. I've never used one of these before, but I think I'm beginning to work it out."

The message lights up once more, instructing the customer to put in a Personal Identification Number.

"What does *that* mean?" asks Snotty. "Does it mean your name, or your phone number, or what?"

"I thought you came here with your mum?"

"Yeh, but I wasn't watching properly."

Behind them, an elderly couple are becoming impatient, coughing and muttering, wanting them to hurry up.

"Sorry," says Snotty. "You can go first. We're not in a hurry."

They let the couple go ahead, watching their every move.

"I've got it now. But we don't know your mother's secret code number," says Sluke. "That's the problem."

"I used to know it," says Snotty. "Now what was the trick? I think it's my birthday, plus the number of our house, add on my mum's age . . ."

"Take away the number you first thought of," says Sluke.

"Now you've made me forget it."

"You don't know it anyway, you wally."

"I did, but it's gone."

"Then that's it," says Sluke. "That Plumber will come and beat us all up."

They go back across the road, looking very dejected, to tell Bessie and Jessie that they've failed.

Very slowly, all four of them start walking home to Snotty's house.

"It's really stupid anyway," says Snotty. "Imagine having to go around all the time remembering your, what was it, Sluke, your Personal Identity Number?"

"You mean your Pin," says Jessie.

"I knew you wouldn't understand," says Snotty. "Far too complicated for girls. They think it's something to do with sewing."

Bessie and Jessie both give him a kick.

"PIN," says Jessie, spelling it out in capital letters. "Now I understand. I saw that word on your mother's notice board, followed by four numbers. I couldn't understand what it meant. I've got it now. Though it's very silly of her not to keep it secret. That's what you're supposed to do . . ."

They all stare at each other. Then as one, they start running back to Snotty's house.

"Thank you, my good man," says Snotty, pulling out a wad of notes from his pocket an hour later.

The Plumber is standing just inside the front door. He looked belligerent at first, but his face has now softened and he is almost friendly.

"It was eighty pounds you said," says Snotty, grandly. Now that things are going well, Snotty is his usual confident, cool, street-wise self.

"No problem," continues Snotty. "Sorry to keep you waiting, old sport. Please accept my mother's apologies."

The Plumber takes the money and hitches up his trousers, shoving his cap to the back of his head.

"Thanks, mate. And if you want any more jobs done, just give me a bell, you know where I am."

"I'll bear that in mind," says Snotty, standing on the steps to watch the Plumber go.

"I say," shouts Snotty, as the Plumber is about to get into his van. "That ladder thing on your roof. How much do you want for it?"

"Can't sell that, mate. More than my job's worth. It belongs to my Governor."

"What about twenty quid then," says Snotty, unpeeling the last of the money he got from the cash machine. "You can tell your Governor it got nicked from your motor when you were on a job," says Snotty. "Kids on this street will steal anything."

The Plumber looks around, thinking. He then jumps on the roof of his van, unties the folding ladder, takes it into Snotty's house, grabs the money and roars away in his van.

Snotty, Sluke, Bessie and Jessie are lying on the football pitch, very proud of themselves.

"You see, it's easy living on your own," says Snotty. "All right, from time to time little things are bound to go wrong, but if you're clever and smart like me, keep your head, as I do, you can soon sort things out."

"Yeh, you did very well there, Snotty," says Bessie.

"Great," says Sluke.

"What about the, er, hole in the ceiling," says Jessie, looking up. "You'll still have to get that repaired, won't you?"

"Oh yeh," says Bessie. "It looks awful."

"I don't intend to have any workmen in this house, ever again," says Snotty.

"Then what are you going to do, Snotty?" asks Bessie.

"It's what *you*'re going to do," says Snotty. "You are the workmen."

"Oh, no," groans Sluke.

"In that storeroom downstairs," says Snotty, "there

are some more sheets of hardboard. Bring them all up, gang. Sluke, go and find that saw and the other tools."

Once again, Snotty gets them working, hammering and nailing. This time he makes them cover the entire staircase up to the first floor.

Then Snotty goes down to the basement and drags out a skateboard, one he hasn't used for a long time.

"That's fantastic, Snotty," says Bessie. "But how will you get up the stairs to come down again? It's too steep and too slippy."

"I've got it all worked out, petal," says Snotty. Sluke sniggers.

From behind the front door, Snotty picks up the Plumber's step-ladder. In the main room he sets it up against the wall, directly below the hole in the ceiling.

Snotty climbs up the ladder, holding his skateboard. He tears away some of the loose plaster round the hole, so that he can easily pull himself through it. He then disappears, but his voice can still be heard.

"From now on," he shouts, "the only way upstairs is by this ladder. OK? It'll give us extra protection. We can always hide the ladder to repel boarders."

"Hey, that's a great idea," says Bessie.

"And when you come downstairs, you all have an option," says Snotty. "You can either slide down, or use the skateboard."

"It's a multi-purpose adventure playground," says Sluke. "You really are turning this house to good use, Snotty. Very constructive, very creative."

"I'm just doing what my mum told me," says Snotty. "She said, *Have fun!*"

8

"When can I sleep at your place, then?" asks
Sluke.

"I'll think about it," says Snotty.

"You're so lucky, being able to go to bed when you
like, stay up all night if you like, play games all night."

"I'd say clever, rather than lucky," says Snotty.

It is Saturday evening. Bessie and Jessie have gone
home. Sluke has hung on, hoping to be invited to stay
the night, but now it's time to go back to his own house.

"It's salad at our place," says Sluke. "Yuck."

"I'm told it's very good for you," says Snotty.
"Remind me, what does it look like? Must be yonkers
since I had salad. Is it that green stuff with slugs crawling
all over it?"

"Oh, shurrup," says Sluke. "All right for you."

Snotty opens the front door carefully, looking around
before he lets Sluke out, checking that Mrs Cheatham
is not about, being nosy.

"See you," says Snotty. "Don't eat too much lettuce."

He locks up very carefully, putting in the bolts, and
goes to get a drink from the fridge.

"I think I'll have an early night," says Snotty to himself. "Get some beauty sleep. Though how can I be
improved?"

He takes a quick shot at the far goal, and scores another cracker. Upstairs he has a go on one of the Space Invaders, and puts a film on the video. All the lights are on, as usual, and there is music belting out from all his stereos.

Over the last couple of weeks, he has gone to bed later and later, playing games for so long that he has gone straight to sleep from exhaustion at about one or two in the morning. Now the novelty of staying up is wearing off slightly. But only slightly.

His mother always insisted that he went to bed at eight on school nights, and nine at weekends.

"Really stupid. I told her over and over again, but she never listened. You should be able to decide your own bed-time. Stands to reason. You should be able to eat when you're hungry and sleep when you're sleepy. That reminds. I haven't eaten for about, I dunno, an hour . . ."

He goes back downstairs and gets out of the fridge a giant carton of ice-cream. It is absolutely solid. His mother, if she were at home, would make him wait till it started to soften a bit, but Snotty can't wait.

He forces open the kitchen cupboard and takes out an electric carving knife, one of his mother's presents last Christmas. She has never used it, because she maintained it was the silliest present she had ever been given.

Snotty was warned never to touch it, but now he plugs it in and slices up the ice-cream. "Another great invention."

Next he tries it on a Mars bar, which it slices beautifully, and then a Kit Kat, but the chocolate breaks into pieces. He tests it on a corner of the wooden cupboard, a knobbly bit that sticks out and has ruined quite a few of Snotty's best shots on goal. The blade of the knife breaks in half.

"That's it then," says Snotty. "Might as well chuck it out. She never used it anyway."

He takes it to the dustbin outside the front-door steps.

"Don't worry, Tiddles! I'm not going to attack you."

Tiddles is Mrs Cheatham's black cat. She is hanging around the dustbin, staring at Snotty, looking alarmed at the sight of his electric saw. She dashes behind the dustbin and disappears.

"Stupid cat," says Snotty. He has never liked it, or the way that Mrs Cheatham fusses over it. He throws the carving knife into the dustbin and goes back up the steps and into his house.

He takes his plate of frozen ice-cream slices to bed and sucks them while he watches television and listens to his stereo. Eating in bed, unless he is ill, is strictly forbidden and his mother would never allow frozen ice-cream so late at night because it might lie on his tummy

and keep him awake.

It takes him a while to go to sleep, but not because of the ice-cream. It's the fault of some crisps. Last night he took three packets to bed with him, and he must have spilt a lot. They are making him so itchy that he has to get up and shake his duvet. Out of it falls a Bounty bar.

"So that's where it's been. I thought somebody had nicked it."

He gets back into bed munching.

"Mum did have her uses. I could have blamed her for pinching it, if she'd been here. Ah, well, you can't have everything."

With that, he falls asleep. The lights are still on, the music still playing, the game machines still humming, but for an hour he sleeps very soundly. He dreams of scoring a hat trick for Spurs. The crowd goes mad and the rest of the team rush to hug him.

He wakes up with a start. It feels as if something has touched his face: something soft and wet.

"I was dreaming, of course," he thinks.

"The Spurs team were kissing me. Imagine playing for Arsenal, and having all those ugly mugs kissing you . . ."

He curls into a ball under the duvet, smiling to himself. He would have told Sluke that joke, if Sluke'd been here.

It takes him a while to get back to sleep. The music and the machines and the lights are proving a bit of a nuisance. Up to now, he has enjoyed them. He has liked their company, though he has not quite admitted that to himself. Nor has he admitted that he has not wanted to go to sleep in the dark, not in this big house, all on his own.

"Oh, no," he yells as the bedroom curtains suddenly move.

He pulls the duvet right over his head, waits for a few moments, then slowly takes a peep at the window.

"Must be the wind. That's all. How stupid of me. No, hold on. The window's shut. I closed all the windows in the house. What can it be?"

He sits up, watching the curtains. Nothing happens. They are quite still.

"I must have imagined it. It wasn't a ghost. At least I don't think it was."

By saying it out loud, letting any ghost who happens to be around know that Snotty knows it's not there, he hopes it will go away.

"Not that I believe in ghosts," he says, putting on what he hopes is his bravest face.

He waits for the curtains to move again. He is daring any ghost to make its presence felt. Nothing happens.

"Right, that's it. Good-night, Snotty, good-night."

He lies down and closes his eyes, very tight, trying to force himself to sleep.

As a little boy, when he couldn't sleep, he would go down to his mother's room, saying he wanted a drink of water, or to go to the lavatory, or he wanted her to find his gaga cloth. This was an old bit of towelling he took to bed every night, sucking the end of it. He had it for years and years.

"Now where is it? In my drawers? Under the bed?"

He gets out of bed and falls over with a crash. He has tripped on a plastic football.

"What idiot put that there? It wasn't there when I came to bed . . ."

He rubs his legs where they hurt, then stops, realizing what he has said.

94

"Look, ghosts, if you want to play football, do it downstairs, please, not up here."

Snotty is speaking very loudly, to keep up his confidence, but he is beginning to worry. The house seems to be full of echoes and strange creaks tonight, in spite of the noise from all the machines.

Suddenly the curtains move again and Snotty shrieks in terror. He takes a big swing at the plastic football, kicking it straight into the curtains.

There is a screech, and out walks Tiddles. She sees the football and runs after it, thinking this is a game.

"You little beast!" yells Snotty. He chases her round and round the room, until she flies down to the next floor where he pursues her round the machines. She escapes into the bathroom. Snotty quickly locks the door on her, hoping it will take her some time to realize the only escape is through the hole in the floor.

Snotty rushes to the stairs and slides down on his bottom in record time. He is waiting below when Tiddles appears nervously at the top of the ladder.

"Gotcha, you little trouble-maker."

Seizing Tiddles by the scruff of the neck, he carries her to the kitchen door into the back garden.

"Oh, no, it really is a ghost this time!"

Over the garden wall, an eerie-looking figure in white is staring at him. The face looks luminous and shiny, not human. Snotty throws Tiddles down and darts back into the kitchen.

"Tiddles, my little darling, come to Mummy. Where have you been, Tiddles . . ."

It is Mrs Cheatham in her nightdress, her face covered in some sort of night-time make-up.

Snotty slams the back door, bolts it securely and goes back upstairs to bed.

This time, he turns most of the lights off, except for one outside his bedroom, which his mother always leaves on. And he switches off a few of the machines.

Soon he is asleep. He dreams he has scored the winner at Wembley for England, but he runs off to a corner flag so that no one can kiss him.

"May I speak to Sluke, please?"

Snotty is up bright and early, eating his breakfast of crisps and chocolate, plus Coke. He has dialled Sluke on his cordless telephone, another new purchase on his mother's Visa card.

"Oh, hello, Nottingham," says Sluke's mother. "This is early for you."

"Well, I have to get up and make the breakfast on Sunday morning. Help my mum and that."

"Oh, I wish Lucas was as good as you are. How is your mum? I haven't seen her for a while."

"Fine, fine," says Snotty. "I'm ringing 'cos she says could Sluke come and play today, and stay the night, if he wants to."

"Is your mum there?"

"Still in bed," says Snotty.

"It won't be a bother for her, will it, having Lucas?"

"No, we've bags of room in our house," says Snotty. "But I think my mum's going to fix a sleeping bag for him in my room. Just in case he gets lonely."

"He is a bit of a scaredy cat," says Sluke's mother. "But don't tell him I told you . . ."

"Don't worry," says Snotty. "I'll look after him. Byee . . ."

9

It is Monday morning. Snotty and Sluke are staggering out of Snotty's house, still discussing who really won the video game, and before that who played best at table tennis, and even earlier how Snotty managed to cheat at darts when he was playing on his own, while Sluke was asleep. Snotty had arranged a Decathlon event for Sunday night – ten games going all through the night.

Sluke looks at his watch and groans. School started ten minutes ago.

"It's all your fault," says Snotty, starting to run.

"Don't blame me," says Sluke. "You said you wouldn't go to sleep. You said you would wake me up."

"How could I?" says Snotty. "I fell asleep."

"I'm knackered," says Sluke. "And it's Maths first thing, isn't it?"

"*Was* Maths first thing," says Snotty.

"Oh, good, we'll miss it," says Sluke.

"Oh, bad," says Snotty. "It's that creep Banks. He gave me a final warning last week."

They keep running, something they both find very hard. Sluke is too awkward and gangly to run very fast and Snotty usually starts to wheeze. Not having slept makes it even harder.

They rush through the school gates panting, straight

into the arms of a stocky, unshaven, leather-jacketed
figure. He grabs Snotty by the scruff of the neck.

"You're that kid Snotty, aren't you?" says the figure.

"No," says Snotty, trying to get free.

"I know you," says Sluke. "You're called Raffy.
You're in the Sixth Form."

"Well done," says Raffy. "I'm glad to see that even
scruffy First Years recognize the all-time super stars in
this school. Do you want a coconut or a goldfish?"

"Thanks," says Sluke. "But we're late, actually."

"Leggo," says Snotty. "You're hurting."

"Sorry, old son," says Raffy. "I thought that sleeve
was empty. Didn't realize there was an arm in it . . ."

"Ha ha," says Snotty, pulling his little bony arm free
and giving it a rub to bring it back to life.

"Honestly, I'm sorry," says Raffy, putting on the charm. "Didn't mean to hurt. Can I assist in any way? Hold your pens? Mop your tired little brows? Carry your bags?"

Raffy is leering and pulling faces at them, trying to be funny.

"Look, gerrout the way, eh," says Snotty. "We'll get a detention if we're late."

"I just want to ask you one thing," says Raffy, "because I know we're gonna be very good friends!"

"Whatcha want?" grunts Snotty, remembering he is at school now, so nothing must be given away.

"It's about your house," says Raffy slowly, watching for any reaction.

"Dunno what you're talking about," says Snotty blankly. "I'm not in a house. Mrs Potter has stopped them. I was in one at my Primary school, Raleigh it was called, or was it Drake. Sluke, what house were we in at Brookfield?"

"I've got this girlfriend, right?" says Raffy. "In fact quite a few Sixth Formers have got girlfriends. And we need somewhere to rave – you know, to groove out."

"Dunno what you're on about," says Snotty.

"Look, now and again we hold parties, and we think your house would be a brilliant place for the next one. Don't worry, there wouldn't be more than a hundred and fifty of us. We won't sell tickets!"

"Hey," gulps Snotty, "look at the time! My mum will already be at school. She's got an appointment this morning with Mrs Potter."

"What?" says Sluke, but Snotty quickly gives him a kick. Raffy for once looks confused. Perhaps he has made a mistake, perhaps this kid really has got a mother around.

"You are called Snotty, aren't you?" asks Raffy.

Snotty shakes his head. Raffy is beginning to think that the name Snotty does sound improbable. And this kid he's been pestering does look a bit half-witted. Someone living alone would have to be pretty smart.

Snotty heads down the corridor of the New Building, straight for the office of Mrs Potter, the Head Teacher at St Andrew's.

"Lucas Mudd," mumbles Snotty to one of the secretaries in the outer office. When Raffy hears this name, one he vaguely remembers hearing before, he decides he may have picked the wrong kid.

"See you then," says Raffy. "But don't forget what I said."

"Ugh," says Snotty.

"What do *you* want?" says the secretary to Snotty.

"I found this ruler and it's marked Lucas Mudd," mumbles Snotty. "Just thought I'd hand it in."

"This is not Lost Property," says the secretary. "You know where that is. Next, please."

Sluke has been trying to listen outside the Head's office. When Snotty reappears, they both walk back to their classroom.

"What are you doing with my ruler?" says Sluke. "You must have pinched it, you pig."

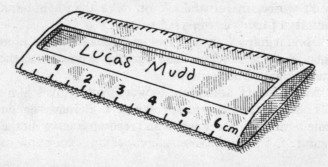

Later that morning Snotty and Sluke are sitting at the back of their History class, their work books in front of them. Their brows are furrowed in concentration, their eyes narrowed. It is a new pose they are working hard to perfect. What it means is that no work is being done.

"All your fault," snarls Snotty.

"Get lost," says Sluke.

"Must be," says Snotty. "Who else would go around telling people my secrets?"

"Don't look at me," says Sluke.

"Well, it wouldn't be Bessie or Jessie, would it? I can trust them. You've got a Big Mouth, you have."

"I ain't told no one. Honest, Snotty. Not one person."

"Huh," grunts Snotty.

"I don't even know Raffy."

"Oh, yeh, you were the one who said you recognized him, trying to be Big."

"Well, I am," says Sluke, "compared with you. You're just a runt."

"You're just a load of rubbish."

"And you're a little blob of rat's pee," says Sluke.

"Shurrup, you snot bag."

"Crawl back into your sewer, you cretinous creep."

Under the desk, Snotty aims a kick at Sluke, his best friend, while in return, Sluke directs a kick at Snotty, his best friend. The desks crash over and their work sheets and papers fly everywhere.

"I might have known it was you, Lucas," says Miss Eager, their History teacher, coming to see what the commotion is about.

"Sorry, Miss," says Sluke. "Wasn't my fault."

"Then who else caused it?" she says, looking straight through Snotty, as if he wasn't there. Snotty smiles to himself. His disguise as a non-person, non-pupil, is working. She picks up Sluke's work sheet. It is blank, apart from his name on top, Sluke Mudd.

"I know your name is Mudd, ha ha ha," says Miss Eager. Sluke has heard this joke ever since he met his very first teacher, way back in nursery-school days. He puts on a long-suffering look. "But I thought your first name was Lucas?"

"It is, Miss," says Sluke.

"So where does Sluke come from?"

"Dunno, Miss," says Sluke.

"Don't be silly. You must know."

"Dunno."

Before he can help himself, Snotty is opening his mouth, breaking his new vow. It is the row with Sluke that has done it. He is determined to get him into more trouble.

"It was when he was little and used to answer the phone," says Snotty. "People would say, 'Who is it?' and he would say 'S'Luke'. It just sort of stuck . . ."

"Thank you, er," says Miss, trying to remember Snotty's name. "Thank you, Birmingham."

"Huh," says Snotty, putting his head down, hoping to disappear from sight once again.

"Well, if writing Sluke Mudd has not exhausted you too much," says Miss, sarcastically, "perhaps you might carry on and start the work sheet I gave you twenty minutes ago. Otherwise, it's a detention."

As she walks back to her own desk, Snotty gives Sluke another nudge.

"And at dinner-time," says Miss, examining some papers on her desk, "I would like you to come to see me, er, Nottingham Bumstead . . ."

Snotty is prowling round his empty form-room, waiting for Miss Eager. He has missed playing football in the playground, and going to Fred's for his dinner, all because of her.

Miss Eager is Snotty's form teacher, as well as his History teacher. She is new to the school, and quite young, and as eager as her name, but so far Snotty has managed to have very little to do with her.

"Why did I open my big mouth?" moans Snotty. "If I'd kept quiet, none of this would have happened."

Snotty kicks a few chairs, bangs a few desk lids.

"What am I saying? It's his stupid fault, that idiot Sluke."

"Please pick those chairs up," says Miss, coming into the room. She is holding a cup of tea and eating a Bounty bar.

"You know we can't afford new furniture," she says, "not in this age of Cuts."

"Huh," says Snotty, picking up the chairs.

Miss Eager goes to her desk, unlocks her drawer and gets out several files.

"It seems to me that you have done very little home-

work for a very long time," she says, looking through her lists. "If any. Is that true?"

"Dunno," grunts Snotty.

"I've spoken to several teachers, and none of them can remember you handing in any written work recently. I have certainly not had a History essay from you in two weeks."

"Huh," says Snotty.

"Is that all you've got to say for yourself? Is there a reason why you can't do it? Are there problems I should know about?"

"Huh," says Snotty.

"You look as if you didn't get much sleep last night."

"I didn't," says Snotty, biting his lip the second he has blurted out this admission.

"Why not?" says Miss, rather alarmed.

"Just couldn't. I had things to do."

"What sort of things?"

"Just things. Ten things. Really hard . . ."

"What sort of ten things?"

"Like sort of tests . . ."

"Who gave you these ten tests to do?"

"No one," says Snotty. Miss stares at him for some time, looking again through her folders.

"Well, this can't go on."

"No, Miss," says Snotty.

Miss Eager is feeling slightly more sympathetic, now that Snotty has confessed his lack of sleep. Snotty thinks about explaining the Decathlon: how he and Sluke had to play one-a-side football, followed by all-star skateboarding, darts, table tennis, two video games, cards, snooker and blind-folded sliding down the stairs, just to make the last test really hard, though they never actually got to it. Then he decides Miss would not understand. That would just lead to further stupid questions.

Instead, Snotty tries to look even more tired, as pathetic as possible, so that she will be kind to him, but he spoils the whole effect by suddenly laughing.

Sluke's head has appeared in the window of the classroom door, and he is making stupid faces behind Miss Eager. He is signalling to Snotty with his arms and face that he has been eating chips, yum yum, with lots of ketchup, wow, then a milk shake, really good. Snotty can interpret everything.

"What's so funny?" asks Miss.

"It's lack of sleep," says Snotty, recovering his serious expression. "It sort of makes my face go funny, I can't control it, can't do anything really, especially not homework. I think I might have caught a bug or

something . . ."

"Then you must see a doctor. I'll suggest it to your mother tomorrow evening . . ."

"What?" says Snotty, alarmed.

"Your mother," says Miss, again consulting her folder. "It is the First-Year Parents' Evening. I see she came last term to several school functions, but not this term for some reason. I'm sure all your teachers will welcome a word with her tomorrow night. It will give us all the chance to find out exactly what has gone wrong with you and your homework . . ."

"Tomorrow?"

"Oh, stop being so silly. You have had the notice for ten days. I gave them out myself. And it's on the Bulletin Board."

The door opens, without a knock, and in walks Raffy.

"Hi, Liz," says Raffy to Miss, very bold. "Sorry to barge in, but it's about my UCCA forms. I think I will apply to do History at Cambridge after all. Give them the benefit of my brilliance."

"Just give me one more second, will you, Raf," smiles Miss. "I have here someone who at present is being rather less than brilliant, at History or anything else. Not one essay given in for three weeks . . ."

"Tut, tut," says Raffy. "Kids these days, eh?"

"Right," says Miss, turning to Snotty again. "When I see your mother tomorrow night, let's hope we can get to the bottom of all this nonsense . . ."

At the mention of the word "mother", Raffy gives Snotty a long, hard look. So he did get the wrong kid after all.

Miss nods her head, indicating that Snotty can now go. She turns to Raffy, all smiles.

Snotty walks out. On the surface, his blank expression is once again firmly in place. Underneath, he can feel panic creeping over him.

"What am I going to do now?" thinks Snotty. "How can I get my mum to turn up when I don't even know where she is . . . ?"

10

Snotty and Sluke are playing one-a-side football, very slowly, neither of them betraying any interest in who will win. Bessie and Jessie are upstairs, disco-dancing to three different jukeboxes, showing as much emotion as metronomes.

Every TV in the house is blaring away, performing loudly to empty walls. Every video game is winking and twinkling, eager for punters who never turn up. Every VCR is turned to red, hot and eager, desperate to be fed. Every computer is impatient to be switched on. Every board game, every ball game waits in anticipation, so excited you can almost hear them squealing "Play Me, Play Me". But tonight there are no takers.

"What am I going to do then?" says Snotty, kicking the ball idly up in the air, aiming at nowhere in particular. It disappears through the hole into the bathroom. "Right, the game's over."

He flops on the floor. Sluke goes to the fridge, hoping that some liquid refreshment will lead to mental stimulation.

Jessie and Bessie come down, sensing the football game is over. They arrived late, having done their homework first, and Snotty wouldn't let them join the football game.

"Look, stop stuffing your stupid face," says Snotty to Sluke. "I want some help. What am I gonna do tomorrow?"

"Use your dummy," says Sluke. "Wrap her up, take her to school and say it's your mother. Tell Miss she's got a bad cough and can't speak."

"Don't be silly," says Snotty.

"I could make a clockwork dummy, fully automated," says Sluke.

"We know you're an electronics genius, Sluke," says Bessie. "But not that clever."

"Only one problem," says Sluke. "It would take me about ten years."

"Has Miss Eager ever seen your mum?" asks Jessie.

"No, 'course not," says Snotty.

"I just asked," says Jessie. "Miss Eager has been here all this term."

"Yeh, but my mum hasn't been to school this term."

"In that case, how about Sluke dressing up as her for the Open Evening tomorrow," says Jessie. "He could wear her clothes and a big hat. That worked when you went to the bank, didn't it? Everyone thought you were with your mum."

"You mean with some old tramp," says Snotty.

"Well, no one stopped you," says Bessie. "So it *did* work."

"Worth a try," says Sluke. "I don't mind being androgynous again."

"What's that mean, Sluke?" asks Bessie.

"He doesn't know," says Snotty. "He read it in the *Daily Mail* fashion pages."

"Why don't you try it, Snotty?" says Jessie. "Miss Eager will never know it's not your mum."

"I thought you at least would show some sense," says Snotty. "Look, it's in the Main Hall, right. There will be about thirty teachers sitting at their little desks. Plus Old Ma Potter on the stage. Right?"

"So?" says Bessie.

"So a lot of them know what my mum looks like," continues Snotty. "They saw her last term, several times, didn't they? When they see me come in with this jerk, dressed like an old dosser, they'll smell a rat. Or in this case, smell Sluke. He's always had a bit of a pong."

"Ha ha," says Sluke, flatly.

All four of them sit and stare into space, careful not to catch anyone else's eye.

"The thing is," says Snotty, "I do want her back sometime . . ."

They all nod their heads wisely.

"But until she comes back, I want to be on my own. I want to have this house to myself. I don't want to be sent . . ."

Snotty doesn't finish his sentence. He is not quite sure what could happen to him, but he knows he wouldn't like it.

"Up to now," says Snotty, "it's been brilliant. I've been managing fine. I'm fine. The house is fine."

"The house is fine," repeats Sluke.

They all nod vigorously. Jessie looks up at the hole in the ceiling, then quickly turns her gaze the other way, but finds she is looking at the boarded-up kitchen unit. Then she sees the scribbles on the wall. So she closes her eyes, still nodding.

"Everything is fine," says Bessie.

They all mean it. They all want Snotty to continue living in his own home by himself. The house has completely changed their lives, become a refuge whenever their parents are annoying, unbearable or just boring.

"How about a note, written from your mum," says Jessie, "saying she's unwell and can't come."

"That's an idea," says Bessie.

"Hmm, it might work," says Snotty. "But they'd be suspicious."

"I don't see why," says Jessie.

"Well, I have done a few notes, over the past few weeks," admits Snotty. "Please excuse Nottingham from Cross Country, PE, RE, PSU, CDT, Maths, History, you name it, she's excused me. Yours and oblige, Zoe Bumstead (Mrs). I always put Mrs in brackets. Dunno why."

"Hmm, a mistake," says Jessie.

"If it's too dangerous to impersonate her body," says Sluke, "because people know her, and too dodgy to write a letter in her handwriting, because you've done that too often . . ."

"Look, just get on with whatever you're going to suggest," says Snotty.

"What about trying to impersonate her voice?"

Sluke is looking at the answering machine. He switches it on and listens carefully.

"Hi, it's Zoe Bumstead here. Many apologies. I've got the usual panics and dramas and catastrophes and some sort of dreaded lurgy, so I'm sorry I just can't make it to the phone at the moment! If you want Nottingham, he should be in from school soon. Unless he's late. You know how he loves school! I hope he won't be kept in, well not for too long! If you have any messages, speak slowly. Here is a silly old bleep . . . Byee."

"Don't mess around with that," says Snotty. "I need that. Everyone thinks she's still here, when they ring up and hear it."

"I might have an idea," says Sluke.

"Oh, yeh," says Snotty. "Your potty boffin ideas never work."

"Give him a chance, Snotty," says Bessie.

"It's too late," says Snotty, mournfully. "Miss Eager will find out everything tomorrow."

"We'll think of something," says Jessie, hopefully.

"Not much point," sighs Snotty. "I've had it."

"Oh, don't give up," says Bessie.

"I knew it couldn't last anyway," says Snotty, sadly. "That Raffy bloke has obviously heard something. The word must be getting around."

"We haven't told anyone, have we?" says Bessie.

"No, but I bet it's all gonna come out now," says Snotty. "They'll stick me straight in prison or something. And that will be it . . ."

The Main Hall of St Andrew's Road School is crowded for the First-Year Parents' Evening. Each teacher is sitting at a separate desk, his or her name and subject on a card in front of them, while lines of parents patiently queue up, waiting to be seen, waiting to hear the worst, or the best, about their offspring.

Most of them have their sons or daughters with them, though in some cases it is hard to tell who is with whom. Many of the boys and girls are desperately trying to pretend they have never met their parents before, that they are not with them, turning their backs, wandering off, looking the other way, making long-suffering faces at their friends.

"Didn't we tell you not to wear those horrible boots," whisper Jessie and Bessie to their mother, hissing out the words, hoping no one else can hear.

"Remember, Dad," mutters Sluke. "I don't want you to open your mouth at all."

Sluke's father and the twins' mother are smiling, exchanging pleasantries as they stand in the same queue, waiting for Miss Eager, ignoring their children's remarks, waving to other parents across the Hall.

Snotty is at the end of the same queue. He is on his own. He never seems to get any nearer the front; other parents and children somehow get ahead of him while he hangs back, as if in a dream.

Sluke and his father are finished quickly. They look very pleased. Miss must have said some nice things about Sluke. All his father had to do was nod.

They have now done all the teachers, so Sluke tells his father he can go. Sluke says he wants to get a Coke from the coffee bar run by the Parents' Association, then he will make his own way home.

When his father has gone, Sluke heads for the Sixth-Form Common room. A girl on her way out asks him what he wants. Sluke says he is leaving a message for Raffy in his pigeonhole.

When she has gone, Sluke goes straight to the pay telephone on the Common room wall. He is holding what looks like a tape recorder. He dials a number.

Once Sluke has left the Hall, Snotty edges out of the queue and goes to Mrs Potter's office.

There is only one secretary on duty, ticking off a long list of parents' names. The phone rings on another desk.

"Not again," she says. "Some fool keeps trying to get through, but whoever it is gets cut off every time."

Snotty nips round her desk and picks up the phone.

"St Andrew's Road School here," says Snotty.

"Thanks," says the secretary.

"Oh, it's you, Mum," says Snotty. "I've been waiting here for you all evening. What kept you? Oh no. How rotten. You want to speak to Mrs Potter? The secretary won't do? Well, I dunno. I'll try. It is almost the end of the evening. OK then, if you insist . . ."

"What is it?" says the secretary, looking up.

"She wants to speak to Mrs Potter. Sounds important."

"Well, go and fetch her, boy . . ."

"Hold on, Mum," says Snotty, putting the phone down carefully. "I'll just go and get Mrs *Potter* . . ."

"No need to shout, boy," says the secretary, but Snotty is already on his way.

In the Hall, Snotty dashes up to Mrs Potter who is just finishing with the last parent.

"Mrs Potter, urgent call for you, personal," says Snotty. "In your office."

Mrs Potter quickly shakes hands with the parent, nods at Snotty and gets up from her desk. Snotty follows her into the corridor.

"There's no need for you to come with me, thank you," says Mrs Potter.

"It's my mum, you see," says Snotty. "And the line is bad."

When Mrs Potter picks up the phone in the office she is rather breathless, something that always happens when she hurries, as she is slightly overweight.

"Yes, this is Gloria Potter speaking."

"Hi, it's Zoe Bumstead here. I've got some sort of dreaded lurgy, so I'm sorry I just can't make it to school at the moment. I hope I won't be kept in, well not for too long. Nottingham should be in school. You know how he loves school! He is a silly old bleep. Many apologies. Byee . . ."

Snotty has heard every word, mainly because he knew what words to expect.

"Well, I am sorry to hear that," says Mrs Potter, putting down the phone, half smiling, turning to Snotty. "Who's your form tutor?"

"Miss Eager," says Snotty.

"I'll tell her tomorrow that your mother rang. Do give her my best wishes for a speedy recovery."

Snotty is waiting for the lift to go up to Sluke's flat. He missed him at school, so he has decided to come round

to his place and thank him.

The lift door opens and out comes Raffy with a girl. Snotty manages to duck behind some other people so Raffy does not see him, but Snotty hears the girl moaning at Raffy for having taken her to such a silly place.

Snotty goes up to the fourteenth floor, where he knocks at the door of Sluke's flat. It is opened almost at once by Sluke's father, looking very angry.

"Oh, it's you," he says. "I just had some joker from your school, trying to push his way in. What's going on?"

"I dunno," says Snotty.

"And he had some girl with him. They wanted to have a party here. Is this your idea of a joke?"

"Nuffink to do with me."

"Better not be," says Sluke's father.

"Is Lucas in?" says Snotty, politely. "Please . . ."

"No, he isn't back yet. But you can take all this rubbish with you. That joker said it was a present for someone called Snotty. That must be you. I certainly don't want it cluttering up our place."

Mr Mudd hands Snotty a plastic bag full of papers, and shuts the door.

Snotty waits till he is outside on the pavement before he examines the contents. They are all History essays, written when Raffy was in the First Year. Almost all have been marked "A for Excellent Work". Raffy must have been offering them as a bribe.

"Just what I need," says Snotty. "That solves my History homework for the rest of this year . . ."

I I

It's Sunday afternoon in Snotty's house. Everything is in its place, orderly and organized, just as Snotty has arranged it.

On the top floor, the stereos and jukeboxes are belting out their various musics and madnesses. On the floor below, the video and computer games are on the move, hoping that their turn will come.

On the ground floor, Snotty and his friends are lying on a huge pile of cushions, taking a well-earned break from their physical exertions, stuffing their faces with ice-cream, milk shakes and bars of chocolate.

They have played two-a-side football, Snotty and Jessie against Sluke and Bessie this time. The game ended in a draw, a rather noisy, argumentative draw, but at least honours were even.

"The easiest thing of all," says Sluke, "was to change 'Here is a silly old bleep' into 'He is a silly old bleep'. I just had to shave the 'r' off 'here'."

"Stop showing off," says Snotty. "We've heard how you did it."

"Oh, it was brilliant," says Bessie.

"Yeh, but he might have mucked up the whole tape," says Snotty.

"No chance," says Sluke. "Before I started editing it,

I made a copy on my tape-to-tape machine. Then I got my slicer out: a pair of scissors, Sellotape, quite simple really, if you know how. You don't need all those fancy editing machines."

"You are clever," says Bessie.

"The hardest bit was dropping in the word 'school' in place of the word 'phone'. A bit dodgy. A few of the inflexions weren't quite right, but I don't think Mrs Potter noticed."

"That's 'cos I told her it was a bad line," says Snotty.

"No, it was the bleep joke," says Sluke. "That was my master stroke, 'cos it made her smile, I bet."

"Right, that's enough," says Snotty. "You're a genius, so let's forget it, eh. Shall we have some chips now?"

All Snotty's meals begin with ice-cream, cakes or chocolate, the theory being that you might as well fill up first on the things you like best, then move on to secondary delights, such as chips and burgers.

From above, there is the sound of hammering and

banging, then a few shouts, but all of it blurred, thanks to the other noises in the house.

"What was that?" asks Bessie.

"What?"

"All that screaming and banging."

"Oh, must be the video I've got for us later," says Snotty. "I put it on to warm it up."

"You don't need to warm videos up," says Sluke.

"That was a joke, dum dum," says Snotty. "Anyway, who's going for the chips? Don't all rush. OK, I'll go, you lazy lot."

"That makes a change," says Sluke.

"When I come back," says Snotty, "I want you, Sluke, to have organized a treasure hunt for us. OK? Right round the house. Really good clues. As you are so clever."

"I'll need paper for the clues," says Sluke.

"No problem," says Snotty. "You can write the clues on the walls, if you like."

"A treasure hunt sounds a bit babyish," says Jessie.

"Fine, then you needn't play," says Snotty. "I want it to be a Monster Obstacle Treasure Hunt, with a really good treasure at the end. Here, Sluke, this ten-pound note can be for the winner."

"Oh, I'll play then," says Jessie.

"I used to love treasure hunts when I was little," says Snotty.

"That wasn't long ago," says Sluke.

"But my mum only ever did them in the garden," continues Snotty, ignoring Sluke. "She wouldn't let me have one in the house, in case it got mucked up."

"Well, we can't muck up your house any more, can we," says Jessie.

"You are lucky," says Bessie. "It's a great house."

"Right, I'm off," says Snotty. "Lock the front door properly behind me. Just in case. Wait for the special signal, OK? Don't answer the phone. And don't let anyone in."

Half an hour later, Snotty is walking home. He has taken his time, because he decided to have an extra Cheeseburger first, just to give himself enough energy to carry back all their orders. He is going up the steps to his house when the neighbouring front door opens. It is Mrs Cheatham.

"Didn't you hear me banging?" she says.

"Scuse me," says Snotty, looking dumb.

"I've been banging on your wall."

"Oh, I don't mind," says Snotty. "I mean, some people might complain about neighbours banging on their wall, but it doesn't worry me. Honestly. Any time you want, Mrs Cheatham. Feel free. Shout and scream as well if you like . . ."

"I was shouting at *you*, you stupid boy," says Mrs Cheatham.

"Well, not very loud, 'cos I didn't hear it."

"No wonder! With all that noise in your house. It's gone on for weeks now. I don't know how your mother puts up with it."

"Oh, she likes it," says Snotty. "Anyway, I've got to go in. She's waiting for these things . . ."

Snotty takes out his front-door key, forgetting that the door is locked from the inside. When it doesn't open, he gives a bad-tempered knock. He has forgotten to give the special signal.

"Where is she then?" says Mrs Cheatham, stepping over smartly from her own front door. "Why isn't she answering, hmm?"

"She'll be working," says Snotty. "Look, you can see her up at her window."

"Huh," sniffs Mrs Cheatham, stepping back. Her long sight is not so good, but she can make out some sort of figure, which could well be Snotty's mother.

Close up, thanks to her reading spectacles, which she happens to be wearing, she can see perfectly well. She looks again at Snotty, appraising him all over, and notices how untidy and scruffy he is, even more so than usual. He also looks pale and unhealthy, with rather a lot of spots.

"How is your mother, anyway?" she asks. "I haven't seen her for weeks. She hasn't gone away, has she?"

"No, she's inside, I told you. She's fine. Well, she

had a bit of a lurgy . . ."

"A what?"

"You know, just a bit of flu really."

"And I suppose you've got it now. You don't look very well."

"Nothing wrong with me," says Snotty. "Look, you don't have to wait here. I can get in all right. My mum will be down in a minute to open the door. So thanks. Byee. Cheers. See you . . ."

"I just want a few words with your mother."

"I've told you, she's working."

At last, Snotty remembers the code that he created. He gives the correct sequence of knocks on the front door, then taps on the window. Someone can be heard unlocking the door from the inside.

"Oh, Mrs Cheatham," says Snotty, suddenly all polite and concerned. "I think that's your phone ringing."

While Mrs Cheatham leans back to listen at her own door, Snotty swiftly pushes open his door, sending Sluke, Jessie and Bessie flying. Snotty manages to get in before Mrs Cheatham can see the state of the house, catch a glimpse of what he has done to the stairs, or see what Sluke has done to the floorboards in the hall. While Snotty has been out, he has taken six of them up. That is the first obstacle, to catch Snotty. Sluke plans to win the ten-pound treasure.

Snotty hopes Mrs Cheatham will not have seen any of these changes. He slams the door quickly. Then he turns round and falls straight through a floorboard.

"You were silly, Snotty," says Jessie.

"Oh, yeh, blame me," says Snotty. "You sound just like my mum."

They are all sitting on the floor eating the chips and burgers bought by Snotty. As they finish each packet, they roll the debris into a ball and kick it up to the hole in the ceiling, trying to reach the bathroom. It's a new game Snotty has invented, which might or might not be included in the next Decathlon.

Around them, on the floor, is lined up an assortment of condiments – tomato ketchup, brown sauces, vinegars, mustards. Snotty's mother allows none of these into her house. She considers her meals good enough to stand on their own, with no need for extra seasoning. Besides, she can never bear to have such smells in her house. But at present it is not her house. Snotty is in charge.

Snotty takes a large bottle of tomato ketchup, gives it a good shake, then pours great dollops of it over his last chip.

"Let's see how far it can be fired," says Snotty. He lays the plastic sauce container at an angle on the floor, aiming it at the fridge door, and jumps on it. Sauce splurts right across the room, making a direct hit on the fridge.

"Yet another new game I've thought of," shouts Snotty. "I bet I could turn it into a TV panel game. What do you think, Sluke?"

"I think you've just ruined one of my treasure hunt

clues," says Sluke. "I wrote it on the fridge door. Now you won't be able to read it."

"Then we'll lick it off," says Snotty. "You should have thought of that one, Sluke. It could be an extra obstacle for your treasure hunt. Or my new TV game show . . ."

"Not a bad idea," says Sluke. "I've done a few sound clues. So we could have invented the world's first Audio Visual Tactile Treasure Hunt."

"Tactile?" says Snotty. "I don't want any tacks in my feet, or any tiles."

"You are silly," says Jessie. Both girls look rather shocked by Snotty's sauce-bottle game.

"Stop saying that," says Snotty. "I'll wipe the mess up before we play football again."

"I mean what you said to Mrs Cheatham," says Jessie. "You should have apologized the minute she started complaining. You should have promised to turn the noise down."

"Why?"

"To keep her quiet."

"I don't mind her noise, why should she mind my noise?"

"Well, she might report you."

"To who?"

"To whom," corrects Jessie.

"To whit?" says Snotty.

"To woo," says Sluke.

Snotty and Sluke start flapping round the room, pretending to be owls, convulsed by their own wit.

"She could report you to the Noise Abatement Society," says Bessie, when they have settled down again.

"Oh, you've really got me worried now," says Sluke.

"I'm well scared. Not sure I'll be able to do the treasure hunt for shaking."

Sluke and Snotty start laughing again, pretending to shake with fear.

"Did you never think of informing the police?" asks Jessie, quietly.

"You mean about our shakes?" says Snotty.

"About your mother."

"Why?"

"Anything could have happened to her," says Bessie.

"She's all right," says Snotty, sitting down. "Anyway, it's hush hush."

"How do you know?"

"I just know."

"But it's weeks since she disappeared," says Jessie. "Aren't you worried?"

"No, not really. She's been off on projects before. She once went for the night to film in Wigan."

"I can understand you not telling anyone at first," says Jessie, "thinking she might just be away for a few days. But I mean, all this time, it's a bit sort of spooky . . ."

"That's true, Snotty," says Bessie. "She could be in danger. She could have been kidnapped. Someone could be holding her, anywhere in the whole wide world . . ."

"She wrote me that note, didn't she?" says Snotty. "That shows she wasn't kidnapped. She went of her own free will."

"How do you know?"

"I just know. And she left me her purse and her credit cards for me to use. That's all worked out, hasn't it? No one's complained, so everything must be OK."

"That doesn't quite follow," says Bessie.

"If she went of her own free will," says Jessie, "why

didn't she take her purse and credit cards with her? Surely she would need them?"

"Not if she's gone with a friend," says Sluke.

"Who says she's gone with a friend?" says Snotty, quickly, glaring at Sluke.

"Nobody, just a suggestion," says Sluke.

"I'll make the suggestions about my mother," says Snotty. "Just you keep your long nose out of it . . ."

"Sorry," says Sluke.

"It is funny not having heard anything at all for weeks," says Jessie. "Not a letter or a card. That's if she is OK . . ."

"Look, so what if I tell the police she's missing?" says Snotty, suddenly getting angry. "So they come round here, right? They take over this house, strip it all down, looking for stupid clues. Then they lock it up empty, and stick me in a home or something. How does that help me? Or help you?"

"You're right, Snotty," says Sluke.

"I'm sure she is OK," says Bessie, "wherever she is."

"Come on," says Snotty. "Let's start the treasure hunt . . ."

In the middle of that night, round about one o'clock, when Snotty is in bed, exhausted after the treasure hunt, he begins to worry.

"Jessie was probably right about Mrs Cheatham after all," he thinks to himself. "Jessie's worse than my mum. She was always right."

Snotty rolls out of bed and looks round the room.

"Now where's my best felt pen? Who's pinched it?"

As he lives on his own, there are not many other people who can be blamed for pinching things. His bedroom is covered with old clothes, comics, magazines, video films, toys, games, bottles, cans, sweets, chocolates. Nothing has been tidied up or put away for the last couple of weeks.

"Who left all this junk here?" says Snotty, as he throws garments and toys around. His normal way of looking for something is to kick everything in the air, hoping the missing item will miraculously fall at his feet.

"Oh, I can't find those stupid pens. Well, she probably wouldn't be able to read my rotten handwriting anyway."

Snotty goes into the next room, his mother's office. This is the one room he has not dared to touch.

He switches on her word processor, her Amstrad PCW 9512, which she often used to let him play on. He puts in a disc, presses C for Create, and starts typing.

DEER MISSUS CHEATEM . . .

Snotty stops to think. Is she married? Was there ever a husband? She has lived next door for as long as Snotty can remember, but always on her own.

I AM SORRY ABAHT ALL THE NOYSE AND THAT BUT OWING TO ME NOT BEING QUITE IN THE PINK AS OF THIS MOMENT IN TIME MY SUN NOTTINGHAM MITE HAVE BEEN A BIT NOSIER THAN USUAL.

Snotty stops again. He wonders if he is capturing his mother's tone, or her wit. It doesn't sound quite like her.

WE HAVE HAD LORRA PANICS AND DRAMAS AND LURGIES RECENTLY! AS YOU MIGHT HAVE NOTICED. THERE HAS BEEN A LORRA BANGING – AND NOT ALL OF IT FROM YOU! BUT THIS WILL ALL STOP FOURTH WIT. I PROMISE. NOTTINGHAM IS VERY WELL AND SO AM I VERY WELL AND I HOPE YOU ARE.
YOURS SINCERELY,
ZOE BUMSTEAD.

Snotty has written this letter very quickly, letting his

inspiration have full flow, knowing there will probably be a few spellings that are not quite right. Spelling has never been his best subject. In fact he never has had a best subject.

"Now, does sincerely begin with a c or an s?"

Snotty is not too worried, as he knows his mother's machine has a spell check. He studies the keys, looking for the appropriate symbol, but can't find it. He presses a few knobs, but nothing happens, so he goes back to the Menu, to see the list of possible things he can do next.

Onto the screen comes the headline ZAMBEZI, followed by a list of words. Snotty can read Livingstone, Victoria Falls, Tanzania, but none of it makes sense to him.

"What was she writing all this for?" thinks Snotty. "Isn't that a river somewhere? Or is it the name of some lousy jazz record? Huh. Potty."

Snotty yawns, and remembers it is the middle of the night. He has vowed to be on time for school this week, just to show any suspicious teachers that he is being well looked after.

He brings back his letter to Mrs Cheatham onto the screen, then presses P for Printing. When it has been printed, he puts it neatly in an envelope and goes outside to shove it through Mrs Cheatham's letter box. Then he goes back to bed.

12

Snotty is walking along his street, another school day over, another A for an excellent History essay.

He ducks down as he passes Mrs Cheatham's front window, in case she is looking out for him, then quickly runs up the steps to his own front door. There he stops, looking alarmed.

"Someone has been trying to get in," thinks Snotty.

To an ordinary passer-by, all looks normal. Snotty opened the shutters before he left for school, so that no one might think the house is empty. He only has them closed during football matches.

There are no milk bottles on the step. Snotty paid the bill and cancelled the milk straight away. Snotty hates milk. There are no newspapers sticking out of the letter box, another sign which might attract nosy parkers. Snotty cancelled them as well. He collects the comics that are his only reading matter.

"My chewing gum has gone," thinks Snotty.

He always puts a very small piece in the keyhole, where the Chubb lock goes, before he leaves for school.

"Ah, here it is on the ground. Someone has been trying their own key, or someone's been banging on the door and made it fall out."

He opens the door carefully. The hall seems OK,

much as usual. Sluke was made to put back the floor-boards after the treasure hunt. The staircase looks the same, inviting as ever, the slide ready to be used.

Then he sees on the hall floor an official-looking post-card, the address in red, from Camden Borough Council.

Snotty picks it up, smells it, turns it over and reads it.

I have called twice today and been unable to gain entry.
Could you please ring me at this number.
Yours Faithfully
  M. PRATT TEAM LEADER

"Hmm, now what can this mean."

He looks worried at first, then his face breaks into a smile.

"It must be for the Camden Under-Thirteen football team! I've been picked at last! The Team Leader wants me. My brilliance has been recognized."

Snotty is still feeling pleased with himself when Sluke arrives, followed not long afterwards by Bessie and Jessie.

All three of them have done their homework first, and had their tea, though that does not stop them offering to help Snotty to finish off an ice-cream cake from Marine Ices, one of their specials.

Snotty announces that he has been saving it – "because this is a special occasion."

"What's happened?" says Sluke. "You've had a bath?"

"You've cleaned the fridge," says Jessie.

"I've been spotted in the school playground," muses Snotty, hardly listening to their jokes. "I wouldn't be surprised if the playground is full of scouts tomorrow."

"You're not joining the Boy Scouts, are you?" says Bessie. "We used to be in the Brownies."

"Only for half an hour," says Jessie.

"I'm certainly not signing for Arsenal," continues Snotty. "Load of rubbish. It's Spurs or nothing."

"I wouldn't try signing anything," says Jessie, "not with your handwriting."

"*Come on you Spurs!*" chants Snotty, running round the room, taking imaginary shots. "*Snott-ee, Snott-ee, Snott-ee, Born is the Ki-ing of Whi-ite Hart Lane!*"

"What is he on about?" says Sluke, turning over the pages of the *Dandy* and *Beano*, both of which he has read five times already.

"Our indoor pitch," says Snotty. "That's what's done it. That's why I've improved so much in the last couple of weeks. If my mum had only let me do it yonks ago, I would be playing for Spurs already."

"Who says you're going to play for them?" asks Bessie.

"Read this," says Snotty, throwing her the card. "The invitation is not actually from Spurs, not at the moment. It's from the team boss of Camden. But it's the beginning of the Big Time. *Wem-ber-lee, Wem-ber-lee . . .*"

Jessie picks up the card.

"It's from Camden Social Services. I recognize the address. We once went there about Meals on Wheels for our Gran."

Snotty looks slightly puzzled for a second, but soon recovers his good humour.

"So I don't mind playing for Camden Social Services First Eleven. I'm not proud. The Team Leader wants me, that's what matters. *We hate Nottingham Forest . . .*"

"*We hate Nottingham Bumstead . . .*" starts Sluke in reply.

Snotty grabs him round the waist in a pretend rugby tackle.

"Gerroff, man," says Sluke. "If you're gonna play for Spurs, you'll have to get used to rival fans shouting nasty things at you."

They roll over and over, then come to a halt in front of the fridge, banging against it so that the door opens and several cans fall out.

"Half-time," says Snotty, opening a drink.

"A Team Leader is just someone in charge of a team of Social Workers," explains Jessie.

"Yeh, but it must be pretty important," says Sluke, "if a Team Leader wants to see you."

"I wonder why," asks Bessie.

"Perhaps that woman next door has informed on you," says Jessie. "I said you should have been nice to her."

"I'm always nice, to everyone," says Snotty. "Anyway, clever clogs, I took your advice. I wrote her a letter this morning, really creeping to her."

"You wrote it?" asks Jessie.

"Yeh, but from my mum, of course. I'm not that stupid."

"That's it then," says Jessie. "That explains everything."

"I don't think you should have done that, Snotty," says Sluke, shaking his head.

"So what? I don't care."

"You will," says Jessie. "If you get put in care."

"Why should that happen?"

"That's what they do," says Jessie, "if they find out you have been abandoned."

"I haven't been abandoned," says Snotty. "Don't be daft."

"Or they put you in an orphanage," adds Bessie.

"I won't go," says Snotty.

"You would have to," says Jessie. "They have a lot of power, Social Workers. If they decide you're loony, they can put you in a place for loonies. They issue a certificate for you, and that's it."

"You mean like a GCSE?" asks Snotty.

"It's not funny," says Jessie.

"If they say your parents can't look after you," says Bessie, "they can just take you away from your parents."

"But I'm better off here than anywhere else," says

Snotty. "I'm not in any harm, and I'm not harming anyone."

"Tell that to the Social Worker," says Jessie.

"Get lost. I'm not letting no Social Worker into this house."

The phone rings and they all jump.

"Don't move!" shouts Snotty. "Nobody is to answer that phone."

They sit in silence while the answering machine clicks on, playing the old message from Snotty's mother. After a few minutes, Snotty switches on the play-back, to see if anyone has left a message.

"I'm sorry you are still out, Mrs Bumstead," says a brisk female voice. "It is Marion Pratt here, Social Services, Area Seven. According to certain information we have received, it is most important that I talk to you and your son. If I am unable to gain entry to your house in the next twenty-four hours, I may be forced to use certain legal powers at my disposal. However, if you could suggest a time when we could all have a little chat, then I should be most obliged. You have my card. Ring me as soon as possible. Thank you."

"Cheeky beggar," says Snotty. "Who does she think she is? I'm not seeing her."

"You'll have to, in the end," says Bessie.

"The best thing is to put it off as long as possible," says Jessie. "She said twenty-four hours. Let's make it a bit longer. Why don't you tell her to come at the end of the week, on Friday? Say your mum might be back by then . . ."

"Hmm," says Snotty.

"Then on Friday, just be polite, and say she's had to pop out somewhere."

"Ugh," says Snotty.

"Tell you what," says Jessie. "I'll write a little note on your mum's machine. My spelling is much better than yours."

"What will you say?" says Snotty.

"Something simple. 'Thank you for your note. Sorry I was out. Please come here at six o'clock on Friday.' That's all."

"Ohhh," groans Snotty.

"Better than the police breaking the door down and carting you off," says Jessie.

Snotty is in the bath, his first for over two weeks, and his last, so he maintains.

There is only half an hour to go before Mrs Pratt arrives, not long to wipe away so much dirt, dust, grime, left-over food, dribbles of endless sweet drinks and tomato ketchup stains.

"Good job we had this bath mended," says Sluke.

"I'm getting out now," shouts Snotty.

"Oh, no, you're not!" Sluke's hand appears over the side of the bath and pushes Snotty down.

"Pig," says Snotty, sliding into the water again.

Sluke is on his back, rolling to and fro on Snotty's jeans, trying to press them. Snotty, of course, gave his mother's iron away.

"This isn't gonna work," says Sluke. "But at least they're clean. I washed them myself."

"If they're still wet, I'm not putting them on."

"Didn't you have a sailor suit when you were little?" says Sluke. "I'm sure I remember it. Be good if you put it on. Mrs Pratt would be very impressed."

"Up your bum," says Snotty.

"No need to be rude – and remember that when Mrs Pratt is here! Right, out you get, my boy," commands Sluke. "There's a good dog."

Sluke has a big bath towel ready.

On top of the snooker table, which is now lying on the floor, Sluke has also lined up baby lotion, talcum powder and assorted potions.

"You're not drying me," snarls Snotty.

"Well, can I trust you?" says Sluke. "You have to be all lovely and fresh and smelling nice for Mrs Pratt. You know it's our only chance of keeping you out of the nick."

"Get lost," says Snotty.

"Nope," says Sluke. "I'm staying here, to watch you dry yourself properly."

"Did you buy all this stuff?" asks Snotty, wrapping the towel round himself.

"Yup," says Sluke. "I got them all on your mother's account at Patel's. We want you to smell sweetly . . ."

"Any Daddy's Sauce, or HP? Those are the aromas I'd prefer."

"Don't mess around," says Sluke. "You've got to look as if you've been cared for. You know it makes scents. Gerrit?"

"That's very good," says Snotty. "For you. OK, I'll have the Lily of the Valley, that one over there. Give it to me . . ."

Sluke leans over to get it. Immediately Snotty dashes past him out of the bathroom, still wrapped in his towel, on which he slides down the stairs.

Jessie and Bessie are working hard, scrubbing and rubbing, washing and sploshing, cleaning and clearing the football pitch.

"Get out!" they both shout as Snotty arrives, clutching his towel round him. "Don't come in here dripping water."

They have managed to get the worst of the marks off the walls, put back the rugs, the paintings and the sofas in their proper places. The kitchen unit has been unboarded, though it still looks rather battered, after being hit so often by a football and kicked by angry feet.

"You haven't found an iron, have you?" says Sluke, coming into the room with Snotty's jeans.

"Out! We're still cleaning in here."

"You sound like my mum," says Snotty.

Sluke puts the jeans neatly on the floor, then goes out into the back garden.

"We've forgotten the ceiling," exclaims Jessie, looking up. "She's bound to notice it."

"Oh, no," moans Bessie. "Can't we disguise it, paint it or something?"

"You can't paint over a hole," says Snotty.

"Then cover it with a carpet or something."

"You don't have carpets on the ceiling," says Jessie.

"It could be a new fashion," says Snotty. "That would impress her."

Through the back door, Sluke can be seen pushing an old garden roller. He gets it into the kitchen, then rolls it backwards and forwards over Snotty's jeans.

"What *are* you doing, you stupid fool?" shouts Jessie. "That roller's filthy. Look at the mess. You've ruined the floor as well as Snotty's jeans."

Sluke stops, staring down at the mess he's made. Slowly, he wheels the roller back into the garden.

"Now what am I going to wear?" says Snotty. "That's my only pair of jeans."

"You *must* have another pair," says Jessie.

"Nope, nothing."

When Sluke reappears Bessie and Jessie jump on him. Together they pull off his trousers, leaving him in his underpants.

"Gerroff, stoppit, ouch," yells Sluke. "I've heard about girls like you."

Sluke slinks into a corner, crossing his legs and trying to hide the fact that he is wearing old-fashioned Y-fronts, rather baggy, once worn by his father.

"Oh, stop moaning, Sluke," says Jessie. "It's all your fault Snotty's pants are ruined. He'll have to wear your jeans now."

"But what about me?"

"It doesn't matter what you wear," says Bessie. "You're not meeting the Social Worker."

"Here, put these on," says Jessie, throwing Sluke's trousers at Snotty. "Go and get dressed properly. And make sure your other clothes are clean."

"I can't wear these," says Snotty. "They're about ten sizes too big for me."

146

Jessie pulls out a large pair of scissors from a kitchen drawer. Carefully she cuts three feet off each leg of Sluke's jeans.

"Oh no!" shouts Sluke. "My mum will kill me. What am I gonna do now?"

"No need to worry," says Jessie. "When the Social Worker's been, you can have them back."

"They're ruined now. What will I tell my mum?"

"Just say you got savaged by a Rottweiler," says Snotty, disappearing up the ladder.

"Look, shut up and put these on," Bessie says, handing Sluke a pair of lime green floral shorts, belonging to Snotty's mother.

"That ladder," says Jessie, still cleaning up. "It does look a bit funny."

"And the hole in the ceiling," says Bessie. "It's sort of weird."

"Mrs Pratt will think the place is falling down."

"And those walls still look scruffy," says Bessie.

"Mrs Pratt will think no one is caring for the house."

"Then she'll think no one is caring for Snotty," says Bessie. "Hmm."

"We'll have to use the upstairs room instead," says Jessie. "Snotty's mother always took visitors there."

"Come on, Sluke," says Bessie. "We'll have to move quickly. All those pinball machines and stuff will have to be shifted."

They go into the hall, then stop. They had forgotten their major refurbishment. The stairs are impassable. "No one could climb that," says Sluke. "Unless they use ice picks or crampons."

"Mrs Pratt will have to use the ladder," says Bessie, "and squeeze through the hole in the ceiling like we do."

They all look at each other, frowning and shaking their heads.

"Hammer, screwdriver, plyers, Sluke," announces Jessie, briskly. "We'll have to take down the whole slide."

"We've only got an hour before she comes," says Bessie.

"As long as Snotty keeps out of the way," says Jessie, "we should make it."

"I heard that," shouts Snotty from the top of the house. "Someone come and help me on with my sailor suit . . ."

13

"How long do you think your mother will be, Nottingham?" asks Mrs Pratt.

She is sitting in the posh drawing-room on the best sofa. Bessie and Jessie dragged it up from the basement at the last moment. It is not quite as dust-free as it might be.

"Long?"

"How long. Your mother?"

"She's taller than me," mutters Snotty, "but not as tall as Sluke, but then he's really tall . . ."

"I mean how long before she returns?"

"Not long, she's just popped out. Sorry about that. Would you like some tea?"

"Oh, that would be very nice," says Mrs Pratt, getting up. "Let me help."

Snotty pushes her back into her seat.

"I can manage," says Snotty. "My mother has left *a tray*. I'll just go downstairs and get the *tray*."

He shouts out the word *tray*. This was the signal for the girls to get it ready.

"Lovely," says Mrs Pratt, getting quickly to her feet the second Snotty leaves the room.

She moves very quickly, for a large woman, rushing to examine the mantelpiece for any cards or invitations,

then to the desk for any letters.

Mrs Pratt is just about to open a drawer when she feels Snotty's hand on her arm.

"Don't let it go cold," says Snotty.

"Goodness, that was quick," says Mrs Pratt, moving across the room to sit down in the easy chair.

On a little table beside her chair Snotty has placed a huge tray of cakes, scones, biscuits, little vol-au-vents and an apple tart. Jessie and Bessie have been sitting outside the drawing-room door with the tray.

All of the cakes and goodies have been bought at
Marks and Spencer, but Jessie has carefully taken them
out of their containers. She has cut them into odd shapes
and sizes and put them on Snotty's mother's best Portug-
uese plates, so that they look home-made.

"Goodness, this is a treat, I don't usually eat in the
afternoon. You didn't bake these, did you?"

Mrs Pratt watches Snotty carefully.

"No way," says Snotty.

Mrs Pratt smiles.

"My mum did them," says Snotty. "This afternoon."

"Your mother did? She must be a very clever
woman."

"Huh," said Snotty.

"I understand she runs her own business, and looks
after you, all by herself."

"Hmm."

"What is her business?"

"Dunno, really," says Snotty. "She sort of writes
things. I think. And answers the telephone. She does a

lot of that."

"Do you have any relations living nearby?"

"No, have you?"

"Oh quite a few, actually," says Mrs Pratt, looking at some notes. "And of course you have a very kind neighbour next door. She presumably keeps an eye on you, hmm, I mean an eye on things? Mrs Cheatham, I see . . ."

"That old bat," snarls Snotty. "If she's been telling you things . . ."

"What sort of things might she tell us, hmm?"

"Load of lies, probably."

"Oh, that's not kind," says Mrs Pratt, taking another cake.

"Haven't you finished yet?" says Snotty, rather rudely.

"Not quite, my dear."

"Ugh," grunts Snotty. He hates being called "my dear", almost as much as "darling", or "love", or, worst of all, "petal".

"Your mother is a long time," says Mrs Pratt.

"Spose you'll want some more tea," sighs Snotty, grudgingly.

"It's a most interesting room," says Mrs Pratt, taking more tea. "I do like the one-armed bandit machines."

"They're my mum's," says Snotty. "She collects them."

"And the Space Invaders?"

"She collects them as well. She collects funny things, my mum. Now, haven't you had enough tea, eh?"

"Actually, I must use your bathroom," says Mrs Pratt, suddenly standing up.

"You can't do that," says Snotty very quickly.

"Why not? Haven't you got one?"

"Yeh, but someone's in it."

"Your mother, perhaps?" says Mrs Pratt, smiling.

"Yeh, I mean, no. It's broken, see. We're waiting for workmen."

"I'm sure I can still use it," says Mrs Pratt.

Before Snotty can stop her, Mrs Pratt pushes him aside and marches out of the drawing-room.

Mrs Pratt opens the first door on the right, which happens to be the bathroom. She is just in time to see Sluke disappearing through a hole in the floor.

"Good gracious!" exclaims Mrs Pratt, letting out a

little scream. "Who was that?"

"Dunno," mumbles Snotty, following after her. "Perhaps you imagined it."

"It looked like a boy in rather outlandish clothing to me."

"Well, you probably know more about that than I do."

"What *do* you mean by that, pray?"

"I mean you're a Social Worker, yeh. You know all about loopy people, don't you. And you go around stealing boys, don't you, giving them certificates and that, really rotten, if you ask me. I dunno what the Government's coming to, allowing people like you . . ."

"What are you babbling about?" says Mrs Pratt. "I distinctly saw a youth going through that floor."

"Oh, yeh, him," says Snotty. "He's part of the building firm. I know, it's terrible. They use slave labour these days. It's worse than sending them up chimneys. It's exploitation. You should be investigating that, instead of coming round here, keeping innocent people away from their homework. I gotta lot to do, see. So if you've finished, then I must get back to my work, if you don't mind . . ."

Back in the drawing-room Mrs Pratt picks up her files. She looks at her watch, thinking hard.

"Your mother *is* a long time," says Mrs Pratt. "I don't think I can wait much longer."

"Good," says Snotty. "I mean, OK, fine, yeh, whatever . . ."

"That was a nice tea," says Mrs Pratt. "And you do seem to be doing well. I tell you what. I'll just give it five more minutes."

They sit in silence. Snotty has tried his best to be charming so far, but he decides now the quickest way to get rid of her is to say nothing.

The five minutes are almost up when the phone rings.

"Don't answer it!" says Snotty.

Mrs Pratt looks bemused. Snotty stays silent.

"Oh, I see," says Mrs Pratt. "That must be the answering machine I keep hearing. It's always the same old message, I've noticed."

"Ugh."

"If you're here, why don't you answer it?"

"S'boring," says Snotty. "It's always for my mum."

The phone continues to ring. They both stare at it. Snotty is willing it to stop. Mrs Pratt is trying to work out what it all means.

The answering machine is on the phone downstairs. Upstairs, the phone is just an extension. All the same, thinks Snotty, it should stop ringing when the answering machine takes over. For once, he must have forgotten to switch it on. At last, it stops ringing.

"Snotty," shouts a male voice, booming up from the bottom of the stairs.

Snotty pretends at first not to hear, but the shout is repeated. He knows it is Sluke, putting on an adult voice. Slowly, he walks to the drawing-room door.

"Whatcha want?" shouts Snotty, wearily.

"It's your mum on the phone," replies Sluke.

Mrs Pratt picks up the phone in a flash, before Snotty can get to it.

"Hello, Mrs Bumstead," says Mrs Pratt, smiling. "Is it Nottingham you want?"

"Please," says Snotty's mother.

"Are you all right, by the way?" asks Mrs Pratt.

"Of course. Just got a bit delayed at Victoria . . ."

"Give us it," says Snotty, snatching the phone. "Mum?"

He puts the question suspiciously, convinced it is one of Sluke's electronic tricks.

He listens carefully, looking first worried, then puzzled. It is all very strange. He can clearly hear his mother's voice, if a bit faint.

"Just got a few seconds," says his mother cheerfully. "We're going back on the river now. Then we're setting off home. Should be with you in a couple of days. I'm fine, everything's fine. Look after yourself and I hope you're having fun. Love you . . ."

The phone goes dead. Snotty turns to Mrs Pratt, looking even more confused. It definitely sounded like his
mother, but where is she?

Mrs Pratt, still smiling, is picking up her briefcase.

"Well, that was a lovely tea. I don't think I need come
back for a while."

"Ugh," says Snotty.

"But perhaps next time I may have the pleasure of
meeting your mother . . ."

"Ugh," grunts Snotty. "You'll be lucky."

Snotty follows Mrs Pratt down the stairs and sees her
out of the front door.

"Look, I've told you every word," says Snotty.

The four of them are all downstairs, arguing over
what's left of the cakes and biscuits.

"Where was she ringing from?" asks Sluke.

"I dunno," says Snotty. "Timbuctoo, for all I know."

"Has she got business in Timbuctoo?" asks Sluke.

"Do you want thumped," says Snotty, glaring at him.

"No, just thanks," says Sluke, "for picking up the
rotten phone."

"If I find out it was you, Sluke . . ."

"No, honestly, I recognized her voice as well."

"That's brilliant news," says Jessie. "It means she's
safe and well, so we don't have to tell the police."

"And it means you won't be bothered by Mrs Pratt,"
says Bessie.

"Yes, but she'll have to make a report," says Jessie.
"That's what they have to do. And she'll probably come
again in a week or so. I know their sort."

"But Snotty's mum will be back by then," says Bessie,
cheerfully.

"Anyway, it means we can carry on living here," says
Sluke. "I mean *you* can carry on living here, till she
comes home. And that means we can carry on visiting
you . . ."

"Well, I don't really know what it means," says
Snotty.

"I do," says Jessie. "It means two-a-side. Me and Bess
will play you two. Close the shutters. Barricade the sink.
The winner finishes off the rest of the cakes . . ."

LONDON BOROUGH OF CAMDEN
SOCIAL WORKER'S REPORT SHEET
(strictly confidential)

Department of Social Services

Name of person or family *Nottingham Bumstead*

S.W. name: *M. Pratt (Team Leader)*

Internal Memo: To all Members of the Team.

See files, A. Cheatham (Mrs), and observations.

I visited Nottingham Bumstead today at his home and had a fruitful talk with him, and with his mother (tho' this was on the phone). The arrangement of the house seemed slightly odd, e.g. large hole in bathroom floor, strange workman only partly clothed, but the house appeared clean and organized. I partook of tea. The boy seemed healthy and well cared for, co-operative enough, as much as they ever are at that age, and appeared not to be in any moral or physical danger. However, I suggest that a member of the team makes a visit once a month, as a precautionary measure, just to cover ourselves, as I suspect there is something unusual going on, viz. his mother's absence.

YAOUNDE

HILTON

Hi, Snotty, my petal! Got delayed and still in Africa. Am now in Cameroon. No, they don't speak Scottish here, ha ha. Sorry phone call so short, but will try again, some time. The job's going well, really exciting, will tell you all soon. Hope you get special tickets for Spurs I have arranged to be sent to you. Look after the house, look after my credit cards, and make sure you don't lose them, dum dum, and most of all, look after your silly self. Lots of love, from your silly . . . *Mum*

SNOTTY BUMSTEAD
AND THE RENT-A-MUM

To Fred and Edward,
my Carlisle United Friends

I

Snotty and the Milkman

I

It had been one of those long boring days which schools specialize in: non days, in which nothing happens. Each hour, each minute, each second lasted for ever, so it seemed to Snotty, but now that it was over the day was slowly sinking out of sight, ready to join all those other millions and trillions and squillions of school days from the past which have all been forgotten.

"Going, going, going . . ." said Snotty to himself, closing his eyes. He had left the noise and squalor of Camden High Street and was nearing the quieter, more dignified if rather run-down terrace where he lived. It was part of his ritual every Friday, when another week was in the bag, down time's plughole, to close his eyes on the home stretch, walk with one foot in the gutter and at the same time swing his Spurs bag round his body. This was to ward off any creatures from outer space who might be about to fly down and attack him, any beasts from under the earth who might be about to rise up and eat him or, most horrible of all, any stupid

Arsenal fans who might be lying in wait with a leg outstretched.

Two monster Fourth-Year youths, each about seven feet high, shaven heads, boots the size of goal posts, with six bellies between them, appeared across Snotty's path. They looked like giant whales, out searching for plankton, or First Years, whichever might be the smaller. Snotty froze, then melted into the gutter, disappearing out of sight, or so he hoped. They sailed on, oblivious of minor plant life, attending only to their Walkmen.

"I bet they're on steroids," thought Snotty. "Or double All Bran. If only their brains had grown as much as their bodies."

He never said this sort of thing to their faces at school, not being daft, not wanting to provoke them. Snotty's aim in the playground was to keep a profile so low that he would appear flat and therefore non-existent, part of the tarmac landscape.

That afternoon, at break, three even bigger, cleverer, smarter kids, all Sixth Formers, had grabbed him in a corridor and cross-examined him about "accommodation possibilities". Snotty had acted dumb, saying nothing, managing to wriggle out of their sight and into his own classroom.

Miss Eager, his class teacher, she'd also been a pain all day. She'd said his work sheets were messy, his homework late once again, but he was not unduly worried. He was beginning to feel he could deal with her. Deep down, it was obvious, she quite liked him. So Snotty liked to think. Anyway, tonight he would get Sluke to do his homework for him, in his best joined-up writing. Sluke owed Snotty a few favours. Probably ten thousand, at the last count.

Mrs Potter was more of a worry. She was Head of St Andrew's Road Comprehensive and a very busy woman, running a school with fourteen hundred pupils and one hundred staff. Or was it the other way round? Snotty could never remember. Compared with his primary school, it was like being in a jungle.

"Dunno why she's after me," said Snotty to himself, still swinging his bag. "If I was Head, I'd be too busy bossing around one hundred staff. I wouldn't be bothered with any of the boring pupils."

Snotty had met Mrs Potter's secretary just as he was leaving the school gates. She had asked him about his mum: was she OK, was she in good health? Snotty knew the secretary by sight, but he had always assumed she could not possibly know him. Had he not kept his head down for almost two terms? She must be secret police, or a witch. What a cheek! Asking about his mum. She'd actually stood in front of him, waiting for his reply. He'd given her his usual mumbles, put on his best glazed look. It appeared to satisfy her.

Slowly and surely, as Snotty reached his own street, all the aggravations of the school week began to disappear. Very soon his other life would take over. His lovely house, arranged for his pleasure. His lovely evening meal, also arranged for his pleasure, when and how he liked it. It was a secret world, known to nobody at school. Apart from Sluke, his best friend, and of course Bessie and Jessie, his other best friends. No one else knew about Snotty's secret life. As far as Snotty was aware. If anyone ever found out, that would be it.

"Going, going, going," repeated Snotty, still to himself, his eyes closed, carefully counting out his footsteps.

"GONE!" yelled Snotty.

He gave a final twirling, whirling swing to his bag, sending it as far above his head as possible. This was a sign that he had at last banished for ever the moans and groans, the slings and arrows of another draggy week. He was on home territory.

At once he could feel his body relaxing, his mind easing, his face, if only just, taking on its smiling mode. At school, Snotty liked to think he offered a blank face to the world. He believed no one in authority knew he existed. He was a spy, going under cover, trying not to register on their consciousness. Now he was about to become a real human being once again.

There was a strange sensation of weightlessness in his arms. This was unusual, not his normal Friday coming-home feeling. Had some form of extrasensory perception taken over, now that he had thrown away the shackles of the day? He opened his eyes, trying to work it out, looking up into the heavens. His precious Spurs bag had totally disappeared.

"Oh, bloody hell."

"Language!" said Mrs Cheatham, his next-door neighbour, hurrying past him, giving a little shudder as if not wanting to associate with him, but a few steps ahead she paused, unable to resist another chance to tell him off.

"Yes, you are observant," sneered Snotty to himself. "I was using language. Not talking Algebra. Or talking Basic. Have a house point."

Mrs Cheatham glared at him, not quite understanding what he'd said, then she marched on, disappearing up the steps into her own house.

The street appeared deserted. No sign of people, or of his bag. Snotty looked in the gutter, just in case anyone might be crouching there, such as Arsenal fans, the gutter being their natural home, ha ha, he said to himself, without smiling.

At the other end of the street, Snotty noticed that the milkman had parked his float half on the pavement. Mrs Cheatham was usually alert to this crime, getting up petitions, considering it a hanging offence, but today she had missed it.

Snotty narrowed his eyes. Only that day, he'd learned in biology that this does help you to see better, thanks to the retina letting in more light, or is it more dark. Anyway, by straining both eyes he could clearly see that hanging from the top of the milk float's frame was his Spurs bag. It must have twirled itself round the strut, while his eyes were closed; then the float must have moved off silently, being electrically powered, without him hearing it.

"Give us back my stuff!" shouted Snotty.

He'd raced down the street and had now shoved his head angrily into the milk float.

"Excuse me," said the milkman vacantly, without looking up, sucking a pencil and studying his order book.

"I want it back at once!" Snotty was in a mild temper tantrum, the sort he'd often had when he was little, stamping both his little feet.

"Did I hear shouting?" said the milkman calmly, still writing.

"Your stupid milk van has stolen my bag!"

"Try a citizen's arrest," said the milkman. "Feel free to take my milk float into custody if you must, but I'd be obliged if you could wait till I've finished this round, if you don't mind."

"My rotten bag, it's caught up in the top of your thingy, and I can't get it down," said Snotty.

"I suppose we could wait," said the milkman, putting down his pencil, "till you've grown big enough to get it down by yourself, but that might mean a long wait, perhaps for ever . . ."

"Ha ha," said Snotty. That was the sort of infantile remark he had to put up with from Fourth Years all day long, the sort of cheap jibes he didn't expect from an adult, or someone pretending to be an adult. The milkman had always appeared a bit stupid to Snotty, though his mother had always liked him.

"So what happened, Snotty, my petal?" said the milkman smiling. "Tell it slowly. In words of one syllabub . . ."

"I was coming home from school, right, minding my own business, right, my eyes were closed, right, no no, not closed, I was just finking, yeh, working out this stupid homework we have to do, when all of a sudden . . . *ouch!*"

The milk float had moved forward, suddenly but silently, almost running over Snotty's right foot, his best foot, the one with which he had scored fifteen indoor goals (and that was only last night's match).

"Stop messing around," yelled Snotty, running to keep up with the float. "You've got my bag. Up there. Look!"

In his mirror, the milkman looked where Snotty was pointing. He stopped the float and got out.

"Why didn't you tell me the single most vital, most mega, most sonic, most stratospheric fact about your bag, you dum dum . . ."

"What's that?" asked Snotty, as the milkman stretched up and got down his bag.

"*Tott-ing-ham, Tott-ing-ham!*"

The milkman was swinging Snotty's bag above his head and going through a selection of Spurs chants, as heard on the terraces, some of them not repeatable in respectable company. Snotty could see the imprint of Mrs Cheatham's upturned nose, flat and squashy and wrinkled, as she watched from behind the net curtain of her basement window.

"If only you'd told me you were a Spurs fan," said the milkman, handing Snotty his bag and getting back into his milk float.

"Thanks," said Snotty.

"No problem," said the milkman, driving away. Then he slowed down and stuck his head out.

"But there could be one problem for you," he continued. "I haven't been paid for three weeks. If I don't get the money tomorrow, you could be for it, my lad . . ."

Oh no, thought Snotty, just as things were going so well, just as he was looking forward to a great weekend, just as he was about to get safely inside his own house.

If he couldn't pay the milkman's money, his Big Secret would come out. Then Snotty's world might totally collapse . . .

2

It was 29–29 in the Spurs-Arsenal final. Snotty had scored all the goals for Spurs so far, and taken every throw in, free kick and penalty. He had organized the tactics and made every refereeing decision. Well, it was his game, his pitch, his house. Jessie, the only other member of his team, who was playing goalie, felt pleased to be on his side, as they were bound to win. They usually did. Snotty was also in charge of the score.

Around the walls he had chalked up previous scores, going back now for weeks and weeks.

Sluke and Bessie were playing for Arsenal, and doing very well, considering that Bessie was really a Spurs fan, and considering the odds stacked against them, such as Snotty's habit of creating new rules when it suited him.

"Off the fridge counts as in," shouted Snotty, watching his own shot bounce off three walls, hit the fridge and sneak under Bessie's body. He then did a lap of triumph round the whole of the pitch, cheering himself all the way.

While he was still celebrating, Sluke got the ball, dribbled up field, and took a shot at Jessie. He stubbed his toe on a floorboard, sending the ball straight up in the air, but by luck he managed to collect it when it bounced down, despite not wearing his spectacles, and hammered it in.

"That hit the ceiling," yelled Snotty, as Sluke went off on his own lap of honour. "No goal."

"You said the ceiling was part of the field of play," protested Sluke, a tall, thin, gangling boy. He threw himself down on the floor, saying he was fed up with Snotty changing the rules.

"Yeh, but not that part of the ceiling," said Snotty. "Put your specs on, Four Eyes. You hit that rose thingy."

This was an elaborate piece of plasterwork in the middle of the ceiling, highly decorated, part of the original Victorian house. Snotty was not worried about doing it any artistic damage. The problem was that bits of it were now starting to fall, getting in people's eyes, such as Snotty's, when he was about to score.

"OK then, I'll count that as in," said Snotty. "As I'm in a good mood. That's thirty-thirty. Half-time. We'll have the refreshments now."

Sluke got up off the floor at once and opened the fridge. All it contained were cans of Coke, filling every shelf. He handed out two to each player, then three to himself, as he was extra exhausted.

"Ah, this is the life," said Snotty.

"Wish we had a pitch like this," said Sluke.

"Wish we had a house like this," said Jessie.

"Wish we had a pitch *and* a house like this," said Bessie.

The whole ground floor of Snotty's house had been converted into an indoor football pitch, all furniture and carpets removed, all paintings taken from the walls and, while play was in progress, all windows shuttered from the inside. The kitchen sink had been boarded up and the freezer and the dishwasher put in the basement. Snotty no longer needed to wash dishes, or wash anything. "When all you eat is take-away, all you do is throw-away." That was one of Snotty's favourite new sayings.

Only the fridge had been retained, and proved very useful. Not just for emergency rations but for shooting practice when Snotty was on his own, waiting for the others to come round for their evening match.

The ground floor had been made open-plan many years ago by his mother, which was fortunate, but Snotty had had to organize a bit of extra building work, enlarging the gap between the kitchen and the living room. Sluke had done that, being bigger and marginally stronger than Snotty, but Snotty had provided the hammer, plus instructions, comments, jeers.

"Just gonna play a few machines," said Jessie, getting up, still holding her Cokes.

"Yeh, think I'll listen to something groovy," said Bessie.

Jessie went upstairs to the first floor which had been completely rearranged as a GAMES area, filled with Space Invaders, computer games, video games, electronic toys and remote-controlled cars. There was also a large snooker room which had previously been a bathroom, Snotty's mother's pride and joy. The bath had been covered over with a snooker table. Snotty no longer had baths, and intended never to have one again, so there was no need to have an old-fashioned, stupid, pointless bathroom.

The top floor was devoted to MUSIC: either listening to it, with the help of stereos, jukeboxes, CD players and endless loudspeakers, or trying to create music. Snotty had bought an electric guitar, mail-order of course, and a large drum kit, also mail-order. So far, he had still not managed to put the drum kit together.

"Come on down, you two," shouted Snotty. "Winning goal."

"You said it was half-time," said Sluke. "That means we should play the same length of time as the first half. If we're just playing to the winning goal, that means we'll be finished in no time."

"Don't be a pavement," said Snotty.

"I think you mean pedant," said Sluke.

"I mean pavement," said Snotty. "Just right for jumping on." Which he did, landing on Sluke's back. They rolled over on the floor.

"Oh, no, it's not wrestling now, is it?" said Bessie.

"Right, it's our turn to be strikers," said Jessie, picking up the ball. "You two are goalies, when you've stopped messing around."

Sluke and Snotty finished their wrestling, then got up and went in goals, cheering on their respective strike forces. Bessie scored first, putting Arsenal in the lead, and therefore the winners, but Snotty changed the rules yet again, saying it was first to forty.

They played for another hour, finishing with the score fifty-fifty, an honourable draw.

"I'm knackered," said Sluke, collapsing on the floor. Somehow he managed to crawl a few metres across the floor, just making the fridge and getting himself another Coke.

"I saw that," said Snotty. "Pass them round, you greedy beggar."

They all lay on the floor, exhausted, sipping their drinks in a contented silence.

"Any word from your mum?" asked Jessie at length.

"No. Why should there be?" said Snotty, rather sharply.

"Just wondered, you know, if she's safe."

"Course she's safe," said Snotty. "She'd tell me if she wasn't."

Sluke lay on his back, examining the ceiling rose, trying to work out the logic in Snotty's remark. He decided to say nothing. The whole subject of Snotty's mum was very complicated, and very cloudy. He did not want to enquire too much. He wanted her to be safe, of course, but he didn't want her to return, not just yet, when it was so brilliant, so marvellous, being able to play every evening in Snotty's house.

Snotty's mum had brought Snotty up by herself, having separated from Snotty's father many, many years ago. In the past she had often gone off for a few days on location, as she worked in the film world, leaving Snotty with an au pair or a baby-sitter.

Several weeks ago she had had to go off suddenly on a secret and very hush-hush project. Snotty was now older, First Year Comprehensive, so she hoped he'd cope on his own. She'd left him some money, her credit cards, and a note telling him to use her cards to pay the bills. He was "in charge of the house" with a mission "to enjoy himself".

After the first two weeks on his own, with no word from his mother, Snotty had started to re-organize the house on the lines she had clearly suggested (Snotty decided) so that he could enjoy himself.

There had been one phone call from her, and one letter, not saying much, but reassuring Snotty she was alive and well. The letter, sent from somewhere in Africa, was pinned up on the wall beside the football scores. It said she was sending him some tickets, but they hadn't come yet.

The only real problem was that various busybodies, such as Mrs Cheatham next door, and Mrs Potter, his Head Teacher, were becoming convinced that all was not well, that something funny was going on, that a boy of Snotty's age should not be left in that big house on his own.

The other more pressing problem was that Snotty had promised to take them all to Marine Ices, once the match was over, but he suddenly realized he had run out of cash.

3

Jessie and Bessie were standing on either side of the Midland Bank corner, keeping a look-out, ready to give the warning sign, should anyone or anything untoward happen.

Sluke was wearing a long coat and an old trilby hat, both found on a skip. He was standing right in front of the cash-dispensing machine, his arms out wide, hoping to make himself and his coat look as big as possible. In front of him, like a baby kangaroo in a pouch, was Snotty, stretching up, trying to put his mother's bank card into the slot.

"Hurry up," hissed Sluke. "You haven't forgotten the PIN number, have you?"

"Don't be stupid," said Snotty.

He was useless at remembering most things mathematical, but he had memorized his mother's number. After all, he had been using it every weekend for some time now. He never took too much cash out at any one time, just in case he got mugged or burgled, only enough for the week ahead. Any urgent items for the house, vital things like the latest computer-programmed jukeboxes, another Nintendo, or a fourth TV, he bought over the phone by VISA card, quoting his mother's number.

"There's something wrong with this stupid machine," said Snotty.

"There's something wrong with stupid you," said Sluke.

"Belt up, Four Eyes."

"Shurrup, shorty."

"Heh, you two," hissed Jessie, watching them from the corner. "Stop squabbling."

"Not my fault," said Snotty. "This machine. The card keeps on coming back out again. I dunno why. I'll try it one more time . . ."

Just as he was about to put it in, he felt a body landing on top of him, a young, muscular body, fresh from a hard game of indoor football. It was Jessie. In one action, she had knocked him flat and taken the card from his hand.

"You're going to lose it, you idiot," she said. "They only reject it so many times, then they keep it."

"How was I to know," said Snotty, getting up. "And that hurt."

"So what we gonna do?" said Sluke. "I'm starving."

"This is more important than your rotten stomach," said Jessie, examining the card. "You did use the right PIN number, Snotty?"

"I'm not a complete idiot," said Snotty.

"Yes, just an incomplete idiot," said Sluke.

"Shurrup, you," said Snotty.

"Of course," said Jessie, looking at her digital watch, "now I get it."

"Is the bank closed, then?" asked Snotty.

"No, it's the date. Look, it says it's only valid till the thirtieth of the sixth. That was yesterday. You'll have to get a new one."

"How do I do that?" asked Snotty.

"I'm not sure," said Jessie.

"Oh, no," said Sluke. "What we gonna eat?"

"How we gonna *live?*" said Snotty. "That's much more important. Everything will collapse if I can't get any more cash out."

"I think my stomach's collapsing," said Sluke. "I'll probably get anorexia and fade away . . ."

He looked at his own watch. Not to check the date but the time, in the hope that he might get back to his own house for supper. Snotty went on moaning.

"I need cash to buy food, to buy Coke, to buy cereals, all that sort of stuff. It's gonna ruin everything . . ."

"I think I'll have to go," said Sluke. "I promised my mum I would be home tonight. She's getting a bit worried, you know, about me being out all the time . . ."

24

"Good riddance," said Snotty. "You're no help at all."

"Actually, we have to go as well," said Jessie and Bessie together. "But don't worry, Snotty. We'll think of something. We're bound to find a solution. We'll come round to your place tomorrow morning. OK? Byee."

"Ugh," said Snotty, turning away, feeling very miserable.

Half-way home he remembered what was happening tomorrow morning.

"The milkman! That's all I need. He said he wanted paying tomorrow morning. Or else. Oh, no . . ."

4

Snotty, Sluke, Jessie and Bessie were all sitting on Snotty's indoor football pitch, having ice-cream for breakfast, as they did most Saturday mornings. In the old days, Snotty's mother had made him a fry-up on Saturday, followed by croissants, which Snotty had quite liked, but he much preferred ice-cream. Especially now he had his own supply, made on the premises, without him having to do any work.

"What's in this lot, Jes?" asked Snotty.

"Bit of Mars bar, touch of curry-flavoured crisps, hint of French fries, dawb of Big Mac, just a squish of HP tomato sauce, nothing exotic this time, Snotty."

Jessie, Bessie and Sluke took turns on Saturday morning, going down into the basement where Snotty had installed his large, state-of-the-art ice-cream-making machine which he had acquired through a mail-order advert. He had bought this, not hired it, because he was sure his mother would be very pleased by this addition to the house. Most of his acquisitions, such as the games

25

and music machines, were hired, just in case his mother should not deem them essential to their domestic well-being, if and when she returned.

Every Saturday one of the girls or Sluke made a fresh load of ice-cream, producing seven new and exciting varieties so that Snotty could work his way through them each morning, just to top him up, get him off to school in a good mood. The following Saturday all four of them finished off anything still left, before making a new load.

Snotty was the Supervisor, Officer-in-charge of Ice-cream, and he therefore did not do any of the hard work. He'd dreamed up the project, bought the machine, and he ordered the milk, eggs and double cream which the milkman delivered every Saturday morning. Normally Snotty hated milk, and had cancelled it after his mother left, till he saw the advert for the new wonder ice-cream-making machine.

"Well, that's the end of this lot," said Sluke, scraping his empty dish then licking it. "Could be the last lot for ever."

"I'll think of something," said Snotty.

"He won't leave this week's stuff, if you don't pay him," said Jessie.

"You can't pay him by VISA," said Bessie. "My mum tried that. Cash or cheque only."

"I've told you, I'll think of something. Don't panic."

There was a loud knocking at the front door. Snotty was the first to jump up – going straight behind the fridge to hide. He had been trying to be offhand and not worried about the problem of paying the milkman, but he was far more concerned than the other three. It wasn't the thought of the ice-cream making coming to an end but what the milkman might do about the unpaid bill. Would he report Snotty to the Social Services, or the police?

"I'm not in," whispered Snotty. "Tell him I'm not in."

"You don't even know who it is yet, you dum dum," said Sluke.

"Why should you presume it's a he anyway?" said Jessie. "Typical male assumptions."

"Go and see who it is, will you," said Snotty. "It stinks behind this fridge."

"I'll go and find out," said Bessie, getting up and going down to the basement. Carefully she looked up and on the steps she could clearly see the squat figure of Mrs Cheatham.

"No problem," said Bessie, coming back. "It's old Ma Cheatham. What should we do?"

"Just ignore her," said Snotty, stepping out from behind the fridge.

There was a deep rumbling noise. They all looked round the room, trying to work out where it had come from.

"She's breaking the door down!" said Snotty. "Call the police! No, no, hold on, *don't* call the police!"

"That was you, Sluke, wasn't it?" said Bessie, pointing at Sluke's stomach.

"I can't help it," said Sluke. "Inanition. You lot got most of the ice-cream."

"Liar, you had most," said Jessie.

"Not my fault anyway," said Sluke. "Those stupid crisps. You shouldn't have used curry flavour. They always upset my tum. In fact my mum thinks I could be getting an ulcer. You can, you know, even young people can get ulcers. I think it's stress, pressure of modern life, too much school, if you ask me . . ."

"Oh, shurrup, you old moan," said Snotty. "Your only problem is greed. We've got more important problems to worry about. How we gonna pay that stupid milkman."

"Perhaps if I talked to him nicely," said Jessie. "If I explained that your mother was out for the moment, and you were ill in bed, suffering from stress, there's a lot of it around, he might take sympathy and not want his money for another week?"

"No chance," said Snotty. "He said he wanted paying today, or else."

"I could dress up as Else," said Sluke. "Or your mother."

"Go back to sleep," said Snotty.

"Perhaps you could give him something in exchange," suggested Bessie, looking round the empty room.

"He can't have the fridge," said Sluke. "I've just worked out how to use it for scoring."

"And he can't have any of the new games," said Snotty. "They're all rented."

"How about an IOU?" said Sluke.

"He's stupid, but not that stupid," said Snotty.

"Actually, he's not stupid," said Jessie. "He's got a Ph.D."

"Is that the make of his milk float?" said Sluke. "I thought it was a BMW."

"No, it means he's a doctor," said Jessie.

"Perhaps he could look at my tum," said Sluke.

"What's he doing working as a milkman," asked Snotty, "if he's a doctor?"

"Not a medical doctor," explained Jessie. "A doctor of philosophy. My mum knows all about him. He went to Sussex University, got a degree in philosophy, but can't get a job."

"I'd rather be a milkman than hang about all day being philosophical," said Snotty.

"If he's so clever then," said Sluke, "perhaps he can solve the problem. Let's just tell him the truth. Explain what's happened. See if he can work out a way of helping us."

"Clever people still want their money," said Jessie.

There was the sound of more loud banging on the front door. Once again Bessie went down to the basement to see who it was.

"It's OK," she shouted. "It's only the postman."

Snotty looked surprised. He did not get letters, never had done, for the simple reason that he never wrote any. The post for his mother was now drying up, apart from various magazines she subscribed to, paid for in advance. That was where Snotty had seen most of his mail-order offers.

Snotty waited for the sound of the letter box being pushed open and then the postman going away, but the banging continued.

"You'll have to go," said Jessie. "It could be a big

parcel, something really good."

"No, it's always rubbish," said Snotty.

"I didn't see him holding anything big," said Bessie. "Could it be a registered letter?"

"Perhaps from your mum?" said Sluke.

Snotty's face brightened at this suggestion. He jumped up, ran to the front door and unlocked it.

"Master Nottingham Bumstead?" said the postman, a pencil between his teeth, rummaging through bits of paper. Snotty did not normally acknowledge his real name, but he was excited by the thought of what the postman might have for him.

"Sign here," said the postman, looking down at little Snotty. "If you *can* write."

Snotty signed and was handed a registered envelope, covered with African stamps. He closed the door, fixed all the bolts, and tore open the envelope. Inside was a letter, and another envelope, containing some sort of card. First he read the letter.

> *Hi, Snotty, my little cabbage! Still on location, still very hush hush, now in Botswana filming in the Okavango delta. I can't spell it either! Hope all is well with you. All well here, but so secret I can't tell you nuffink else, or* THE STAR *will get vee cross as no one must know where he is or about his project to* SAVE THE WORLD *(eat this letter after burning it). I have arranged with the Bank to keep paying all standing orders and credit cards, so donta worry, my sweet.* THE STAR *sends you his own special ticket as enclosed. Have fun. Love from your silly old Mum . . .*

Snotty raced to tell the others that his mother was safe and well.

"Heh, this is brilliant," said Jessie and Bessie when they had each read the letter.

"Where's this ticket she's on about?" said Sluke. "Let's have a look."

"It'll be for some boring film," said Snotty. "She gets a lot of these preview tickets for crappy films."

Sluke opened the other envelope. Out of it fell a card, embossed with the name and coat of arms of Tottenham Hotspur, F.C. It was a ticket for one of their private Executive Boxes, to seat eight people, the sort which includes food, refreshments, TV, waitress service, plus private parking, and other facilities.

"You lucky beggar!" said Sluke.

"No interest to you, Sluke," said Jessie. "You don't follow football, being an Arsenal supporter."

"We can come with you, can't we, Snotty?" said Bessie. "We're both Spurs fans."

"You can all come," said Snotty. "And so can another Spurs fan I know . . ."

5

There was still an hour to go before kick-off. Tottenham High Road was already crowded. Lines of away supporters were marching along the pavement on one side of the road, escorted by police, some of them on horseback. Traffic on the road itself was almost stationary as cars, buses and taxis tried to move forward inch by inch.

On the other pavement, it was mainly Spurs supporters, good-humouredly walking to the match, or standing talking, waiting for friends, watching the passing show, shouting at the Man. U. fans on the other side of the road.

"'Scuse me, folks, urgent delivery," yelled a voice from the top of a milk float, cleverly making its way through the Spurs supporters, half on and half off the pavement.

It was Sluke, self-appointed look-out, directing the driver from above, pointing out gaps in the crowds.

In the driver's seat sat the milkman with Snotty beside him, clutching his Executive Box ticket.

At the back of the float, sitting on a pile of milk crates, were Bessie and Jessie, waving to the crowds and holding up their Spurs scarves.

"Come on you Spu-urs," they shouted in unison. Those pedestrians who had been a bit annoyed to find a milk float pushing through them were amused to see Bessie and Jessie, true supporters, who had managed to get an unusual lift to the match.

"It's brilliant you inviting me along, Snotty!" said the milkman, carefully steering round a hot-dog salesman. "Never been in an Executive Box before. In fact I've never had a seat before. When I was a student, I always stood on the Shelf."

"How long you been a Spurs fan, then?" asked Snotty.

"All my life," said the milkman. "It came with my mother's milk."

"You mean your mum was a milkman?"

"Good one, Snot," smiled the milkman, swerving to avoid another hot-dog salesman.

"Even at Brighton, I used to come up to follow Spurs," he continued. "You tend to inherit the team you support. You're born with it, then you follow it, through thick and thin. Only fans are truly loyal. Players and managers will move anywhere, changing their clubs, depending on the money."

Snotty wondered if he should reveal they had an Arsenal fan on board, namely Sluke, who could be about to change his club, thanks not to the money but the thought of a flash Executive seat.

On the roof, Sluke had suddenly found himself with

a Spurs scarf which had appeared in his hand by accident. In the other, by intent, he was holding a hot dog, which he had managed to acquire just as they were passing the last hot-dog stand.

"Heh, Doc," shouted Sluke, banging on the roof with his Doc Marten boots. "Don't go so fast. I never got no ketchup that time. Heh, that way, over there. I can see fried onions . . ."

At the main entrance to the West Stand the crowds were thickest of all, with security guards and police making sure that people without tickets were not admitted. A lot of the crowd were simply hanging around, hoping to see the players arriving, or to spot any famous fans.

"Move it," snarled a very bossy security guard, banging on the front of the milk float, then he turned to salute one of the Spurs stars purring forward in a Jaguar, lifting the barrier to let him drive into the private car park.

"I said move it," he repeated, banging on the milk float again.

"What's he on about?" said Sluke. "We're the fastest movers in all North London. Faster than Ernie. The fastest milk float in the West. Do you remember Ernie, Doc? You're educated . . ."

Sluke started to sing, swaying in time to his own tuneless tune. He had become carried away with all the crowd excitement, and also three hot dogs and four Cokes.

"Get down off that van, son," said the policeman, coming over. "What's going on here?"

"This milk float's blocking the entrance," said the security guard. "Should be banned, if you ask me, bloomin' stupid, delivering milk round here of a Saturday afternoon."

"Actually, I am not delivering milk," said the milkman, in his best Ph.D. accent. "I happen to be delivering VIP guests."

"On your bike," said the security man.

"No, it is a milk float, your first guess was correct. Jolly well spotted."

"You think you gorra lot of bottle, don't you, clever dick," said the security man.

"Right again," said the Doc. "Skimmed or semi-skimmed, the choice is up to you."

"Oh, got a right joker here," snarled the security guard.

"Just move on, please," said the policeman. "You're holding up the traffic."

"Nottingham, be kind enough to show the officer your ticket."

Snotty got out his envelope. The policeman and the security guard both looked suspicious as Snotty carefully opened it and pulled out his Executive Box ticket. The moment they saw the card, their expressions changed.

"This way sir," said the security guard, indicating a small gate for them to walk through. "Sorry about that."

"One moment," said the Doc, holding Snotty by the arm, restraining him in his seat. "Our Executive Box ticket does include parking, if I'm not mistaken, hmm, is that not so, ah ha, my good man?"

The security guard slowly lifted the barrier and let the milk float glide through. The Doc parked it between a white Rolls Royce and a red Ferrari, telling Sluke and the girls to jump down carefully.

"Make sure you don't leave sticky fingerprints or make any scratches on my milk float. It is my best one."

All five of them strolled over to a private entrance to the Executive Boxes. At the carpeted doorway, the milkman gave a wave to the security man who had tried to stop them, beckoning him over, as if perhaps he might be about to give him a tip.

"I say, Mr Security Man! Do keep an eye on my motor during the match, there's a good chap. I don't want anyone breaking into it, or pinching any mementoes, especially that one there . . ."

Snotty was not listening. He had raced up the carpeted staircase to his Executive Box, followed by Sluke, Bessie and Jessie. They couldn't get over the size and luxury of their special box, with its kitchen, TV, video, telephone, sofas, chairs and their own waitress, waiting to bring anything they might want.

Spurs beat Manchester United 3–2, a great match, enjoyed by all, especially five people in one of the best Executive Boxes. They ordered food and drink non-stop during the match and watched repeats of all goals on the video at half-time. After the game, the Spurs goal scorers came into their box to shake hands with them personally.

The players were a bit surprised to find that the SUPER-STAR SINGER who owned the box was not there, but they were pleased to find four such young, enthusiastic and highly knowledgeable supporters, all four clearly long-time Spurs fans, judging by their scarves, plus their terribly intelligent, long-haired older friend who said he was their personal chauffeur.

When they eventually staggered out, having eaten, drunk and celebrated in style, the milkman led the way back to his milk float. He checked to see if the memento was still intact, the one he had noticed early and had asked the security guard to keep an eye on.

The Spurs bag belonged to Snotty, who had insisted on taking it to the match. Being Snotty, he had then forgotten all about it, leaving it under the seat where he had been sitting beside the driver. It was not there. Someone had fixed it outside the milk float, hanging it from a strut. Doc milkman left it blowing in the triumphal breeze as they drove home. He said he had enjoyed the afternoon so much that Snotty need not pay his milk bill for the next month.

When they got to Snotty's house, Snotty invited them all in for ice-cream. Including the milkman.

2

Doctor Snotty

I

Sluke was first up on Monday morning. He had spent the weekend at Snotty's, with his mother's permission, and had risen early to prepare a little treat for Snotty – ice-cream in bed.

Sluke's mother had told him to be as helpful as possible, to act like a good guest or he wouldn't get invited again, to do what Mrs Bumstead told him, go to bed when she said and try to help in the house. She hadn't actually spoken to Mrs Bumstead herself, but she had heard her voice on the answering machine. Mrs Bumstead sounded as cheerful as ever, saying she would be back soon.

This was an old tape made by Snotty's mother months ago. Snotty had followed it up by ringing Sluke's mother himself, pretending to talk to his own mother in the background, saying, "Yes, Mum, OK, Mum, I'll tell her you really do want Sluke to come for the weekend, because he's your favourite guest!"

Sluke went downstairs and decided to give himself a

little treat first, as he was a bit tired, having been ever so helpful all weekend, especially to himself. This time he helped himself to two double helpings of ice-cream.

While he stood in his underpants eating his ice-cream, his tummy gave a little rumble, but it didn't worry him very much. Then his underpants began to feel a bit tight. That didn't really worry him either. He had been guzzling a lot over the weekend.

He had slept in his underpants, even though his mother had sent him with his pyjamas, freshly washed. Snotty had sniggered when he saw them. Since his mother had been away, Snotty never used such soppy things as pyjamas, preferring to sleep in his clothes. He worked out that it would save the human race months and months of their lives, if only people didn't waste time getting undressed every night.

"Where you been, fatso?" said Snotty as Sluke came back into Snotty's bedroom, carrying the ice-cream. Snotty was in his bed, surrounded by toys and games plus emergency chocolate and crisps in case of night-time starvation.

Sluke's bed was a mattress on the floor, an island in a sea of chocolate wrappers and crisp packets, signs of the emergencies they had both had to contend with over the weekend.

"Doing things for you," said Sluke. "As always."

Sluke appeared tall and thin when dressed, but now Snotty could see he was getting a slight tum. Snotty enjoyed getting at him for his eating habits, making Sluke furious, because he hated the idea of being fat.

"Before you start stuffing yourself once again," said Snotty, "I need some comics. OK. Chop chop. You know where they are."

Sluke groaned but went downstairs to the games floor. He didn't mind the odd errand – it was little enough to pay for the privilege of staying at Snotty's, though he knew that Snotty liked having him there. During the night Snotty had confessed that he sometimes did get a bit scared, sleeping in this big house all on his own.

Sluke went into the bathroom, avoiding the hole in the floor which they would have to get mended before Snotty's mum came back, *if* she ever came back. He opened the glass door of the shower which was stacked from floor to ceiling with Snotty's comics, including *Dandy*s and *Beano*s he'd first read when he was seven years old. Snotty almost preferred old comics to new

42

ones, knowing in advance the bits where he was going
to laugh.

Sluke gathered up enough comics for both of them,
and went back to Snotty's bedroom.

"Ah, this is the life!" said Sluke, dropping on to
his mattress again. He flicked through the comics while
licking several empty chocolate wrappers, just in case
there were any scraps hiding inside, any gungy bits still
lurking. Then he inspected the empty crisp packets,
putting his tongue inside each one to suction up any
scrinchy, inchy bits.

The phone rang on the floor below. Sluke had his head inside the last crisp packet, but he dragged himself out of it and headed for the bedroom door, wanting to save Snotty the bother of getting up.

"Don't answer it!" said Snotty. "I've left the answering machine on. No one rings me at this time of morning."

"What time is it, anyway?" said Sluke, looking for his watch amidst the mountain of wrappers and empty ice-cream plates. "Oh, no. Eight o'clock. We're gonna be late for school. Come on, Snot, move your bum."

"Move yours," said Snotty, "if you can . . ."

It didn't take Snotty long to get up. He was already in his clothes and as for washing his face or cleaning his teeth, he had given that up long ago, though he had managed a quick once-over before going to the Spurs Executive Box. Bessie and Jessie had forced him to, saying that he was beginning to pong.

Sluke took much longer. He was having trouble with his jeans, trying to fasten them behind a jukebox, so that Snotty wouldn't see him and jeer.

As they came down the stairs, they could hear someone at the front door. They stopped, listened, waited. Through the letter box came two envelopes, both addressed to Zoe Bumstead, Snotty's mother. Snotty picked them up and examined them.

"You can't open them," said Sluke. "They're for your mum."

"She said I could," said Snotty. "She said I was in charge of everything. I'm in loco thingy, that thingy Miss Eager was telling us about."

"Loco parentis?" asked Sluke.

"Sounds like it," said Snotty.

"I think that stands for loco meaning lunatic," said Sluke. "So that's about right . . ."

But Snotty was not listening to Sluke any more, so he missed this joke at his expense.

"Brilliant news," said Snotty, tearing open one of the letters. "My mum's new bank card has arrived. It'll last for the whole of next year."

For a moment he looked slightly worried. The thought of his mother being away for as long as that had not struck him before. In the night time, on his own, he told himself she would be back soon, perhaps in a week or so.

"Excellent," said Sluke.

"Now for the bad news," said Snotty, reading the other letter. "Mrs Potter wants to see my mum. She wants her to ring and make an appointment."

"Not so excellent," said Sluke. "But don't worry. We can put her off. You can say she's got a cold."

"Yeh, but I know Mrs Potter. Never trusted her. She's after me. She'll keep asking, saying she's got to see my mum. Then what do we do?"

"Has she ever seen your mum?"

"No, when I went for my interview, we saw Mr Jones, the Deputy Head."

"Then I could go as your mum," said Sluke. "She'll never know."

"Don't be stupid, you fat idiot," said Snotty. "You couldn't fool anyone."

"'Course I could," said Sluke, dancing around the hall, putting on a squeaky voice, pretending to be Snotty's mum. As he danced, he banged against the inside of the letter box, a very big letter box, the biggest in the street, which Snotty's mum had had enlarged especially to take all the books and film scripts which were sent to her for her work.

Through this large letter box came a very large arm covered in tattoos, which grabbed hold of Sluke.

"Ouch, stop it, leggo!" shouted Sluke.

"Open this door, Lucas!" said a very angry male voice.

Sluke managed to unlock the door, while still being

held by the tattooed arm.

When the door opened the owner of the arm, who happened to be Sluke's father, picked him up bodily, carried him down the front steps and threw him into the front passenger seat of a large articulated lorry, which had been left with its engine running.

"Thanks for the weekend, Snotty," yelled Sluke as the lorry drove away.

Then he was gone.

2

Snotty was not allowed out at lunch time, not even to the school cafeteria. He sat in his form room by himself; he was supposed to be writing out some extra history work Miss Eager had given him. At least she hadn't reported him to Mrs Potter.

" 'Snot fair," said Snotty, staring out of the window. He'd been staring for most of the time so far and had not yet started his work. "I was only ten minutes late. What's ten minutes when you have to spend thousands and thousands of minutes at school? I bet I've done a million minutes already.

"Let me see. Let's say six hours a day in school from the age of five, that's three hundred and sixty minutes a day five days a week, oh, and nursery school, now when did I start nursery school . . ."

"That's good, Nottingham," said Miss Eager, coming through the class-room door. "Glad to see you are properly occupied for once."

She'd had her lunch and had come back to do some marking at her own desk.

"Heh, I thought I told you to redo your history," she said, looking at his book.

47

"Maths," said Snotty. "I'm doing Maths. Just trying to get ahead with this new calculating and stuff."

"Then don't. I told you I want your history written up neatly before the bell goes, or you'll be in detention all week."

Snotty began copying out his history, very slowly, till he noticed Sluke's face pressed up against a window behind Miss Eager's desk, making faces at him.

Sluke had arrived just in time for school, thanks to his father taking him in his lorry, though why his father had suddenly come for him was still not clear to Snotty.

Sluke pulled up his shirt and pointed at his stomach, indicating what a big school dinner he'd had, seconds of everything, yum yum. Snotty could see funny red marks all round Sluke's waist. Probably where he'd spilt his jam roly-poly. Sluke was a messy eater.

Sluke was now pretending to be sick, writhing in agony, then pointing at Miss Eager's head, as if he was being sick all over her. Snotty tried hard not to laugh; he knew Miss Eager would give him another detention if he did.

"I think someone wants you, Miss," said Snotty, hoping Miss Eager would turn round and catch Sluke.

"Just get on with your work!" she said, without looking up.

Behind Sluke, Snotty saw Mr Jones creeping up on him. For the second time that day a large hand took

48

hold of Sluke, lifted him off the ground and carried him away.

3

"So why did your dad come for you this morning?" asked Snotty as he and Sluke walked home after school. They were late out. Sluke had got himself a detention from Mr Jones and Snotty had nobly waited for him.

"He didn't believe I was at your house," said Sluke. "He'd come to check."

"Where could you have been?" asked Snotty. "Spending the weekend at Buckingham Palace with the Queen, or at Ten Downing Street with wazzisname?"

Snotty was very good on football teams, points gained, goals for and against, position in league, best players, best reserve players, but he was not so up-to-date when it came to politics and politicians.

"My dad says I can't stay with you again," said Sluke.

"What?" exclaimed Snotty.

"He says my mum was worried about me all weekend."

"That's stupid," said Snotty. "He saw you were with me. He knows you stayed at my house. What's the problem?"

"He thinks there's something funny going on."

"He's been looking in the mirror, has he?"

"That's not funny," said Sluke. "You leave my father alone."

Sluke's father was rather hefty and overweight, with sitting in his lorry all day, driving up and down the motorways. Sluke did not like attention drawn to his father's weight, preferring to boast about his father's strength.

"So what's your mother worried about then?" asked Snotty.

"Dunno," said Sluke.

"I know," said Snotty. "I bet you been moaning to her about your stupid stomach, ain'tcha?"

"Well I do think I might have an ulcer growing.'

"Don't be stupid," said Snotty. "You just put it on."

"She keeps on asking me what I eat at your house, what sort of diet, is your mum a veggie, does she eat raw lentils, or seaweed, dunno why."

"Well, tell her the truth," said Snotty. "We just eat normal things. Ice-cream and sweets, crisps and Mars bars, stuff like that. You can tell her I sometimes take you out for hamburgers and chips, pizzas and things, all dead normal stuff . . . no hang on, don't say I take you out. She'll wonder where we get the money from."

When they arrived at Sluke's block of flats, they pressed the lift button for the fourteenth floor. As usual, the lift took a long time to come and when it did, out stepped Mrs Mudd, Sluke's mother.

"I was just coming to look for you," she said. "Why are you so late, Lucas?"

"Late? I'm not late."

Mrs Mudd looked at Snotty suspiciously; she thought he was a thoroughly bad influence on her beloved son.

"Miss Eager wanted us to help with the school play," said Snotty. "She's making the sets. It opens on Friday."

"Well, you're not helping on it any more, Lucas," said Mrs Mudd. "I'm taking you for an X-ray at the Royal Free on Friday. I'm worried sick about that stomach of yours."

"Oh, Mum, it's nothing, Mum," said Lucas.

"That's what you say now, but every time you've been at Snotty's, it's moan moan moan. What have you been eating there?"

"Food," said Snotty. "Just food."

"I've been trying to ring your mum all day, but all I get is that answer phone. Tell her I'm coming round this evening to see her. About nine o'clock. I'm going to get to the bottom of all this . . ."

"She's away," said Snotty quickly.

"But she was there at the weekend," said Mrs Mudd. "Wasn't she?"

"Oh, yeh, it was just this morning. She had to rush off, to Africa I think, dunno really, but just for the day really."

"To Africa, for the day? What *is* going on?"

"Dunno. Never been to Africa. Supposed to be hot, lot of animals and that . . ."

"I mean in your house. What on earth's happening there? Lucas can't keep away from it."

"Nothing," said Snotty.

"That's what you say," said Mrs Mudd. "Well, *you*'ll be in this evening, won't you?"

"Er, yes," said Snotty, hesitantly, wondering what was coming.

"Then that'll do for a start. I'll just have a look around, even if your mum hasn't come back from her day trip to Africa," she said nastily.

51

"Er, what is it you want to see?" asked Snotty.

"Your kitchen," she said. "That will do for a start. Come along, Lucas. I want you inside, at once!"

With that, she marched Lucas into the lift, which shot away to the fourteenth floor.

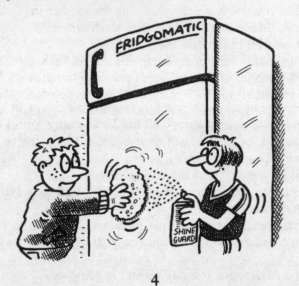

4

Snotty had tried to have a game of indoor football with Jessie and Bessie, but they'd given up. He couldn't concentrate, worrying about Mrs Mudd's arrival in just an hour's time.

Playing with only three people didn't work anyway, now that Sluke was grounded. They'd tried one against two, and the one player always got hammered. One against one had led to quite good games, with the winner playing the other one, but that had caused arguments. Snotty wanted to play in every game, even when he was beaten. It was his pitch, his ball, his rules.

For this evening, the rules had been changed slightly. Hitting the fridge, from any angle, had been banned. Jessie had cleaned it up, inside and behind, in readiness for Mrs Mudd's inspection. The sink had been unboarded and washed down.

"Do you think we should bring the cooker in?" asked Bessie. 'Make it look like a real kitchen?"

"Can't be bothered," said Snotty.

The cooker had been dragged into the back garden in the first stages of Snotty's conversion of the ground floor into a football pitch. It was now looking decidedly dirty.

"What about bringing some of the old kitchen stuff up from the basement?" said Jessie.

"Boring, boring," said Snotty.

"Just to make it look more like, you know, a kitchen?" suggested Jessie.

"This *is* our kitchen," said Snotty. "We prepare our meals here."

"How?" asked Bessie.

"We open the fridge, open our mouths, and prepare to eat. Anything else you want to know?" said Snotty.

"But you don't actually do any cooking in this kitchen," said Jessie. "Anyone can see that."

"Oh, stop wittering on," said Snotty. "OK then, if it makes you happy, we'll call this the dining room."

"Then she'll want to see the kitchen," said Bessie.

"You two are driving me potty," sighed Snotty. "Look, I'll say the kitchen is locked up. My mum always locks up the kitchen when she goes out. Keeps the mice in, ha ha."

"If you make that sort of joke, she *will* get worried," said Bessie.

"All we have to do is show her the fridge, right," said Snotty. "Just show her how amazingly clean it is, OK?

53

That's all she's worried about. She thinks we're poisoning her precious Lucas, giving him food that's gone off. Nothing goes off in this house. It's straight down Sluke's gob before it can go off, or go anywhere. Now just shurrup, you two, eh. Can't you see I'm reading?"

"So that's why your lips are moving," said Jessie.

Snotty was reading some of the magazines which had come for his mother over the last few weeks. They had been left lying all over the place, but this evening Jessie had gathered them into a neat pile, trying to tidy up.

Snotty flicked through a copy of *Private Eye*, saying it was childish, then *Variety*, maintaining it was in a foreign language, and then *The Stage*, reading all the adverts for auditions, hoping to find something that might suit him.

"Think I'll be a famous actor when I grow up," said Snotty. He paused, looking mournful. "*If* I grow up."

"What's to stop you?" asked Bessie.

"I'll probably get put in prison or shoved in a home, and just wither away."

"Now you're being pathetic," said Jessie.

"I'm not. If the Social Services find out about me living here on my own, they could do anything."

"But they won't find out."

"Oh, yeh? Mrs Mudd will probably report me right away, once she's seen this place."

"We won't let her in," said Jessie. "We can all hide and pretend no one's at home."

"She'll only come back tomorrow with Mr Mudd. You've seen the size of him. He'll push the door in. Big fat lump. No wonder Sluke is scared he'll end up like him."

"You shouldn't make comments like that," said Jessie. "People can't help their size. You're being sizeist."

"People make comments about my size all the time," said Snotty. "But then they're all stupid."

"You shouldn't call people stupid either," said Jessie.

"Oh, shurrup, stupid," said Snotty, throwing a magazine at Jessie.

"Well, if you *are* going to let her in," said Bessie, "I'd better tidy upstairs as well. She'll want to poke around everywhere."

Snotty returned to reading *The Stage*. Jessie was turning over the pages of *Private Eye*.

"Graduate, twenty-three, six feet high, strong, hard-working, adaptable, seeks challenging work," said Jessie, reading out one of the adverts. "Anything legal considered, the more bizarre the better. Own car."

"What's bizarre mean?" asked Snotty. "Does he want to work in a shop?"

"No, he wants something unusual," said Jessie. "Perhaps you should hire him as your bodyguard, to stop people like Mr Mudd getting in. You could do with a strong man about the house."

"It's a mum I want," said Snotty. 'Not a man."

Bessie returned, holding a bundle of clothes, dirty dishes, comics and bits of toys she had found lying around.

"Where should I put these, Snotty?" she asked.

"Don't care," said Snotty, rudely.

"Are these your pyjamas?" said Bessie.

"No, they're Sluke's," said Snotty, looking up. "He's forgotten them, the dum dum. Straight in the dustbin. He's not my best friend any more."

"They look a bit small for Sluke," said Bessie, throwing them at Snotty, catching him on the head. "Sure they're not yours, Snotty? Or do you still wear a Babygro . . ."

"See, that's just typical of the stupid sizeist comments I have to put up with," said Snotty.

"It was only a little comment," said Jessie.

"Yeh, they are small," said Snotty, examining the pyjamas. "The waist is two inches smaller than me. Yet he's twice my size. And weight. They must be killing him."

"How stupid," said Bessie.

"His jeans are too tight for him as well," continued Snotty. "I saw him struggling into them this morning. No wonder he's got a red mark round his middle. You should see the size of his belly."

"But he's always boasting how thin he is," said Jessie. "Saying he's never going to be fat like his dad. It doesn't make sense."

"Oh, yes, it does," shouted Snotty, jumping up, throwing his magazine on the floor. "I think it could explain everything . . ."

5

Snotty was sitting at his mother's word processor, staring at the blank screen. He'd found a disc with some space on it and had pressed C for Create. He was holding his hand to his head, looking very Creative.

Bessie was wrapping the pyjamas up neatly, using some pretty wrapping paper she had found in Snotty's mother's desk. Jessie was looking along Snotty's mother's shelves for a dictionary.

"Dear Mrs Mudd," wrote Snotty. "I just gorrin in from being in Africa tonite and my house is very excellent and imakulate and my son Snotty I mean Nottingham has been a very good boy and I am sorry to hear your Sluke has been poorly cos on accont of his stumake which I fink personally is a load of kodswallop. Is his stoopid pantz, if you arks me, yours and oblige, Mrs Bumstead (Mrs) . . ."

Snotty stood up to get some of his mother's headed notepaper, ready to put it into the printer, but Jessie pushed him back into his seat.

"That's rubbish," she said. "That won't do at all. You can't even spell the simplest word."

"W-O-R-D," said Snotty. "Anyway, you don't have to, clever clogs. It's got a Spellcheck, see. You just press this, and it gives you the right spelling. I was gonna do it later, if you hadn't been so bossy, after I'd finished Creating, after I'd let it all flow."

"Oh, yeh," said Jessie, pushing him off the seat. "You know you're the worst in the class at English. I'll do it."

Jessie deleted Snotty's letter and started again.

DEAR MRS MUDD,

she began to type.

"Copycat," said Snotty. "I done that."

"You did that,' said Bessie.

Jessie continued the letter.

I AM RETURNING LUCAS'S PYJAMAS WITH NOTTINGHAM, HE LEFT THEM OVER THE WEEKEND. I HOPE HE IS FEELING BETTER.

I THINK I KNOW THE CAUSE OF LUCAS'S STOMACH CRAMPS. HE IS WEARING UNDERPANTS AND JEANS

WHICH ARE FAR TOO TIGHT FOR HIM. I KNOW HOW
BOYS GET THESE THINGS INTO THEIR HEAD, INSIST-
ING ON CERTAIN ITEMS OF CLOTHING WHICH ARE
FAR TOO SMALL FOR THEM, ESPECIALLY WHEN
THEY HAVE A TENDENCY TO OVEREAT. THEY WANT
TO PRETEND THEY ARE THINNER THAN THEY ARE.
IT IS A COMMON PSYCHOLOGICAL PROBLEM. RED
MARKS ON THE ABDOMEN ARE THE USUAL SIGNS TO
LOOK FOR. THERE IS A LOT OF IT AROUND . . .

Jessie stopped typing and told Bessie to look up the
hard spellings for her. Then she asked her to see if she
could find a medical dictionary on Snotty's mother's
bookshelves, hoping she might be able to throw in some
technical terms. All Bessie could find was a Hip and
Thigh Diet. So Jessie continued:

I SUGGEST YOU BUY LUCAS LARGER SIZES AT ONCE,
IN BOTH TROUSERS AND UNDERGARMENTS. I ALSO
SUGGEST YOU CUT OUT THE OLD LABELS AND PUT
THEM ON THE NEW CLOTHES, SO THAT HE STILL
THINKS HE IS WEARING THE SMALL SIZE! I AM SURE
IN A FEW DAYS HIS STOMACH PAINS WILL GO.

I AM WORKING ON AN IMPORTANT FILM PROJECT
THIS EVENING, SO I'D BE GRATEFUL IF YOU COULD
COME ROUND ANOTHER TIME. IF YOU DON'T MIND.
YOURS, ZOE.

Jessie read it through, checked the spelling of "grateful" in her dictionary, and then printed it out.

"Heh, that's brilliant, Jessie!" said Bessie.

"Not bad," said Snotty, grudgingly. "But it was all my idea, don't forget. I sussed out Sluke's problem."

"Right, you take it round at once, with the parcel," said Jessie. "She won't have left yet. We've still got an hour. Make sure you give it to her, not Sluke. She'll be so pleased when Sluke's better, she won't worry any more about what's happening in your house."

"I hope so," said Snotty.

"Hold on," said Jessie, as Snotty ran to the front door. "Make yourself look presentable."

Bessie and Jessie grabbed Snotty and dragged him to the sink. They washed his face under the tap, wet his hair and then combed it with their fingers, as neatly as they could.

"There, that looks as if you do have a mum at home," said Jessie.

"Off you go, my little man," said Bessie.

6

Mrs Mudd was just coming out of her flat as Snotty arrived. She didn't recognize him at first. He looked so clean and fresh, and he had a helpful smile on his face.

"Yes?" she said, suspiciously, then she answered her own rhetorical question. "No."

"Excuse me?" said Snotty, ever so hesitant.

"No, you can't play with Lucas. He's not going out. Certainly not to your house."

"My mum sent me with this note," said Snotty politely.

Jessie had even typed out Mrs Mudd's address on the envelope, so it did look very professional. After all, Snotty's mother was a professional woman, as Mrs Mudd knew.

She opened the envelope slowly, then began tut-tutting, clicking her teeth, then nodding her head.

"Lucas!" she shouted. "Come here at once!"

Sluke appeared in the hallway behind his mother, giving Snotty an apologetic smile. She grabbed his wrist with one arm and pulled up his T-shirt with the other, revealing a very fat belly, and some distinct red marks round his waist.

"This could explain everything," she said.

"Yeh, that's what my mother finks," said Snotty.

"She wasn't medically trained, was she?" asked Mrs Mudd.

"She was nearly a Doctor," said Snotty. "Of Philosophy. If she'd passed some more exams, she would have been, the ones set by the Milk Board . . ."

"What on earth are you talking about?" said Mrs Mudd. "Anyway, thank her for her help. I'm sure it will do the trick."

Mrs Mudd closed the door, still holding Sluke by his wrist. As Snotty waited for the lift, he could hear Mrs Mudd telling Sluke she was certainly not buying him new jeans, not at the moment, but he was going on a diet immediately.

3

HRH Snotty

I

It was celebration time at Marine Ices, Snotty's favourite eating place. The restaurant was crowded at Saturday lunch time, but Snotty had booked a table, best one, in a corner, and he, Bessie, Jessie and Sluke had gone through the menu.

A very posh family at the next table, the children in their best clothes, were talking about the Royal Free Hospital, about some event they were going to that afternoon.

"I was quite looking forward to having my X-ray done there," said Sluke loudly, finishing his Spaghetti Bolognese, his third round of garlic bread and his fourth Coke. "Not often they get such fine physical specimens to examine."

Sluke pulled up his T-shirt to expose his ample and unmarked tummy. At the same time, he gave a loud belch. "Pardon, I'm sure," he said.

The posh children at the next table giggled, but their parents told them to eat up their salad and not to stare at silly boys.

Sluke had made a miraculous recovery and there had been no need for him to go to hospital after all. He was slightly disappointed, as he'd planned to have a whole day off school for his X-ray, if not most of next week, but he was very pleased his pains had disappeared completely.

His mother had rung Snotty's mother, full of praise, leaving a message of thanks on the answering machine, saying she was sorry she'd been worried about Lucas staying at Snotty's house. He could now play at Snotty's any time, if of course he was invited.

This morning a large bouquet of flowers had arrived for Snotty's mother, with a note, heaping on more thanks. Luckily, Snotty had been at home to take it in.

"Knickerbocker Glories all round," announced Snotty. "We're so pleased that dear Lucas has made such a sudden recovery."

"It was amazing," said Sluke. "I just woke up yesterday and the pains had gone. I dunno why."

"Perhaps you just imagined it in the first place," said Jessie.

"I didn't," said Sluke. "It was agony. And you lot never believed me."

"It was eating too much," said Bessie. "You'd got too fat, that was all."

"I'm not fat," said Sluke. "My mum's bought me new jeans, but they're the same size as the old pair, so you're sussed."

The other three looked at each other, but said nothing.

"I've got a present for you," said Snotty, handing over a cassette tape. "It's to mark your wonderful recovery. Listen to it in the privacy of your own bedroom. Don't let your mum hear."

"Is it Heavy Metal, head-banging stuff?" asked Sluke. "Raving, rapping, housing, mousing, over the top mega, spega music?"

"No, it's your mum talking," said Snotty.

"Your what?"

"It could catch on," said Snotty. "In fact it might make Number One in the charts, when I've done a bit more work on it."

Snotty had made a copy of Mrs Mudd's voice on the tape, then he had added some backing music, plus the noise of animals eating and the sound of Spurs supporters cheering. He'd then mixed them all together on his new recording equipment, hired on his mother's VISA card.

"I had to do something all week, didn't I," said Snotty. "I got fed up playing football on my own."

Snotty paid the bill, in cash, having been to the cash point. On the way out he ordered monster double cones for everyone, flavours of their choice, so they could have something to walk with, just in case pangs of hunger overcame them on the way back to Snotty's. Once there, of course, they would get started on their own home-made ice-cream. It was Jessie's turn this week.

"I think I'll use real fruit," said Jessie. "None of that

spicy stuff we had last week."

They stopped at the fruit stalls in Inverness Street where Jessie chose the best strawberries, melons, peaches, lychees, and several exotic fruits she didn't know the names of.

"Who says we don't have a healthy diet," said Snotty, helping himself to Jessie's baskets of fruit. "Just you tell your mum what we had today, Sluke."

After the fruit stalls Snotty wandered round the tape and record stalls which covered most of the pavements on the High Street, as they do most Saturday mornings, and bought some African music.

Bessie and Jessie then led the way over the road towards the clothes market. "You need some new stuff for school," said Bessie. "I think that's why Mrs Potter wants to see your mum. She thinks you look neglected."

"Oh, don't mention her!" said Snotty. "She's written another letter to my mum, wanting to see her."

"Heh, this looks good," said Jessie, taking Snotty by the arm. "Just your size."

"I'm not buying any of that rubbish."

"OK, we will," said Jessie. She took the money out of Snotty's pocket while the other two held him tight. "Your mum expects you to look after yourself as well as the house. You've worn those same jeans for weeks, and slept in them by the look of it."

All three of them eventually got Snotty into a new pair of jeans, a proper shirt and a pullover. They then bought him two T-shirts.

By the time they arrived in Snotty's street they were all staggering under the weight of the shopping they had acquired, and feeling the effect of all the food, fruit and ice-cream they had consumed.

It was only when they got to the top of the steps leading to Snotty's front door, that they noticed something strange. The front door was already open.

2

"What do you think's happened?" said Sluke.

He was hiding in a gateway ten doors away from Snotty's house. Beside him was Snotty, crouching behind their piles of shopping. Jessie and Bessie were somewhere down the road on the other side of Snotty's house, pretending to play a jumping game, but carefully keeping an eye out for anyone or anything that might emerge from Snotty's front door.

They had all fled, the moment they saw the open door, scattering like magnetic iron filings. Now they were trying to work out what was going on.

"I bet you left it open," said Sluke.

"Don't be stupid. 'Course I didn't."

"Then it must be burglars," said Sluke.

"Oh, no," said Snotty. "They'll have taken my new recording stuff. It's all hired as well. What am I going to do?"

"Good job the fridge was empty," said Sluke. "Means they won't have stolen any food."

"Oh, shut up about stupid food! That's all you think about."

"Oh, no," said Sluke, peering out from the gateway. "I think the milkman's stuff's been nicked."

"You what?" said Snotty, still crouching, too small anyway to see over the gate.

"Your milkman leaves his stuff on the top step, doesn't he? Every Saturday morning. No sign of it. This is getting really serious. You'll have to call the police . . ."

"I can't," said Snotty. "They'll find out I'm living here alone."

"I wonder if the burglars are still inside," said Sluke, getting a bit bolder and stepping out of the gateway on to the pavement.

"You go and look," said Snotty. "You're bigger than me. I'll keep guard here."

"Actually," said Sluke, coming back into the gateway, "I'll have to get home. My mum expects me for lunch . . ."

"Will you shurrup about food," snarled Snotty, giving Sluke a push.

Above them, the front door of the house opened and

large dog came bounding out, heading not for Sluke or Snotty but for their piles of shopping.

"Here, what are you two doing, messing about on my step?" said an angry-looking man, coming down the steps after the dog.

"Sorry, just resting," said Snotty, getting up. "Been doing some shopping for my mum."

"Oh, it's you, is it," said the man. "Ain't seen your mum recently. How is she?"

"Fine, fine," said Snotty, gathering up the shopping bags and pushing Sluke ahead.

"Well, you'd better hurry home with the shopping," said the man. "Your mum will be waiting for you."

Sluke and Snotty picked up their bags and walked towards Snotty's house, watched by the man. Outside Snotty's front door, they stopped, scared to go any further.

"Heh, I've just thought of something," said Sluke. "Perhaps your mum *is* at home. She's come back, while we've been out shopping . . ."

For a moment, Snotty's face lit up, then he shook his head. "She wouldn't leave the front door open. And her car's not back."

While they waited, neither of them daring to go up Snotty's front steps in case any burglars should rush out, Bessie and Jessie appeared from the other side of the street. They rushed right past the hesitant, cringing figures of Sluke and Snotty, bounded up the steps and through the open front door.

"Cor, they're brave," said Sluke.

Snotty and Sluke listened, then carefully they crept up the steps and peeped into the front hall.

Down the stairs came old Mrs Cheatham, followed by Bessie and Jessie, both smiling.

"How did you know it was her?" asked Sluke.

"We saw her through your top window," explained Jessie. "So we knew it was all right."

"It's not all right," said Mrs Cheatham. "It looks as if an earthquake has hit your house. Where's your mum?"

"Oh, she's not in, then?" said Snotty, putting on his dopey look.

"'Course she's not in," said Mrs Cheatham, resting against the hall wall, completely out of breath. She had managed to go all the way upstairs, despite her problems with her bad legs, her bad eyesight, her bad hearing.

"Are you all right, Mrs Cheatham?" asked Jessie.

"I'll manage," she said. "I'm just shocked by the state of this house. Looks like a bomb has hit. Where is your mother, anyway?"

"She'll be back soon," said Snotty.

"That's what you've been saying for weeks. Who made all this mess? Where did that hole in the bathroom come from? What's happened to your kitchen?"

"Kitchen?" said Snotty, still being dopey. "Oh, my mum's moved all the kitchen stuff downstairs in the basement, you know how she's always moving things around, changing stuff and that . . ."

"I never looked downstairs," said Mrs Cheatham, heading for the stairs, but Snotty blocked her path. Jessie and Bessie brought her a chair to sit on, saying she must be tired going up and down all those steps.

"Would you like a cup of tea?" asked Jessie.

"That would be nice, dear," said Mrs Cheatham.

"We ain't got none," said Snotty, making a face at Jessie. "My mum's given up tea. It's her new ecological diet, brought back from Africa. Save the tea forests. Tea leaves have feelings, you know. Tell you what, have some strawberries."

Snotty pulled a punnet out of a bag and handed it to Mrs Cheatham. Half the strawberries had been eaten and the rest were covered in dog's saliva.

"Ugh, you trying to poison me, or something?"

"Sorry about that," said Snotty, pulling things out of another bag. "Have a pair of jeans . . ."

Mrs Cheatham got up from the chair, pushing Snotty

71

away, and once again headed for the basement stairs.

"Shush," said Jessie, taking Mrs Cheatham's arm, putting a finger to her lips. "We're not supposed to disturb."

"Is your mother working down there, then?" asked Mrs Cheatham.

"Secret project," said Snotty. "That's why she's moved her office down there. Some big film she's on. No one must know about it."

"So she's in, is she?"

"In the pink," said Snotty.

"OK then, I won't disturb her just now," said Mrs Cheatham.

"Is that why you were upstairs, looking for her?" asked Jessie, innocently.

"I was looking for the fridge, if you must know."

"And did you find it?" asked Bessie.

"With a struggle," said Mrs Cheatham. "I've put your milk and stuff in it, so it doesn't go off, you see . . ."

"Thanks awfully, Mrs Cheatham," said Jessie, gripping her arm more firmly and ushering her to the front door, helped by Bessie.

"Tell your mum I'll come back and see her later," she said to Snotty as she went out.

"You'll be lucky," said Snotty under his breath.

3

The music was on at full blast, shaking the whole of the top floor, the music floor of Snotty's house.

Snotty was mixing in some bits of the tape of the new African music he had bought, adding it to his Mrs Mudd record. He was wearing earphones, but he still insisted that the music should be on full blast, to resonate round

the room, or his studio as he now liked to call it.

"You'll have Mrs Cheatham complaining," said Bessie.

"She won't hear," said Snotty. "She's half deaf."

"But she's not daft," said Jessie. "She'll be back soon, demanding to see your mum."

"Yeh, what we gonna do next time?" said Sluke.

"Do wa, boop booop, grug grug, wham bam, dee doom," yelled Snotty, swaying in time to the music.

"I don't think that will impress her," said Bessie.

"Turn that stuff down, Snotty," said Sluke. "I can't hear myself eat."

Sluke had brought up a large bowl of the latest batch of ice-cream hidden under a Spurs scarf so that Snotty would not realize what he'd done. The ice-cream was supposed to last Snotty all week for his breakfast, but he was too busy with his music to notice what Sluke was eating.

Bessie and Jessie were both helping Snotty with the music, contributing ideas, operating the synthesizer, playing bits on the keyboard, harmonizing and humming along. Sluke, being tone-deaf, felt rather out of it, but the ice-cream was helping to keep him occupied.

"What I don't understand," said Sluke, "is how she got in."

"Who?" asked Jessie.

"Old Ma Cheatham."

"You know how," said Jessie. "She has a key for this house. Snotty's mother gave her one, yonks ago, for use in emergencies."

"Oh, yeh," said Sluke, covering his ice-cream with the Spurs scarf, as Snotty was swaying his way, but they were all ignoring Sluke, letting him witter on while they worked on their music.

"I wonder if one of her keys is in this house," said Sluke. "I know, why don't we go into her place when she's out, have a look round. What do you think, you lot?"

"What for?" asked Jessie.

"See if there's anything worth eating."

"What a pig you are," said Jessie, throwing an empty cassette case at him.

"Heh, that nearly hit Snotty's scarf. Have you no respect?"

Sluke got up and wandered round the room looking at musical machines till they pushed him away. Then he found a radio and tried to tune in.

"Soon be time for the half-time results," said Sluke. "See how many goals Crystal Palace are hammering Spurs by, ha ha."

"Put that thing down, Sluke," said Jessie. "Can't you see we're busy?"

Sluke went to the front window and stood there look-ing out, humming aimlessly to himself, muttering from time to time that he was starving.

"We've got to decide what we're going to call our-selves," said Bessie.

"Snotty," said Snotty, taking off his cans for one moment, then putting them on again. "Always thought that was a nice name."

"We've helped as much as you," said Bessie. "Two girls and one boy made the music, so I think we should have a feminine name."

"What about Jes 'n Bes?" said Jessie.

"Sounds like a cowboy and his horse," said Sluke.

"Shurrup you," said Snotty.

"How about calling us Zoe, after Snotty's mum?" said Bessie. "This *is* her house."

"But we'll have to spell it in a new way," said Jessie. "How about Zo-Ee?"

"Sounds groovy," said Bessie.

"Sounds mega," said Jessie.

"Sounds stupid," said Sluke. "You should be working on a way of stopping Mrs Cheatham coming back, not messing about with this crappy music."

Jessie threw another empty cassette case at him but it missed, banging against the window. Then they went back to their music-making.

"Heh, look what I can see," said Sluke. "Coming into your street, Snotty. Amazing. Can't believe it. Your street really is coming up, Snotty."

"You can't catch us that way," said Jessie. "Go back to sleep."

"No, really, come and see," said Sluke. "There's a Rolls Royce in your street."

"So what?" said Jessie. "Cars are really boring."

"It's stopped right outside your front door, Snotty. It's enormous. And it looks as if it's got a sort of flag at the front . . ."

"Look, shurrup, Sluke, we're busy," said Snotty, ignoring Sluke and concentrating on his music. "Jessie, pass me that reel, please."

"Guess what's happened now," said Sluke a few minutes later. "Someone's coming to your front door, Snotty. In a uniform. Can't be that social worker. They don't drive Rolls Royces. Could be the secret police . . ."

From the front door there was the sound of loud knocking, clearly heard by all of them, even on the top floor.

4

"Not in this room," said Snotty, leading the way along the hall, past the door of the open-plan living room. He quickly closed it, hoping they had not seen inside. "There's a phone upstairs you can use."

He was being very polite and welcoming, for Snotty. When the driver of the Rolls had knocked at the front door, saying he had broken down and could he use a phone, Snotty had been suspicious at first, but then he had grudgingly allowed him to come in. The driver had been followed into the house by two ladies, both uninvited.

"An indoor football pitch," exclaimed one of his unexpected guests, who had managed to catch a glimpse of what lay inside the door Snotty had closed. "How marvellous! Just what William and Harry always wanted. Do go and get them, would you."

She turned to her companion, an equally elegant and very well-spoken lady, who went back down the hall and then returned with two young boys.

"You don't mind if they have a game, do you?" said the first lady.

"No problem," said Snotty. "You can play with them, Sluke. They look about your level."

Sluke had followed Snotty down the stairs, to see who had been knocking at the front door, leaving the girls upstairs, still making their music.

Sluke went off to play football with William and Harry, moaning that it wasn't fair, why did he have to get stuck with the kids.

Meanwhile Snotty led the way up the stairs to the
first floor. He showed the driver where the phone was,
apologizing for all the mess, all the toys and games. He
tried to clear a bit of space where the two ladies could
sit down. Several pieces of his mother's better furniture
had been brought up some time ago for the visit of Mrs
Pratt, the social worker, but they were now covered in
comics and sweet papers.

"Sorry about this," said Snotty.

"It's frightfully good of you," said the assistant lady,
staring round, clutching her handbag, as if looking for
something . . .

Oh, no, thought Snotty. She's going to ask for the
bathroom. Not only was it now a snooker room, but
there was the matter of the hole in the floor.

"Er, I don't suppose by any chance," began the assistant lady, "that you have a . . .?"

"It's not working," said Snotty quickly.

"Nothing seems to be working today," sighed the assistant lady. "Our car phone isn't working, the security car got lost, then our car packed up on us."

"Jolly lucky we broke down outside your house," said the leading lady, "or we would not have had the chance to see your marvellous home. So clever, so original, wish we had something like this."

"Easy enough to do, if you've got your own house," said Snotty. "You got your own house, then?"

"Not exactly," said the leading lady. "It belongs to the family. I don't think they'd allow us to do what you've done . . ."

She wandered round, exclaiming at all the toys and games. The chauffeur was on the telephone, holding on, waiting for a mechanic to find something.

"All I was going to ask," began the assistant lady, looking round again, "is if by chance you have another phone? You see we have to contact the Palace."

"There's no score," said Snotty.

"What?" said the assistant lady.

"Nil nil, half-time. Palace have been dead jammy. Spurs missed a penalty . . ."

"You're a Spurs fan are you?" said the leading lady. "William and Harry both love Manchester United."

"So they don't follow football," said Snotty.

"That's one of their jokes as well," said the leading lady. She had now stopped in the middle of the room, listening to the music from above.

"Sounds good," she said, going to the doorway, trying to hear the music more clearly.

"Her Highness likes all music," said the assistant lady.

"Yes, she is tall," said Snotty.

"Is it African?" asked the leading lady.

"Sort of," said Snotty. "We're just working on it. Mixin' a few tracks an' that."

"You have your own recording studio? How exciting. May I go and listen?"

"Come on, then," said Snotty. "But don't touch anything."

Bessie and Jessie each had their earphones on, concentrating on the music. They did not at first hear Snotty and his two visitors entering the recording room.

"These are two of my technical people," said Snotty grandly, waving in the direction of Jessie and Bessie. "I do all the real creative work."

"What a lie," said Jessie and Bessie, turning round when they heard his voice. "It's our group as well."

"I say, what do you call yourselves?" asked the leading lady.

"Zo-Ee," said Jessie.

Jessie stared at the leading lady, Snotty's visitor whom he was now showing round the room, feeling she had seen her somewhere before. Then suddenly she put her hand to her mouth, taking a quick breath, and gave Bessie a nudge.

Snotty went over to the controls, showing off his expertise, winding back the tape to the beginning, to see what the girls had added.

"You don't mind if I listen, do you?" said the leading lady, looking for a place to sit down. The floor was very dusty. Snotty had never cleaned or Hoovered since his mother left.

"Don't sit there," shouted Jessie, just as the leading lady was about to sit down on the Spurs scarf.

"Sacred territory, is it?" she said smiling, carefully picking it up. Underneath she found Sluke's half-empty bowl of ice-cream. He had forgotten to finish it, being too busy watching the Rolls out of the window.

"Have it if you like," said Jessie. "I made it. Full of goodness. Fresh strawberries, melons and lychees."

"Yum yum," said the leading lady.

She found a relatively clean bit of rug and sat on it, listening to the music and eating her ice-cream.

Jessie offered to get the assistant lady some ice-cream, but she declined, standing at the window, watching below where the driver had now opened the bonnet of the car and was doing something with the engine.

"This is fun," said the leading lady, getting up and dancing by herself in time to the music. "Much more amusing than opening the new wing at the Royal Free Hospital."

"Ah," said the assistant lady, just as the tape finished. "He's waving at us. I think the car is fixed. We'd better be going. With a bit of luck, we'll only be ten minutes late. If you are ready, Ma'am."

For a moment, Snotty thought his mother had come back. He went cold, giving a little shiver, then he realized it was the leading lady who was being addressed. Very strange. Surely the other lady couldn't be her daughter.

"Thanks awfully for having us," said the leading lady, shaking hands with Bessie, Jessie and Snotty in turn. "Very entertaining."

The two ladies went down the stairs, followed by Snotty, Jessie and Bessie.

"William and Harry, we're orf!" shouted the leading lady.

Harry appeared at once, but there was no sign of his brother.

"William, where are you?" shouted his mother again.

Snotty went into the football pitch where Sluke was standing alone, caught in the act of changing the scores on the wall, to his advantage of course.

"Where's William?" said Snotty.

"I thought he was with you," said Sluke.

"How could he be?" said Snotty. "We left him with you."

"Stupid kid," said Sluke.

"That's no way to speak about an heir to the throne," said Jessie, coming into the room.

"Didn't notice his hair style," said Sluke. "If he'd been a skinhead, I'd have noticed that, but it was just sort of floppy . . ."

"Oh, shurrup," said Jessie. "Don't you realize you've lost the next but one King of England . . ."

5

They held a meeting in the hall, trying to keep calm and go over what had happened. Sluke at first said that William had just sort of disappeared, just walked out of the room, without saying a word, but he couldn't remember exactly when or why.

"You wanted to play one a side, didn't you?" said Jessie. "That's why you didn't notice when he sloped off, and you didn't care."

"Yeh, well, maybe," said Sluke. "But I thought he'd gone upstairs with you lot, listening to the stupid music and that."

"But he hadn't," said Jessie. "So it's all your fault. You were supposed to look after him."

"Oh, I remember now," said Sluke, "he said he wanted the toilet."

"Oh, I'm sure he would never say that," said the assistant lady indignantly.

"So did you take him to the lavvy?" asked Snotty.

"If anything, William would have asked for the loo," continued the assistant lady, giving a slight shudder.

There then started an argument about correct usage. Snotty, like his mother, always used the word lavatory, though now and again he shortened it to lavvy, which his mother did not care for. In Sluke's house, polite usage was to say toilet. Didn't everyone say toilet, asked Sluke. Royal custom, according to first-hand evidence, preferred the word loo, which is what William would have said. All of this amazed Jessie and Bessie who said they used none of those words. In their house, so they explained, they always used the word bathroom to cover all functions of – er – a bathroom nature.

"Oh, no," shrieked Jessie, "you didn't send him to the bathroom, did you?"

"I didn't send him anywhere," said Sluke. "I just said there's one under the stairs, and one upstairs, that's all I said, if I said anything, but I was busy at the time, scoring this brilliant goal . . ."

They quickly looked in the ground floor lavatory/toilet/loo, which was under the stairs and hard for a stranger to find, as it looked like a cupboard. It was empty.

They then all rushed upstairs to the bathroom, led by Jessie and Bessie. They had been the first to realize the significance of the bathroom. This was where some weeks previously there had been a series of changes, some by intent, such as the bath being converted into a snooker table, one of Snotty's more inspired ideas, and some by accident, such as a flood which resulted in a hole in the floor. Snotty had covered it over temporarily with one of his mother's Indian rugs – and then forgotten it.

Bessie got to the bathroom first and tried the door. It was locked. She banged the handle, trying to force it open.

"Wills, are you in there?" asked his mother, getting down on the floor and trying to look underneath the door. All of them crouched beside her, looking for cracks in the door.

"William, darling, do open the door!" pleaded the assistant lady.

They all listened carefully. At first they could hear nothing, then there was the sound of a window being forced up.

"Oh, no," said Sluke. "He's trying to climb out. He'll break his bloomin' neck or split his head open . . ."

"It won't be the first time," said the assistant lady. "Remember the time he collided with a golf club."

"William, open this door at once!" said his mother firmly, giving the assistant lady a glare.

"I can't," said a faint and rather frightened voice. "It's stuck."

"Well, don't panic, darling," said his mother.

They could hear him climbing down from the window-sill on to the bathroom floor. Bessie and Jessie put their hands to their ears. If he stood on the wrong part of the Indian rug, he could be in more danger than climbing out of the window.

"It wasn't my fault," complained William plaintively. "The door stuck when I shut it."

They could hear him clearly now behind the door. He turned the handle again, but it still wouldn't open.

"I did try to shout for you," said William, "but you were all listening to some music."

"Sorry about that, darling," said his mother.

"I'll just try the window again," said William. "I got it open just now. There's a drainpipe not far away. Looks jolly easy. I'll just move this table on top of the bath so I can climb a bit higher . . ."

"A table?" exclaimed the assistant lady. "On top of a bath?"

"Ouch, urgh, nahhh . . ." yelled William. There was a loud crash.

"Darling, are you OK?" shouted his mother.

There was silence. Bessie and Jessie were sure that he had fallen through the hole in the floor.

"It's all right!" said William suddenly. "I just stood on a snooker ball."

"A snooker ball?" said the assistant lady. "In a bathroom?"

"Oh, stop making inane remarks," said William's mother.

"I'm now on the windowsill," announced William. "If I just lean out a bit further I'll be able to . . . ohhh!!"

"I can't bear it any more," moaned his mother. "Can't someone *do* something?"

"William, just stay on the windowsill," shouted Snotty. "Don't move any further. And don't stand on the carpet whatever you do. Sluke come with me."

Snotty raced downstairs. They got the step ladder from the basement and set it up in the middle of the football pitch. Sluke was sent up the ladder first, to tear away the bit of hardboard that had been tacked over the hole in the ceiling, not for any artistic reasons but to stop their football getting lost. Sluke then held the ladder while Snotty climbed through the hole.

William nearly fell off the windowsill when he saw the Indian carpet rising before him. He'd begun to feel dizzy anyway, at the thought of climbing down the drainpipe.

"This way, Wills," spluttered Snotty, his mouth filled with bits of dust and plaster and his head covered in Indian carpet.

He helped William through the hole and they both came down the ladder. Sluke's attention wandered just as they stepped on the bottom rung; he saw some football scores on the wall he'd forgotten to alter. Snotty, William and Sluke all fell in a heap, but fortunately none of them was hurt.

The noise brought the others rushing down the stairs. William was given a huge hug by his mother – who then proceeded to give Snotty a hug as well.

"Our hero," she said. "What would we have done without you?"

"Ugh," said Snotty, a bit embarrassed at being hugged.

William was brushed down. Snotty was thanked again, and so was Sluke, for playing football with Harry if not William.

As the visitors were walking down the front hall, Mrs Cheatham's eyes could be seen peering through the letter box. She'd watched the Rolls, observed people going inside Snotty's house, heard banging and shouting, windows opening, things crashing, and had naturally come to investigate.

The assistant lady opened the door and walked straight into Mrs Cheatham, sending her sprawling. Both ladies immediately helped Mrs Cheatham to her feet.

"I do hope you're all right," said the leading lady.

"You should be a bit more careful. Bloomin' cheek, coming out of a door without looking properly, who do you think you are anyway . . ."

Mrs Cheatham got to her feet and glared at the two ladies.

"Oh . . . er . . . oh, I don't believe it."

"I say, you are all right, aren't you?" said the leading lady.

"I'm all right, thank you, your Highness, your Majesty, your Excellency . . ."

"Are you sure?" said the leading lady.

Up and down the street neighbours were peeping out, watching the scene on Snotty's front-door step. They'd all spotted the Rolls and, like Mrs Cheatham, had wondered who Snotty's posh-looking visitors might be.

"Once again," said the leading lady, turning to shake Snotty's hand, "many thanks indeed."

Across the road there was a flash as a photograph was taken from the top flat at number 26. At number 24 they had even managed to get out their camcorder.

"It was awfully good of you to have us," said the leading lady. "Great house, brilliant ice-cream, marvellous facilities, and I did love Zo-Ee . . ."

"You've been talking to Zoe?" said Mrs Cheatham.

"Listening to her," said the leading lady. "And I'm sure it's going to be a great project. Goodbye . . ."

6

The *Letter* came second delivery. It meant that Snotty only saw it when he came home from school. It didn't have a stamp, which was the first thing that struck him as fairly peculiar. There was simply a funny red circle and an embossed seal on the back of the envelope.

"Don't just rip it open," said Sluke, coming into the house behind Snotty. "You know I collect that sort of stuff."

"I thought you collected stamps?" said Snotty. "Well, there's no stamp on this, so hard cheese."

"Let's have a look," said Sluke, trying to grab it. "Heh, that's even better! I'll have that for my postal history collection."

"What's that, then?" said Snotty.

"That means envelopes, or covers as we experts call them. It includes the study of different postal markings. This one looks official, because of the red franking. Open it carefully."

"How boring," said Snotty, ripping the envelope

open. "I bet it's from Social Services. That cruddy old Mrs Pratt, poking her nose into my business again."

Snotty's angry face began to turn into Snotty's happy face, as he slowly read the letter. Then he handed it triumphantly to Sluke.

Kensington Palace
London, SW1
    Dear Mrs Bumstead,
    HRH the Princess of Wales has asked me to write and thank you for the hospitality and kindness she received at your house the other day. She was particularly grateful to your charming son "Snotty", hero of the hour, for his help with Prince William. The ice-cream was also much appreciated! Good luck with the Project Zoe. We wish it all success.
    Yours sincerely,
    Lady in Waiting

"That's not fair," said Sluke, when he'd finished reading the letter. "It was me who had to play with those soppy kids. I did all the hard work. You just sat around chatting, listening to your stupid music and eating my ice-cream, which I was saving, so you owe me some. If you ask me, I should get a knighthood, for giving up my ice-cream and playing with those kids."

"It's my house, remember," said Snotty, taking the

letter back from Sluke. "*My* indoor pitch, *my* game, *my* rules which I invented."

"So? I still did all the work. OK then, I'll accept an OBE . . ."

Sluke took a drink from the fridge and sat down on the football pitch floor to study the envelope, examining the franking and the seal.

Snotty suddenly rushed up the stairs, and came down a minute later, moaning and groaning, shouting and cursing, still holding the *Letter* in his hand.

"Who's stolen all the pens in this house?" yelled Snotty, opening drawers and emptying things out.

"I dunno," said Sluke. "It's your house, remember."

"I've *got* to find a pen," shouted Snotty. "This is urgent."

Sluke stood up languidly and fetched Snotty's Spurs bag which Snotty had dumped on the hall floor after school.

"Here's a Biro," said Sluke, producing one from the bag. "You can never find things, can you, Snotty."

"That's red, you idiot!" said Snotty, snatching it from Sluke's hand and hitting him with his bag. "I want a *black* pen."

"Oh, why didn't you *say*?" said Sluke. He slowly took his best black felt-tip pen from a string round his neck.

He kept it hidden there, under his T-shirt, so that people like Snotty could not borrow it.

Snotty laid the letter flat on the hall shelf. Very carefully, he read it through again and then added one small mark – a comma between the words "Project" and "Zoe".

"What you doing that for?" said Sluke. "You're mucking it up, and it's not even your letter."

"Now read it," said Snotty. "It looks as if she's talking to my mum personally, saying 'Good luck with the Project, Zoe,' instead of wishing us good luck with our Project Zoe record."

"Yeh," said Sluke. "I suppose it does. So what?"

"So it looks as if she knows my mum. As if my mum was here when she visited us. Get it? All the nosy neighbours in our street will be convinced that my mum is here. Well, most of the time anyway. Oh, give it to me, you dum dum."

Snotty took the letter to his mother's room and made twenty copies of it on her photocopying machine.

"Take one to your mum," said Snotty. "Let her see it. Flash it around. Feel free."

"What about Jessie and Bessie?"

"Yeh, one for them as well," said Snotty. "And one for Mrs Cheatham. One for that pig with the dog. Two for the people opposite taking photographs. One for Mr Patel to put in his shop window. One for Marine Ices to frame and put on the wall with the letters from other famous people. Oh, yeh, one for the *Ham and High*. It'll probably make their front page.

"We want as many people as possible to know we've had Royal Visitors. It should give us a breathing space for a few weeks. And make us pretty famous."

4

Snotty and the Rent-a-Mum

I

Mrs Potter's ultimatum came on a Wednesday morning. It arrived by recorded delivery at Snotty's house before he went to school. At school a copy of it was put into his hand by Mrs Potter's secretary, who made him sign that he had received it. When he got home from school he turned on the answering machine to find the same message repeated. Snotty's mother was to appear at school a week on Friday at five o'clock, ten days ahead. Or else.

For a day Snotty was in a daze, unable to concentrate his normally incisive mind. Sluke dropped some of the latest flavour of ice-cream on his head, by mistake of

course – Sluke never wasted ice-cream – but Snotty didn't seem to notice.

When Jessie or Bessie mentioned the appointment, he muttered that he would go into hiding, or run away to sea on a tramp steamer (he'd always wanted to be a tramp), or go on the road with a travelling theatre.

He was flicking over the pages of his mother's copy of *The Stage* at the time. And it was this that suddenly galvanized his slumbering mind into instant and brilliant action.

"We'll hire one!" he shouted.

"Hire what?" said Sluke.

"A mum, of course," said Snotty. "This paper is full of people looking for parts. Trained people, who can act. We'll hire one of them to be my mum."

"What if she doesn't look like your mum?" said Sluke.

"That doesn't matter," said Snotty. "Mrs Potter has never seen my mum. As long as she can act like my mum might act, that'll do."

All four of them lay on the floor and spread out the pages of *The Stage*, studying the advertisements very carefully. Jessie was sent to get a sheet of clean paper and a pen, as her handwriting was the best.

They found there were two columns of classified adverts, one headed "Artists Wanted (Professional)", which seemed mainly for exotic dancers to work abroad, and the other "Artists Wanted (Amateur)" which seemed to be for people to act in local theatres or panto-mimes.

They decided to advertise in the professional column, because they would need a high standard of acting to convince Mrs Potter. But they were a bit confused by the exotic dancing.

"What's exotic dancing?" said Sluke.

"Dunno," said Snotty. "But we'd better put it in. Seems to be mentioned in most of the ads."

"OK, then," said Sluke. "Write this down, Jessie: 'Someone to be Snotty's mum and do exotic dancing . . .'"

"Don't be stupid," said Jessie. "We can judge if someone's a good mum, but how can we judge exotic dancing if we don't know what it is?"

"She's right," said Bessie. "And, anyway, Mrs Potter would get suspicious if someone starts doing exotic dancing all over her office."

Once again, they studied all the advertisements, noting that most of them gave exact details, such as age of the part to be played.

This led to further arguments. Snotty maintained his mother was twenty-seven, which was what she had always told him, but Jessie and Bessie said this must be a lie. It would mean she had had Snotty when she was about fifteen, which was ridiculous.

Then there were discussions about what his mother looked like, the colour of her hair, complexion, distinguishing marks. Snotty himself did not seem to be sure what she looked like, at least he couldn't think of the right words to describe her, but then she had been away for many weeks now. In the end Jessie produced the best solution. Applicants must send a photograph. Quickly she wrote down her advert in her best handwriting before anyone could change it:

Wanted: actress to play part of mother, aged 30–40, short season only, but excellent remuneration for the right person. Send photo and CV. Box 124X.

They waited all weekend, then Monday, Tuesday and Wednesday: yet still not one response. By that time they were all arguing among themselves, blaming each other for getting it wrong. It meant there were only two days to go: their last two days of freedom, perhaps for ever, before all was discovered.

"Your fault," said Snotty. "I wanted to put in a phone number. We'd have had lots of replies by now."

Bessie and Jessie had persuaded him that a phone number was a bad idea. If you advertised your real phone number, people could check up on you. Who, for example? said Snotty. Just people, official people, any people, wanting to know what was going on.

Their mother always used a box number when she sold things, which meant that people sent their replies to the newspaper who then passed them on. That way you could study the handwriting, the address, perhaps a photograph, before deciding if the applicant was suitable.

"If we get nobody," said Snotty, "you'll have to do it, Sluke."

"Ha ha," said Sluke.

He often dressed up as an adult, of uncertain sex, when helping Snotty to get money out of the cash-dispensing machine on busy days, but that could not be done very often, or very convincingly. After all, Mrs Potter knew Sluke.

"How about your friend Doc milkman?" said Sluke. "With his long hair and ear-ring, he could easy look like a woman."

"Not like my mum, you pig," said Snotty, giving Sluke a kick.

"Actually," said Jessie, "looks are not the most important thing. It's how you behave yourself, whether you can talk and think and act like a mum. That's going to be the difficult part for any actress."

"So difficult, no one wants the job," moaned Snotty. At that moment there was a gentle knock at the front door, then another, equally hesitant.

"It must be someone after the job," said Sluke, jumping up.

"Don't be daft," said Snotty. "No one knows the address. We gave a box number."

"Perhaps she thinks this is the box," said Sluke. "You have rather knocked the house about."

"Just sit down and shurrup," said Snotty.

The knocking started again; then they could hear someone fumbling with the letter box.

"You can answer it, Sluke," said Snotty, "for giving cheek."

It was Mrs Cheatham on the front step, beaming.

"Is Snotty in?" she asked, all smiles.

"He might be," said Sluke. "Who wants him?"

"Everybody, if you ask me," said Mrs Cheatham. "He's suddenly become so famous. So I hope he can spare me just a few minutes?"

"He's in conference," said Sluke, rudely. "Tell me what you want. I'm his spokesman."

"OK, then, you'll do. As you're so big and strong. You can come and give me a hand."

She stepped over the little wall on to her front steps and through her front door, followed by Sluke. Just inside her door was an enormous grey mailbag, filled to the brim with letters.

"This came this morning when Snotty was at school,"
she said. "Good job I was in. Now can you manage
them, Sluke? I'll just lead the way . . ."

" 'S all right," said Sluke, lifting the bag on to his
thin shoulders, staggering under the load. "I can
manage. Thank you very much."

He staggered across to Snotty's front steps, managing
to stop Mrs Cheatham following him, though she was
desperate to get in.

"What do you think the letters are for, Lucas?"

"For Snotty."

"I mean why is he getting so many?"

"Fan letters, I should think," said Sluke.

"Well, he is ever so famous, since the Royal visit,"
said Mrs Cheatham. "Everybody's talking about him,

saying what a lovely boy he is. I always said so myself.
I remember taking him out in his pram when he was
little, you know, what a treasure. Sometimes I baby-sat,
when his mother was out at a film première, oh, he was
always . . ."

"Thank you, Mrs Cheatham," said Sluke. "Sorry
you've been bothered. And goodbye."

Sluke closed the door, with Mrs Cheatham outside.

Snotty, Bessie and Jessie could not believe their eyes
when Sluke emptied out the mailbag. There were 1,713
applications for the job. Most contained photographs.
All contained phone numbers.

"Cor, where have they all come from?" said Sluke.

"It's because of the unemployment," said Jessie. "I
think every out-of-work actress in the world has applied
for the job."

They started at once sorting through the applications.
Snotty said all bad handwriting had to go. Being a bad
handwriter himself, he didn't want to have to read bad
handwriting. Silly jokes won extra points; his mother
always made silly jokes in letters. As for the photographs, Snotty had the final say on which ones looked
most like his mother.

It took them two hours to make a short list of fifty.
Then they started ringing people, saying auditions would
be tomorrow from four o'clock onwards, could they be
there, yes or no? When ten people had said yes, no
question, they would be there, Snotty was bored and
told the others to put the rest of the letters back in the
mailbag.

"Phew," said Snotty. "I'm knackered."

"The real hard work is to come," said Jessie.

"How do you mean?" said Sluke.

"What on earth are we going to ask them?"

RENT-A-MUM: MULTIPLE CHOICE QUESTIONS FOR ALL
THOSE APPLYING TO ACT AS SNOTTY'S MUM. TICK ONE
ONLY. THANK YOU.

A. When Snotty says, "I'm bored, Mum," do you answer:

  1 Only boring people are bored.
  2 Being bored is part of the growing-up process, so the sooner you learn to live with it the better, my lad.
  3 So am I, Snotty. I know, let's go to the pictures together.

BORED →

B. When Snotty wakes up in the morning and says he feels sick and is not well enough for school, do you:

  1 Groan, then pretend not to hear him, carrying on reading *The Independent*.
  2 Say, "It's your own stupid fault. I told you not to go out in the rain yesterday without a jacket."
  3 Say, "Poor you. Have the morning off, then if you feel a little bit better at lunch time, we'll go to McDonalds."

HAPPY →

C. When Snotty comes home from school and says he has not been picked for the team, do you say:

1 I'm not surprised. You never went to training.
2 I hope that means next time you'll try a bit harder.
3 I think you're right, Snotty. That teacher has always been against you.

UNHAPPY

D. When Snotty says that everyone in his class has got Nintendo/ a TV in his bedroom/ his own snooker table, do you say:

1 That doesn't mean to say you should have one.
2 That's funny, I was talking to Jessie's/Bessie's/ Sluke's mum only yesterday and they certainly haven't got such things.
3 Great idea, Snotty. We'll get one at once, only bigger.

BORED →

E. When Snotty says, "I've nothing to do, Mum," do you say:

1 When I was your age, I only had old saucepans and spoons to play with, but I was always gainfully occupied.
2 Read a book.
3 Here's some money, why not go and get a video from Mr Patel?

F. When Snotty has lost something, do you say:
  1 It's your own fault. You're always losing things. You'd lose your head, if it wasn't tied on.
  2 Now just think back to exactly where you had it last.
  3 Don't worry, it'll turn up if you don't think about it.

HAPPY →

G. When Snotty comes home and says he only got 17% for Maths, do you say:
  1 I'm surprised you got as much as that, the way you revised.
  2 Right, my lad, extra homework from now on.
  3 Heh, that's pretty good. Let's go to Marine Ices and celebrate.

UNHAPPY ←

The idea of having some multiple choice questions had been first suggested by Jessie. She said that to interview ten people was going to be very difficult, in fact it could take hours. They needed a simple method of eliminating the useless ones, the out-of-touch, the dum dums, the horribles, the no-hopers, the old bats, the drears, the humourless or those people only doing it for the money.

"They're all doing it for the money," said Bessie.

"Yes, but we want Snotty to have a mother who also cares, someone on his wavelength, someone he can relate to."

"You're sounding like a social worker now," said Sluke.

"Good," said Jessie. "The lucky applicant might have to deal with a social worker, after she's managed to con, I mean impress, a Head Teacher."

Jessie tried her multiple choice questions on the other three, asking them to tick the answers they would like their ideal mother to give. She altered a few words here and there, refining and rearranging them on Snotty's mother's word processor, then printed them out and made ten copies. Finding ten pens which had not dried up and ten unbroken pencils took almost as long as thinking up the questions.

Together, they then agreed on how they would judge the applicants, depending on which answers they ticked. Once again Jessie wrote it all down, so there would be no arguments later about what they had decided and what sort of mum they were looking for:

UNHAPPY

NUMBER ONE answers. Any applicant ticking even one of the Number One answers would immediately be identified as a bossy boots, horrible, yuck-making, totally unfit for the role of anyone's mother, let alone Snotty's mother. Such people would be eliminated at once. Thank you and goodbye.

BORED →

NUMBER TWO answers. These would indicate a certain seriousness, a certain concern, a certain toughness, but too many of them would count against the applicant. Thank you, don't ring us, we'll ring you.

HAPPY →

NUMBER THREE answers. These were what Snotty would want to hear from his mum. A clean sweep of number threes, and bingo, the job would be filled. Well done, when can you start?

4

All four of them were on their best behaviour at school on Friday, especially Snotty and Sluke. Should either of them be kept in detention then the whole interviewing process would be ruined. It had been agreed they would have equal votes, but that Snotty would have the casting vote in the event of any disagreements.

"I've just realized something," said Sluke, as he and Snotty ran home, both of them quickly out of puff, thanks to all those weeks of ice-cream and chips. "If me, Jessie and Bessie vote for someone you don't like, that means it's three to one, so that's not fair, if you then out-vote us."

"Life's not fair," said Snotty.

"You sound like the sort of mum we don't want," said Sluke. "Saying things like that . . ."

"I was just joking."

"How will we know if the applicants are joking or being serious?"

"I'll know," said Snotty. "I always know with my mum."

There was already a short queue outside Snotty's front door when he got home. Seven out of the ten were sitting on the front steps, some carrying little make-up cases, some a change of clothing. Three of them had been there all the afternoon, as Mrs Cheatham had observed, watching from behind the curtains.

"What's going on?" said Mrs Cheatham, opening her front door the moment she saw Snotty arriving home.

"They're Snotty's groupies," said Sluke. "Now that he's mega famous."

"Ignore him," said Snotty, giving Sluke a thump. "They've come for my mum, that's all."

He'd chosen his words very carefully, so as not to confuse the actresses, who were all listening, hoping to pick up any clues about what might be expected of them.

"She's going to interview them all for a part, is she?" asked Mrs Cheatham. "How exciting!"

Snotty asked the actresses if they could wait a few minutes longer before the auditions started, then he and Sluke went inside.

Five minutes later, Bessie and Jessie arrived. They'd been home first to change out of their school clothes. First they set up a little table in the hall, where Jessie put down a cassette player and laid out the sets of questions, one for each person, to be filled in straightaway, no talking, no conferring, no looking at each other's answers.

Sluke and Snotty got a long bench out of the back garden and dragged it inside, setting it up at the end of the football pitch. This would be where the judges would sit, interviewing the final short list.

Jessie would first eliminate as many of the ten as possible by giving them the multiple choice questions.

At four o'clock exactly Jessie, wearing her best dress and her most grown-up expression, opened the front door and asked all ten of the actresses to come in. She handed each a set of questions and a pen.

"This is stupid," said one. "I hate questionnaires."

"I'm dyslexic," said another.

"My agent never mentioned this," said a third.

"Thank you and goodbye," said Jessie, sharply, putting on her bossiest expression. She had immediately seen that none of the three was suitable. She ushered them to the door, but managed to turn on the charm when she thanked them ever so kindly for turning up.

The other seven were studying the questionnaires. Some were crouching on the hall floor, some sitting on the stairs, some sitting on their make-up cases.

"What a good idea," said one.

"I love questionnaires," said another.

"Cor, this is hard," said a third, opening her case and taking out a cigarette.

"Sorry, no smoking," said Jessie, opening the front door.

"What do you mean?" said the woman, looking angry.

"The part does not call for smoking," said Jessie. "Thank you for coming."

The remaining six settled down to the questions, except for one at the top of the stairs who kept on looking down, hoping to see what the others were writing.

"That's cheating," said Jessie. "Goodbye and thank you."

So that left five.

When they had finished their answers, Jessie took their papers and marked them quickly. One had ticked every first answer, which they had agreed meant instant disqualification. So she was out. Jessie suspected she had not bothered to read the others, she looked so dozy.

One had ticked four first answers out of a possible eight. She looked alert enough, but very grim and serious, the sort who probably agreed with all the first answers, so she was also out.

Now there were three. None of those remaining had ticked any Number One answers, but on the other hand, none had ticked all the Number Three answers. There was all to play for.

"Close your eyes and pick a pencil," said Jessie. She clutched in her hands three broken pencils that she hadn't been able to use.

"Right, you've picked the shortest one, you can come in first. Then you, then you. Is that clear? Right, first one follow me. You two please wait here. You will be called soon. And no listening at the door. Thank you."

Jessie switched on the cassette player on the hall table. Out came the latest Zo-Ee number, featuring Mrs Mudd. This was to relax the two who were waiting and make it harder for them to hear the interviews in the football pitch, just in case they might be tempted to listen under the door. At the same time she had switched on a tape recorder hidden on the stairs, where the two waiting applicants were sitting, to pick up their conversation.

5

The first applicant on the short list was called Maggie. She was short, fat and jolly, and she wore a full-length Laura Ashley skirt. She didn't look a bit like Snotty's real mother, despite the effect produced by her photograph, but she had an amused, inquisitive expression which appealed to Snotty.

"Hello, Maggie!" said Bessie, trying to be friendly. "Thank you for coming."

"Thank you for asking me," replied Maggie, smiling.

"I've got a Christmas question for you first of all," said Snotty. "What's the best way to serve turkey?"

"I'm afraid I'm no good at cooking," said Margaret, giving another smile, not as radiant this time, quickly glancing round the room. She had been to some unusual auditions in her time, but this was one of the strangest settings. However, people often did start by asking trick questions, just to catch you out.

Snotty put a cross against Maggie on his clipboard. He was the only one with a clipboard, taken from his mother's desk, since he was chairman of the Board of Judges.

The Turkey joke was one of his mother's favourites, so old, so pathetic, so unfunny, yet she always laughed at it. Snotty wanted one of his would-be mums at least to offer a silly answer. His real mother always did that, when she didn't know the answer to something.

"I can't even make toast," continued Margaret. "Unless I have a recipe book."

Snotty gave her another cross, not wanting a mother who couldn't cook, but Jessie nudged his arm, whispering that he should use his rubber. It was a joke, dum dum, Maggie was being funny, you're not the only one who can make jokes.

"How much pocket money do you think twelve-year-olds should get?" asked Sluke, trying to appear serious and solemn.

"I don't know," said Maggie. "One pound a week?"

"What time do you think twelve-year-olds should go to bed?" asked Bessie.

"About eight o'clock?" said Maggie.

"If a teacher complains about your son, whose side would you be on?" asked Snotty.

"Goodness," said Maggie. "That is a difficult one."

They all threw various other questions at Maggie, none of them very hard, none of them meant to trick her, but she could answer very few of them.

"Have you any questions for us?" suggested Jessie.

"I'm a bit confused about the part," began Maggie. "Is it for – er – a tele or a film, a play, or what?"

"Thank you," said Jessie. "Could you please wait outside and send in the next one."

Next came Claire, tall, short hair, wearing a boiler suit and high heels. Again, she didn't look like Snotty's mother, or her own photograph, but Snotty was determined not to hold this against her.

"What's the best way to serve turkey?" asked Snotty.

"Excuse me?" said Claire, looking worried.

"Not a bad answer," said Jessie, putting B+ on Snotty's clipboard, the way Miss Eager did on essays, at least on Jessie's essays. Snotty usually got 'See Me' on his, which he maintained meant C.

"Tell me," said Sluke, "how much do you think twelve-year-olds should get as pocket money?"

"It would depend on the financial and socio-cultural circumstances," said Claire, staring into the faces of her four inquisitors, searching for clues. The setting did not worry her, as she liked a confrontational interview, and was used to them, but she would have preferred more information about inner motivation vis-à-vis her character.

"If your son was not invited to his best friend's party, what would your reaction be?" asked Jessie.

"We would have to define first of all the meaning of 'best friend'," said Claire. "Is it a subjective or objective term? A simple value judgement, or based on a long-term one-to-one relationship? In parenting, it is not always viable to . . ."

"Any questions for us?" asked Jessie, bewildered.

"Who is the director going to be, and is it Brook school acting or Stanislavksy?"

"Thank you," said Snotty, yawning. "Next, please."

The last applicant was called Flora. She was of medium size, medium build, with long curly red hair and spectacles. She was even less like Snotty's mother than either of the other two.

"I didn't realize your hair was red," said Snotty, looking at her photograph.

"It can be any colour you like," said Flora, taking off her wig to reveal short blonde hair. "And so can the specs. They came out of a Christmas cracker."

"How much do you think twelve-year-olds should get for pocket money?" asked Sluke.

"Personally, I think all twelve-year-olds should be out earning their own money," said Flora, very solemnly. "Either by going down the coal mines, or pulling ponies along. Failing that, I'm a great believer in them sweeping chimneys."

All four children looked horrified, till Flora burst out laughing. Snotty gave her a big tick. Jessie added an A.

"What about going to bed?" said Bessie. "When should they go?"

"When they're tired," said Flora.

"If your son didn't get invited to his best friend's party," asked Sluke, "what would you do?"

"Hold a party for him the next week – and invite his best friend, and everyone else he's ever known . . ."

They went through all the questions they had asked before, plus a few more, and each time Flora either gave a silly answer which made them laugh or a serious one with which they agreed.

"Any questions for us?" asked Jessie.

"Yeh," said Flora, looking at the goal posts chalked on the wall. "What time does the match start?"

"Oh, we do have one final question," said Snotty as Flora was getting up. "What's the best way to serve turkey?"

"Join the Turkish army," said Flora, walking towards the door. "Boom, boom."

As she reached the door she turned and took an imaginary kick at an imaginary ball, scoring an imaginary goal in off the fridge. She went out into the hall celebrating an imaginary goal.

6

Snotty was standing at the counter in the school secretary's outer office. At a school the size of St Andrew's Road Comprehensive, even the school secretary has an outer office. This was as far as most pupils ever got, to hand in notes, messages or registers, unless they were being called before the Head for some misdemeanour.

"This way, Mrs Bumstead," said a junior, opening the door into the secretary's room and pointing to an old but comfortable-looking sofa and a couple of wooden chairs.

The school secretary was working on a computer and looked up only to give a brief but cold nod to Snotty and then a brief but slightly warmer nod towards the woman with him.

"Mrs Bumstead?" she said, already ticking the name on a list beside her.

"Guilty," said Flora.

The school secretary had been at her desk when the real Mrs Bumstead had first come to school with her son while in his last term at primary school, but that had been a year ago. Hundreds of parents had passed through her room since then, plus thousands of notes, messages, registers and quite a few naughty pupils.

"Nice class of sofa," said Flora, sitting down. "Just as comfortable as I remember from last time."

Snotty had explained to Flora that his mother had been to the school only once, when she and Snotty had been seen by the Deputy Head. He had carefully briefed her on Mrs Potter, on the names of his main teachers, the names of the main buildings, his best friends, but he had not actually mentioned anything about furniture.

"That sofa's new," said the school secretary. "A gift from the Parents' Association. I don't know what we'd do without them."

"Very true," said Flora. "Without parents, where *would* we all be? Non-existent, if you ask me . . ."

The school secretary looked startled, wondering what this parent was talking about. Snotty gave Flora a nudge. He had warned her not to talk unless spoken to directly. That was his well-tried formula for getting through his school life.

Flora was wearing his mother's clothes, complete with one of her floppy hats. This helped to disguise her short-cropped, punk-style blonde hair. She also had on a long-sleeved blouse to hide a tattoo on her upper arm. Even Jessie had not noticed that at the audition. Snotty's mother had not got any tattoos, unless she had acquired one in Africa.

Snotty had briefed Flora on his mother's job, as much as he could, about her film and TV work – something to do with the casting side, as far as he knew. She had gone off suddenly on some secret project in Africa, with some Big Star, to help some sort of Save the World charity.

A little green light lit up on the school secretary's desk. She got up and opened the door into the Head's office.

"This way, Mrs Bumstead," she said.

Mrs Potter was on the phone, giving some instructions, so Flora sat down on a chair in front of the desk while Snotty stood beside her, feeling very small and very worried. He was beginning to sense that Flora was throwing herself into the part rather more whole-heartedly than he had expected. He also did not care for some of her improvisations.

On Mrs Potter's desk were some photographs of children. Flora immediately leaned over and started exclaiming over them, going "Ooh!" and "Ahh!" and "Coo-ee, coo-ee, coo-ee!".

Snotty knew Mrs Potter was a "Mrs", but that had always seemed to him a title, not a marital fact, just as he had called all his primary school teachers "Miss" whether they had been married or not. Sometimes he'd even called the men teachers "Miss".

If he had known any personal details about Mrs Potter, he would have briefed Flora, but he didn't. No, on second thoughts, he would have told her to make no comments or reactions of a personal nature.

Flora was still oohing and ahhing, putting on a range of funny voices, going quite over the top. Snotty gave her a kick on the ankle, hoping she would desist.

"Ooh, cor, luverly, wot a smasher that one is!" cooed

Flora in a joke cockney accent. "Doncha love him?"

Mrs Potter, still on the phone, swivelled round and looked across the desk, wondering who this person was, making all the silly noises.

"Heh, look at this one!" said Flora, now in a deep American accent. "What a hunk."

Mrs Potter put the phone down and picked up some notes in front of her, making sure her five o'clock appointment was with a First Year parent, not some hysterical Sixth Former, suffering from exam fatigue, who had wandered in by mistake.

"Lovely children," said Flora, now affecting a posh English accent. "Are they your own, or rented?"

"What?" said Mrs Potter, still adjusting, putting the phone call from her mind, realizing at last that Flora's pretend kisses were aimed at the photographs on her desk.

"Oh, yes, *les enfants*," said Mrs Potter, smiling. "It is a bit corny, having one's kids on one's desk."

"Oh, it's sweet really," said Flora. "Lots of people do it, in fact I'm thinking of setting up a rent-a-kid business, you know, people who haven't got kids and want to appear caring and loving, they could hire my kids for their family photos. Or say your own kids are horrible and ugly, I could rent you some stunners. Or say your own kids simply refuse to be photographed, which I know a lot of kids do, they can be a pain sometimes, don't you agree, then you could hire my kids, by the hour, by the day, by the metre, well you wouldn't want titchy ones, would you . . ."

"Jolly good idea," said Mrs Potter coldly, glancing at her notes again, and then at Snotty, trying to remember if she had seen him before. He did look rather small, even for a First Year, but he was standing awkwardly,

on one left foot. Had he been injured, she wondered?
The report in front of her did suggest he was not being
properly cared for.

"Then when I've set up that business," continued
Flora, still in full flow, ignoring Mrs Potter's cold stare,
"I might go into rent-a-mum, whatja fink, Mrs P.,
groovy idea, huh? Ever heard of rent-a-mum?"

Snotty glared at Flora. She was now going too far. He
should have signed a contract with her, to play the part
properly, making her responsible if she mucked the

whole thing up. She seemed determined to give things away rather than protect him.

Snotty swung his right foot against her ankles as hard as he could. She gave a yell but managed to grab Snotty's foot and hold on to it, while still talking.

"I have often hired out my own dear Nottingham for photos," said Flora, "in advertising work, and for women's magazines. They often want photographs of the 'surly' child, the obstreperous child, the standing-on-one-foot and glaring child, or even the falling-down-on-the-floor and screaming sort of child . . ."

She let go of Snotty's leg when he least expected it, and he went crashing to the floor.

"Yes, I'm sure there's a call for that sort of thing," said Mrs Potter, checking the report in front of her once again, while Snotty picked himself up.

"You haven't been to a parents' evening yet, have you, Mrs Bumstead?" said Mrs Potter.

"No, and I'm terribly sorry," said Flora, replying in her normal voice at last. "I've meant to each time, and each time it's coincided with panic at work. You know how it is . . ."

"Nor have you managed to see Miss Eager," continued Mrs Potter, "even when she invited you to talk to her informally."

"Guilty again," said Flora, putting on her most demure and humble look.

"The thing is," said Mrs Potter, "Miss Eager has become worried about Nottingham. He has not been handing his homework in on time, his clothes always look unwashed and on occasions he has fallen asleep in class, as if perhaps he has been up all night . . ."

"Ah, the petal," said Flora, giving Snotty an affectionate cuddle. "The thing is, Mrs Potter, speaking mother to mother, which I hope I can, hmm? He's always looked like that!"

Flora smiled, hoping she had softened any further blows or criticisms which might be coming.

"To put it bluntly, Mrs Nottingham," said Mrs Potter, "the signs are that he is being left on his own for long stretches of time."

"On his own?" laughed Flora. "Snotty, I mean Nottingham, is never on his own. He's the most popular boy on the block, always surrounded by loads of friends, the house is always filled with his chums . . ."

"That's what we're concerned about, Mrs Bumstead," said Mrs Potter. "While you are away, which I know you have to be from time to time, because of your work, perhaps he is entertaining too many of his friends?"

"But I love his friends being around," said Flora. "It's only on rare occasions I have to be away, goodness me, then he looks after the place beautifully. Mrs Cheatham, my next-door neighbour, is always saying how kempt our house is. Kempt? Can one say kempt, Mrs Potter? You're the teacher, ha ha."

"That's as may be," said Mrs Potter, frowning at her notes. "But some people are becoming rather concerned."

"Mrs Pratt, by any chance? Well, she was telling me only the other day what a lovely tea he gave her. You do know her, don't you? Social Services. She made a social call. That's why it's called Social Services, boom boom."

"Yes, I know about her call," said Mrs Potter, checking her notes again. "She was not entirely convinced, though she did talk to you on the phone, I believe?"

"She certainly did, and what a lovely conversation we had, but then she is a lovely, caring, wonderful woman!"

"I see she's due to call again next month."

"Oh, I'll be there this time, in the flesh. Every time I'm needed from now on I'll be there, doing my bit, playing my part as a good mother. After all, I need the money . . ."

"What?" said Mrs Potter.

"I mean I need the money from my film work in Africa."

"Yes, I'd heard about that," said Mrs Potter.

"I did think of teaching after I left Sussex," said Flora, "but I knew I wouldn't have the patience."

"Yes, it does take patience," said Mrs Potter, glancing at the clock on the wall. "Among other things."

"Unlike some forms of women's work," said Flora, lowering her voice, becoming confidential, "mine goes in short, sharp bursts. With you, Mrs Potter, I'm sure it must be intense all the time. What problems you must have to cope with, education in crisis, schools under such pressures, opting in, opting out, opting all over the jolly old place! I suspect you hardly see your own dear children during the week, hmm? Hence these lovely photographs on your desk . . ."

Flora picked up the photographs again, but this time she looked at them quietly and solemnly, shaking her head and sighing.

"Working women can so easily miss the best years in their children's lives. So sad, so difficult."

"We all have to make sacrifices," said Mrs Potter briskly.

"Yes, and that often means, from time to time, in little ways, we may neglect our own children," said Flora. "Don't you think, hmm?"

"There is neglect and neglect . . ."

"Any neglect I've been guilty of, and I'm willing to admit it, is now over. The film I'm working on is nearly finished. If you're very good, I'll invite you to the première. How about that, eh, Mrs P.?"

Flora stood up and put one arm round Snotty, smiling broadly. Snotty tried to force out a smile, sensing that Flora had come to some sort of climax in her performance. Then he forced it in again. He remembered he'd taken a vow of non-smiling while on school premises.

"It will be a royal première, will it?" said Mrs Potter with a knowing smile. "Using your royal contacts, of course."

For a moment, Flora looked blank. She felt she'd given a star performance, but here was a line she didn't quite know how to follow.

Oh no, thought Snotty. How could he have forgotten to tell Flora about the Royal visitation? Mrs Potter must have heard about it, perhaps even seen the letter he'd copied. What if Flora now denied having any Royal friends?

"Ah, the Royals," said Flora, thinking hard. "I'll introduce you to some of the Royals I've known all my life."

"That'll be nice," said Mrs Potter, standing up.

"The Grand Old Duke of York," said Flora. "He'll be there, if he's not marching! Old King Cole – we need him there, just to be merry. Boom boom. The Queen of Hearts – she'll be doing some baking for the party afterwards. And if the King in his Counting House can get away, he'll be there as well. It is a children's film, after all . . ."

"Sounds delightful," said Mrs Potter. She shook hands with Flora, signalling that the interview was over.

Then Mrs Potter did a strange thing, something out of character. As Snotty was leaving the room, she gently ruffled his hair. It felt sticky. Had it not been washed for a long time? That was often a sign of neglect. No, it must be some new shampoo.

After they had left the room, Mrs Potter smelt her hand. A mixture of honey and tomato ketchup. Funny shampoo!

7

The next morning, Sluke and Snotty slept in very late. They had been out the evening before, celebrating at Marine Ices with Bessie and Jessie. Then he and Sluke had stayed up most of the night, playing football and watching videos.

"Look at the time," said Sluke, waking up Snotty. He'd got up first and been down to get the last of the tomato ketchup and honey ice-cream. "Gerrup. Flora will be here for her wages at eleven o'clock. Have you got enough cash for her?"

"Don't panic," said Snotty. "I've got plenty."

"Where do you keep it?" asked Sluke.

"Mind your own business," said Snotty.

"I think you should pay her double. She did a great job!"

"Huh, she nearly didn't," said Snotty. "My leg still hurts where she held on to me."

"So that's why you were useless at football last night."

"Yeh, but I still beat you, so there."

"It solves all our problems from now on," said Sluke. "Having Flora as a rent-a-mum. It was a great idea of mine."

"Liar. I thought of it," said Snotty. "I think of everything."

"Well, think of a new ice-cream we can make today. It's your turn."

They went downstairs together. Sluke looked in the fridge, hoping there might be some drinks or other delicacies which he had missed on his dawn raid. The shelves were practically empty, as they were going shopping later, but the freezing compartment looked almost overflowing. Snotty had told him it was full of kidneys and liver, left by his mother.

"Yuck, what a rotten fridge," said Sluke, slamming the door.

"Don't do that, you idiot," shouted Snotty. "I need to get in there. Now I'll have to wait."

"Oh, no; you're not going to make kidney and liver ice-cream, are you? Ugh. Disgusting."

"Heh, not a bad suggestion," said Snotty. "Wish I'd thought of that. You've got a brain cell or two still functioning."

Snotty opened the freezer part and took out a large plastic bag, frozen solid. He held it under the hot tap

for five minutes to let it melt. Out of it he drew a bundle
of ten pound notes, enough to pay Flora, the milkman
and for the Saturday shopping.

"Another of my great ideas," said Snotty.

8

Flora arrived bang on time to collect her wages. She had
a skinhead haircut this time, which appeared to be real
unless it was a skinhead wig. She didn't seem at all
concerned that some of her bank notes were still cold
and stiff.

"Better than handling hot money," she said. "I've
been given some of that in my time, I can tell you, from
dodgy agents."

As she was counting out her money, the phone rang
so she picked it up, still considering she was working,
despite her haircut.

"Zoe Bumstead speaking," she said. "Who's that?"

"Zoe Bumstead," said a faint voice at the other end.
The line was poor and crackling.

"Excuse me," said Flora, putting on one of her silly

voices. "You must have the wrong person, if not the wrong planet. Who are you, where are you, and why are you saying you are me?"

"I'm ringing from Africa," said the voice. "What's going on? I'd like to speak to Snotty . . ."

Flora put her hand over the phone and beckoned to Snotty.

"Oh, no, it must be her," she hissed. "Your real mum."

"Hello," said Snotty, picking up the phone. "Mum?"

"Who else did you think it was?" said his mother. "Old Mother Hubbard? Who was that who picked up the phone?"

"Oh, er, it was Jessie, just being silly."

"Listen, this is just a quick call, only a few seconds," said his mother. "I'm just about to get a boat into the Okavango delta, can't tell you any more details, but this is to say I'm fine and hope you're getting on OK, doing your school work, washing your face, and your hair, and it won't be long now before I'm back, love you, Snotty face . . ."

The phone went dead, just as the front door bell rang. Flora went to answer it.

Snotty sat down, half dazed, rather stunned, but very thrilled to have heard from his mother.

"Good gracious, what an amazing surprise," said Flora at the front door. "This is incredible."

Snotty groaned. He could hear Flora exclaiming and shouting, roaring and laughing. He presumed it was one of her silly tricks so he sent Sluke down the hall to see what was happening, if anything.

Flora was in the arms of the milkman, holding on to him, shrieking and giggling, snogging and kissing.

"After all these years," she said. "We meet again."

126

"Yeh, isn't it amazing?" said the milkman.

"What's going on?" said Sluke.

"We were at university together," said Flora, clinging to the milkman. "My first feller! And he's just as hunky as ever."

"Huh," said Sluke, looking rather embarrassed. "I'll tell Snotty you're here."

Sluke took the milk, sugar and eggs, and went back to the football pitch. Snotty was still sitting on the floor, thinking about his mother's phone call, a happy smile on his face. Sluke told him what had happened.

"Where's the milkman's money?" said Sluke. "I'll pay him."

"No, I'll do it," said Snotty.

Snotty went into the hall followed by Sluke, but there was no sign of the milkman or Flora. Then, through the open front door they saw the milkman sitting in his milk float. Beside him was Flora, her arm round him. There was a burst of peeping on the horn and then the milk float set off, straight down the street, ignoring several neighbours who had been waiting for their delivery.

"I wonder if I'll ever see my rent-a-mum again," said Snotty, closing the door, putting the milkman's money back in his pocket. "Don't suppose it matters. I'll be having my real mum home soon. I hope . . ."

SNOTTY BUMSTEAD
THE HOSTAGE

For Ntefatso Alice Mosheti Ridge of Botswana

I

Snotty and the Tramp

I

Snotty was sitting at the back of the class, trying to look non-existent. He had practised this trick hard ever since he had started at St Andrew's Road Comprehensive, hoping to glide through the first year, if not his whole secondary school career, without being noticed by any teacher. As he was rather small, rather weedy, rather nondescript, this was not too difficult. Snotty had always been easily overlooked by grown-ups.

"Or groan-ups," said Snotty to himself. Despite giving a studied appearance of not being there, Snotty could still talk to himself, enjoying long internal monologues which often made him smile or grimace, which of course he then had to hide. If he was not there, how could he smile or grimace? He quickly wiped his face clean of any expression. A pity about the ice-cream marks. They were still there, left over from his breakfast.

"All people seem to do is groan at me these days," thought Snotty. "Some people have got it in for me, that's what." Then he paused in his reflections. "Am I becoming paranormal? Or do I mean paragliding? Parahandy? No, that's what my gran likes. Panadol? No, that's those stupid pills my Mum uses. Correction. Used to use. I wonder if she still does?"

It was last period on a Friday. The school week was long over, as far as Snotty was concerned. Why didn't they open the cages, let the prisoners out.

Snotty slid deeper behind his desk, almost reaching the floor. He'd better not lie on the floor or he could be taken for leftover rubbish. He straightened up slightly. That could be a mistake. If he fell asleep, and then the bell went, the stupid cleaners might barge in and chuck him in their waste bin.

He stared ahead, not exactly vacantly, but with a sort of occupied vacancy, concentrating hard on absolutely nothing. Apart, of course, from listening for the bell. He had this theory that if you did not look at anyone in

particular, did not catch the eye of any other human being, such as Miss Eager, to mention but one human being at random (who happened to be droning on at that very moment, giving out a list of weekend homework) then the other persons around, such as say Miss Eager, would think you were not there. Eye contact, that was what must be avoided, if one wanted to be invisible.

This had always been Snotty's school rule. But now, because of what had recently happened in his home life, it was even more important for Snotty not to draw attention to himself.

"Zotty!"

Snotty sat upright. Miss Eager was smiling in his direction, holding something in her hand. Oh no. She'd seen him. She'd sussed him out. She was on his trail. It would be the head next, old Ma Potter, who wanted him. Then the Social Services. Then the police. Then that would be it. The game would be up.

A boy at the end of Snotty's row got up and walked slowly towards Miss Eager's desk, looking nervous and embarrassed. No wonder, thought Snotty. If he was wearing state of the art trainers and a black leather designer bomber jacket to school, he'd be feeling pretty nervous. The minute you went into the playground, the giants in the Fourth Year would be after you. It was also said that this new kid had his own barber, his own swimming instructor and his own chauffeur. Poor kid. Who'd want all that, thought Snotty. Well, a chauffeur might be OK, in fact pretty useful. Snotty might hire one himself one day, but having people knowing you had such things, that was the dodgy bit. Better to keep your head down, act ordinary, look scruffy, look non-descript, and appear invisible.

"This letter is for you Zotty," said Miss Eager.

"Special delivery. From your father, I shouldn't wonder, ha ha." She gave a silly smirk, uttered a silly, fawning giggle, and handed the letter to Zot.

Snotty had forgotten this new kid was called Zot. Just the sort of stupid name a pop star would give his son. If he, Snotty, was a famous pop star, and he had a son, he would deliberately call him something dead simple, like John. Nothing wrong with John, as names go. Snotty would quite like to have been called John. Or Tom. Perhaps even Fred. Better than his real name.

This stupid kid's stupid father, the one who was a pop star, had given himself a stupid name, when he'd first become a stupid star. Buzz! – with an exclamation mark. That's what he insisted on calling himself. He'd been born Bobby Bee, so that was the origin of the name. Really stupid, so Snotty thought. Snotty didn't like him, or his crummy songs, but Mums all round the world loved him, thinking that Buzz! was really lovely, really caring, really nice. Ugh, thought Snotty.

"Even my Mum likes Buzz! Says he's one of the nicest stars she's ever worked for. So she says. Correction. So she used to say, actually."

Snotty had not heard from his mother recently, so he didn't know who or what she now liked or didn't like.

Zot Bee was walking back to his seat, holding the letter. "I feel quite sorry for him, actually," thought Snotty.

Zot lived up in Hampstead, in some posh house, and had gone to some crummy little private school, till his dad, the famous pop star, being really caring, really lovely, etc. had sent him down to Camden Town, to Snotty's school, to meet real people, turn into a real person.

"If I had a rich dad, or even just a dad," thought Snotty, "I'd stay at home with my own tutor. Then I'd never have to go to school, ever again . . ."

A smile began creeping across the edge of Snotty's face, totally without permission. It was getting ready to tweak the corners of his mouth, hoping to ignite a twinkle in his eyes then make a dash for his cheeks, but Snotty managed to catch it, just in time. He resumed his habitual blank exterior expression, the one he reserved for school. Inside though, his mind was still tumbling away.

"Now who will I have as my private tutor. Gary Lineker? He's looking for more work these days. Or Gazza, if he can still kick a ball. Perhaps Maradona, if he's free. He was always good in one-to-one situations . . ."

Snotty considered all the other famous players it would be good to have lessons with. He would of course pass on one or two of his own tricks, little ball skills he had

13

acquired, such as in off the fridge. Teaching is supposed
to be a two way process, after all.

"Nottingham Bumstead!"

Miss Eager's sudden yell made Snotty almost fall out
of his chair. She didn't know his nickname, of course,
the one all his friends used, and his mother. He hated
his real name. Almost as stupid as Zot or Buzz! But at
least over the years Nottingham had become Notty and
then Snotty, so Snotty always explained to new kids,
once he had allowed them to become familiar. It could
have been worse. Imagine being called Liverpool or

Manchester or even something truly gross, such as Arsenal.

"Come here at once," said Miss Eager. "I've got something for you."

Miss Eager was now her usual bossy self, no longer smirking and creeping towards that Zot kid.

"I said come here!"

Snotty felt slightly alarmed. What had she got for him? A letter from the School Inspector? A request from the Social Services? A police warrant? Someone was after him, that was clear. He was about to be exposed and then handed over to the authorities.

"Hurry up, boy. It is your turn."

That's it, thought Snotty. He stood up and walked slowly towards her desk.

Miss Eager was bending down, fiddling with something. Snotty wondered if he should make a dash for it now, out of the door, down the corridor and away for ever.

On her desk had appeared what looked like a wooden box. Inside it was some sort of little animal. Miss Eager was now beaming at Snotty, all friendly, all smiles. Her stern expression had just been her little joke.

"It's your lucky weekend, Nottingham," she said. "It's your turn to look after the school rabbit."

Snotty looked furious. He didn't know his school had a rabbit. They'd once had a hamster at his primary school, in the baby class, centuries ago. He didn't think Big Schools had such soppy things as pet animals.

"It must be taken proper care of, but not played with," said Miss Eager. "It is not a pet. It belongs to the Biology Department and they need it back first thing Monday morning. The instructions are here, with all the things you must do . . ."

15

Snotty's face had moved from fury to terror. It was hard enough looking after himself, without having to worry about a stupid rabbit. People didn't realize his situation. There again, the last thing he wanted was for people to realize his situation, or anything else about him.

"I did send your mother a note last week," said Miss Eager, "saying that if it was not OK, to let me know. She did get it, didn't she?"

"Ugh," muttered Snotty, determined to give nothing away. She was trying to catch him out. He must give nothing away.

"So she doesn't mind, does she?"

"Ugh."

"Good, well here it is. Look after it safely."

The bell rang. Everyone jumped up, grabbing their bags, rushing for the door, hurtling into the corridor, hurtling into the weekend, except for Snotty and his three friends.

Snotty stood beside the desk, holding the rabbit

hutch. He was shaking slightly, like a video film which has been suddenly stopped, but the pause button isn't quite working properly.

Sluke, his best friend, had picked up Snotty's bag, his Spurs sports bag, and was standing grinning inanely, quite enjoying Snotty's discomfort.

"What you smirking at?" said Snotty.

"Well, you always used to moan that your mum never let you have a pet," said Sluke.

Jessie and Bessie, who were twin sisters, and Snotty's other best friends, were cooing and clucking at the rabbit in the hutch, trying to attract its attention.

"Ooh you are lucky," said Jessie, putting on a silly voice.

"Snotty's always lucky, in everything," said Bessie. "Just think of his house."

"That's it then," snarled Snotty. "Everything is now ruined. It's part of a trick to catch me. And I bet I'll be caught."

"Don't be so paranoid," said Bessie.

2

It was 18–18 in the world cup final, Camden Town Indoor League, southern section, Snotty's house division. Snotty and Bessie, representing Spurs, were playing Sluke and Jessie, representing Arsenal. They played this game every Friday evening, most of Saturday, and often Sundays as well. That's when they weren't busy upstairs, engaged in one of Snotty's many other exciting games and amusing activities.

The whole ground floor of Snotty's house had been re-arranged for the playing of FOOTBALL. The furniture had been removed, carpets dumped in the cellar, paintings taken from the walls and most of the kitchen declared obsolete, including the sink and the cooker. As Snotty didn't cook, preferring to eat out or exist on take-aways, there was therefore no need to have a cooker. As Snotty did not wash up, there was no need to have a sink.

All that remained in use from the super-duper kitchen which his mother had so carefully designed was her fridge. This was a vital part of the Camden Town Indoor League, southern section, Snotty's house division. In fact they had bought an extra fridge, to even things up and accommodate the extra rations needed during the football games.

Each fridge was considered part of the pitch, meaning you could bounce the ball off it, play one-twos, or score from an obtuse angle by hitting the fridge door first and then into the goal. This often counted as two goals, if Snotty's team happened to be losing.

Snotty often changed the rules, if he happened not to be on the winning side. Sometimes, if the other team scored, in off the fridge, he would say "Ah, sorry, no goal, the fridges are not actually on the field of play. Sorry about that." It was Snotty's ball, Snotty's pitch, Snotty's house, so it was only natural that he could alter the rules of his game.

There was nothing left in the downstairs room which was breakable, apart from the fridges, which so far had survived. To protect the window panes, they always closed the wooden shutters during games, then opened them afterwards. No need to break windows or draw attention to what Snotty and his friends were doing.

Upstairs, Snotty had converted the whole first floor into a GAMES area. The bathroom was no longer a

bathroom, not since the bath had been covered over with
a snooker table. It was now officially the Snooker Room.
Far more useful. Snotty had never liked having baths.

A shame about the hole in the floor, but that had been a minor problem with an overflow, all Sluke's fault, but it added an extra thrill to playing certain shots. You had to be jolly careful not to lean too far back, when holding your cue, in case you disappeared from sight, falling through the hole and ending up downstairs. That counted as missing one shot. (See Snotty's rules, for the playing of snooker.)

Elsewhere on the first floor every possible space had been filled with computer games, video games, electronic toys, space invaders, remote-controlled cars, board games, card games, war games, peace games, end games, anything at all which could conceivably be called a toy or a game.

On the top floor, it was very different. That was totally devoted to MUSIC. Not just the playing of music, with massive stereos, CD's, loudspeakers, juke boxes but the making of music with the use of electronic keyboards, electric guitars, drum kits, and other instruments, plus all the equipment needed for a miniature recording studio. If Snotty and his chums, feeling suitably inspired, hit upon an interesting sequence of notes, or just an amusing sequence of noises, then bingo, they could record it for posterity and for Snotty's mother, to amuse her, on her return. If she returned. It would be proof that Snotty had not been totally wasting his time, and her money.

When she had suddenly left, some time previously, she had not only left behind her bank card, Visa card and cheque book for Snotty to use, but a very nice note telling Snotty "to have fun". He had not taken that literally at first, thinking she would be back in a day or two, no need to change things.

Snotty's mother worked in the film world, and often

Mrs Z. Bumstead   01/96

did go off suddenly on projects, but this time the days had turned into weeks. Snotty had begun to realize he was not having much fun, having to cook boring meals for himself, washing up his boring plates, cleaning the boring kitchen floor, giving himself a bath. She had said have fun, but that wasn't his idea of fun. So slowly he had converted the house to his own needs and uses, his special wishes and personal desires. With the help of Sluke, plus a sledgehammer, he had opened up the ground floor. And with the help of Bessie and Jessie, and his mother's Visa card, he had gone through the various catalogues and ordered a few choice objects to make sure he had fun, fun, fun, on every floor.

"Full time," said Snotty, sinking to the floor. He had said full time would be when someone got to 40 goals, but he'd just scored his side's thirtieth goal, making it 30–29, and so decreed his side had won. Time for a break.

Sluke opened one of the fridges. Every shelf was filled with Coke. No sign of boring things like margarine or milk or cheese.

21

"Oh excellent," said Sluke, quickly helping himself. "So you did buy some more. Excellent."

"Stop saying 'excellent'," said Bessie.

"Well, it's better than saying 'actually'," said Sluke, "which is what Snotty says all the time."

"Actually," said Snotty, "that's the poisoned Coke you just drank. I put arsenic in it, ha, ha."

Sluke pretended to splutter, then finished the can and opened another. "Tastes excellent," he said.

"As you like Arsenal, you're bound to like arsenic," said Snotty.

Sluke took three cans and handed one each to Snotty, Bessie and Jessie, then helped himself to another. When he finished he gave a huge belch.

"Sorry," said Sluke. "Just slipped out."

"You'll be slipping out," said Snotty, "down the street and home, if you don't belt up."

The last thing Sluke wanted was to be sent home. Like Jessie and Bessie, he loved coming to Snotty's house.

"I'm starving," said Sluke, opening the fridge door again, wondering if he should have another can.

"What about the rabbit?" asked Bessie, sipping her drink slowly.

"I'm not eating that," said Sluke. "You know I'm a vegetarian."

"I mean shouldn't we give the rabbit a drink? Didn't it say something on the instructions?"

Snotty got up and they all followed him up the stairs. He'd put the rabbit in his bedroom, when he came home from school, not wanting it hit by a stray football.

On the way upstairs, they stopped to play a few games, turn on a few machines, switch on a bit of music. The rabbit was OK, and appeared fast asleep.

As they came down the stairs again, there was the sound of loud banging on the front door.

"Don't answer it," said Snotty. "It could be the police. We'll pretend there's no one here."

"Don't be silly," said Bessie. "They'll know someone's inside, with all the noise."

The knocking continued. Bessie crept to the front door and listened. Then carefully she peeped through a crack in the letter box.

"It's Mrs Cheatham," whispered Bessie.

"You'll have to open the door," said Jessie.

Snotty opened the door slowly, undoing all the extra bolts which he had put on a few days ago to keep out intruders, such as a couple of pushy Sixth Formers from his school. They'd heard rumours, they said, that some first year kid called Snot had this huge empty house which they thought would be great for parties. Snotty had denied it, saying they'd got him mixed up with someone else. That new kid called Zot, probably. They hadn't pestered him after that.

Snotty opened the door just enough for Mrs Cheatham to see that it was him. Jessie and Bessie stood behind the door, so that she couldn't open it any wider.

Mrs Cheatham was the old woman who lived next door – very nosy, so Snotty thought. She was standing on the step, peering in, holding her black cat Tiddles in her arms.

"I'd like to speak to your mother," she said.

"Ugh, she's not in," said Snotty.

"She never seems to be in, if you ask me," said Mrs Cheatham.

"I didn't ask you," said Snotty.

"Didn't ask me what?" asked Mrs Cheatham.

"Nuffink," said Snotty, putting on his blankest face.

"When will she be back?"

"Soon," said Snotty.

"Where has she gone?"

"Soon," repeated Snotty, a trace of a smile escaping him.

Saying "soon" had made him think of his mother. When he was small, and always wanting things, asking for this, asking for that, when could he have some ice-cream, when could he go out to play, when in other

words he was really annoying, going on and on, his
mother always replied with the same word – soon –
regardless of what he had asked, till he stopped asking.
It became one of their jokes.

"Are you on your own?" asked Mrs Cheatham.

"Wotchamean," asked Snotty, wondering if she'd
spotted Bessie and Jessie behind the door. He didn't

want her to see that he had people in, playing with him. Mrs Cheatham knew Bessie and Jessie's mother and would probably tell her about all the noise and that. They didn't always tell their mother that they were playing at Snotty's house.

"Is there anyone else with you?"

"On the planet, you mean?" said Snotty. "About two billion people, I fink, give or take. Do you know the population will be four billion in ten years time, so Miss Eager says, so we really all have to save trees and fings to stop the ozone layer from getting worse, or something . . ."

"I don't know what you're talking about," said Mrs Cheatham. "Oh, is that your mother? Coo-ee, Zoo-ee!"

Snotty turned round, though he was sure Mrs Cheatham must be about to play some sort of trick on him. His mother's name was Zoe, but Mrs Cheatham could never pronounce it properly, insisting on saying Zoo instead of Zo-ee.

It did look like his mother going up the stairs. Someone was wearing his mother's long Afghan knitted cardigan, which she'd got on one of her travels, and her hand-painted Doc Martens, which she'd done herself. The person appeared to trip slightly, turning the bend in the stairs, but this wasn't surprising, given that the boots had not been tied.

"I thought you said your mother wasn't in?" said Mrs Cheatham.

"She told me to say that, cos she's working, see. Got a lot on, see. Secret film thing. So I've told you, OK? Bye . . ."

Snotty gave Mrs Cheatham a gentle push, easing her out, then closed the door behind her. He ran up the stairs, knowing that Mrs Cheatham would be going out into the road, to stare up at the window of the room which Zoe, his mother, used as her office.

Sluke was already there, taking off Snotty's mother's coat and draping it over a head and shoulders bust which he placed on a chair in front of Snotty's mother's desk. It was near the window, but thanks to the net curtains, only the outline could be seen.

Snotty went straight to his mother's word processor and switched it on, shoving in the Start of Day disc.

"Thanks, Sluke," said Snotty. "Good job you're so tall and skinny, and look like a woman anyway."

"What's wrong with that?" asked Bessie and Jessie together.

"Nothing," said Snotty.

"Pity you don't look more like a man, Snotty," said Bessie.

"Right, you can do the man's job," said Snotty. "You can get the ice-cream."

Snotty made it every weekend, using an enormous ice-cream-making machine which he had bought with his mother's Visa card. Last week he had tried a new flavour. Fried Bacon and Tomato Sauce Ice Cream, which Bessie and Jessie had said was really excellent, though Sluke hadn't eaten much of it. Snotty had also tried Coke and Chips ice-cream which had proved very popular. This weekend he had made a vegetarian ice-cream with carrots and lettuce, a new invention which had been suggested by Sluke.

Bessie went to get the latest batch and took it upstairs to the music floor where they all sat around in Snotty's bedroom, listening to music and stuffing themselves with ice-cream, feeling very pleased that they had fooled Mrs Cheatham.

"This is the life," said Sluke. "You're so lucky, having a house like this, Snotty, organized the way you want it, no one nagging you all the time, bossing you around, having to do jobs and things . . ."

"Isn't it time you fed the rabbit?" said Jessie, a trifle bossily.

"Who cares," said Snotty. "I never wanted it. I got conned."

"Don't say that," said Jessie. "Rabbits have feelings."

"He'll love this," said Sluke, taking his dish of ice-cream over to the rabbit hutch. "Rabbits do like lettuce, don't they?"

The rabbit had quite a lot of the ice-cream, and appeared to love it. So did Sluke and Snotty. They had about six bowls each. Bessie and Jessie were not so keen on the vegetarian ice-cream, preferring fruit or sweets to carrots and lettuce.

28

Around nine o'clock, Bessie and Jessie said they had to go home. Their mother was expecting them. Sluke, who was staying the night, was already fast asleep. Snotty was yawning heavily.

"They always did say that lettuce was soporific," said Jessie.

"Super what?" mumbled Sluke in his sleep.

"Super Spurs," mumbled Snotty, closing his eyes.

"Shhhh," went the rabbit, or it might have been Sluke.

So the girls let themselves out, remembering first to switch on the answerphone, leaving it set so that if anyone rang, Snotty's mother's voice would be heard, saying she was out, but please leave a message, and she would be back SOON . . .

3

Snotty woke up about three in the morning. Some strange noise had disturbed him. He looked around his bedroom, his eyes getting used to the half dark. It was never completely dark in Snotty's bedroom because of the street lamp outside. His mother had always been pleased they had a lamp right outside their front door, the better to deter burglars. The better to attract burglars, so Mrs Cheatham argued. It meant they could see to do their burglaring, so she always said.

"Grunt, zzzzz, grunt, zzzzz," went the noise.

It seemed to be coming from the floor. Snotty looked over the side of his bed. Had some strange animal crept in while he was asleep? No sign of any animal, or even a human. Just a large bundle of old clothes by the look of it.

"Sluke, you pig, shurrup snoring, will ya," shouted Snotty.

Sluke was deep inside his sleeping bag on the floor beside Snotty's bed, snoring loudly. Despite Snotty's shouts, he didn't move. In the end, Snotty got out of bed and gave him a kick.

'Goal!" mumbled Sluke, half asleep, peeping half a head out of his sleeping bag.

"Your rotten snoring woke me up," said Snotty.

"It wasn't me," said Sluke, his head disappearing again, going straight back to sleep, but this time he wasn't snoring.

Snotty got into his bed again but couldn't get back to sleep. He tried counting Spurs home goals this season, then the away goals, but still couldn't drop off.

There was a scratching sound, a sort of rustling and then more scratching, like someone tearing paper, or eating crisps. That must have been the sound that woke him up, not Sluke's snoring.

"It could be Mrs Cheatham's new lodgers," thought Snotty, "having a riotous party next door. That would explain it."

But as he listened, he became convinced that the noise was in his own house. He could hear a sort of soft padding, as if someone was coming towards him, up the stairs. Then it stopped, and seemed to go the other way.

This time he was worried. Could it be a ghost? Or a burglar? One of the reasons he invited Sluke to stay with him so often was to keep him company, stop him worrying, which of course he didn't tell Sluke. He liked to pretend it was a huge favour, letting Sluke stay.

"Stupid Tiddles," moaned Snotty. "That'll be it. I bet it's that stupid cat. She must have got out of Mrs Cheatham's arms when I wasn't watching."

He got out of bed and gave Sluke another kick.

"Gerrup, Sluke. It's that stupid Tiddles. It's in our house. I want you to go and catch it."

Sluke eventually woke up, poking all of his head out of his sleeping bag.

"You what?"

"There's a stupid animal in the house."

"I know," said Sluke. "Your stupid rabbit." Then he went back to sleep again.

"Of course!" Snotty had forgotten all about the rabbit. He smiled at his own stupidity. He got out of bed and went to look at the rabbit, just to check it was all right. The hutch was empty.

"Oh God," moaned Snotty. "Now look what you've gone and done, Sluke."

Snotty switched on the bedroom light and started looking for the rabbit, shouting at Sluke to come and help him. There were so many musical machines and instruments on the top floor that the rabbit might be hiding anywhere.

"It could be sitting in that sound box, rabbiting on," said Sluke.

31

"Just look, don't make stupid jokes."

There was no sign of the rabbit, so they went down to the next floor.

"Oh God, you stupid fool," said Snotty. "You forgot to turn that off."

"Not my fault," said Sluke.

Snotty's mother's word processor was flickering away, throwing a greenish light round the room. Snotty switched it off.

Downstairs, on the football floor, there was no sign of the rabbit either.

"I never wanted that rabbit," said Snotty, for about the hundredth time. "I was tricked into it. I was set up. And I fell into the trap."

"Don't be stupid," said Sluke. "How could you be trapped by a rabbit?"

They then went into the hall and Snotty noticed at once that the bolts had not been put in place on the front door. Bessie and Jessie had gone out last, so naturally he blamed them, though he should have remembered and told them to do it, if he hadn't fallen asleep.

"It's a dodgy door as well," said Snotty, putting the bolts securely in place. "My Mum always worried about it. Anyone with a bit of plastic could easily force it open . . ."

"Like Tiddles you mean," said Sluke. "The cleverest cat on the block."

"Shurrup you. For that you can go in the basement. The rabbit must be there. I'll keep watch."

"For what?" asked Sluke.

"So's the rabbit doesn't run passed you, dum-dum."

Snotty was nervous about going down to the basement. He had hardly been in it, not since they'd moved all the spare carpets and paintings and furniture and pots and pans down there from the kitchen to create the football pitch.

"Go on, don't just stand there looking stupid," said Snotty.

"All right," said Sluke, but all he did was move his big feet a few metres down the hall. "I'll stand here looking stupid instead . . ."

"Right then, you can go home," said Snotty, pretending to unbolt the front door.

"OK then, I'll have a quick look, but that's all. What's the stupid rabbit's name?"

"I dunno," said Snotty.

"Didn't you look at that tag on his ear?"

"What tag?" asked Snotty. "I never saw no tag."

"Double negative," said Sluke. "Miss says you shouldn't use them."

"Get down there," said Snotty. "Or else."

"I'm going," said Sluke.

He opened the wooden door under the stairs, leading down into the basement, propping it wide open with Snotty's Spurs bag. Then slowly he went down the steps.

Snotty waited. There was silence for a long time. Then he could hear Sluke making little noises, going "Puss puss puss," as if he was trying to catch a cat. Then he started going "Woof, woof, woof."

"What do you say to a rabbit?" said Sluke, reappearing. "Bunny, bunny, bunny?"

Snotty pushed him back down the steps, telling him to stop messing around.

Suddenly, there was a huge roar and a lot of crashing and banging, followed by a lot of swearing, the sort of language Sluke did not normally use. Snotty smiled, then his face froze. The voice swearing had not been Sluke's. It was a man's voice, with a Scottish accent.

Should he make a dash for it? Unbolt the front door and get out quick, going for help of course, not to leave Sluke on his own. Or had it been one of Sluke's jokes, putting on a silly voice?

Sluke eventually staggered up the steps, carrying the rabbit in his arms.

"Champion, champion," said Sluke, looking triumphant. "I caught both of them."

"You what?" asked Snotty.

"Come on," shouted Sluke down the stairs. "I've got hold of the rabbit. He won't bite you."

Behind Sluke emerged a very old, very scruffy man,

unshaven, with matted hair and dressed like a tramp.
He stood in the hall and looked around, rather dazed,
rubbing his eyes and blinking. Then he stared at Sluke,
and the rabbit in Sluke's arms, and began to smile.

"If I'd kent it was just a wee rabbit," he said. "Och,
I thought it was a monster rat."

"Yeh, you weren't half scared," said Sluke. "Hiding
in that corner. You looked terrified to me."

"Just cautious, son, just cautious. I didn't want to
harm a wee timorous beasty, oh what a panic was in her
breasty . . ."

"What're you on about?" said Snotty. "And what're
you doing in my house anyway?"

"This is Arlington House, isn't it?" said the man,
slyly looking round.

"If my mother heard you saying that," began Snotty,
then stopped himself.

Arlington House, which was only a few streets away,
was a special place for homeless people and down-and-
outs.

"Where is your mither, anyway, my wee man?" said the tramp. "Perhaps she'd let me stay the nicht?"

"Not likely," said Sluke.

"How did you get in?" asked Snotty.

"The sneck wasn't on the door. I just pushed it. Verra easy, when you know the way."

"Right, now you're on your way," said Snotty, unbolting the front door. "I'll hold the rabbit, Sluke. You get him out."

Sluke, who was as tall as the tramp anyway, led him down the hall and out of the door, pointing out which way to go for Arlington House.

"Do you believe his story?" said Snotty, when they had safely bolted the front door again.

"How do you mean?"

"That he was a tramp, and not a burglar."

"'Course he was a tramp," said Sluke. "Smelled like one anyway."

"You would know," said Snotty.

"Anyway, there's nothing to worry about," said Sluke. "It was just an accident he got in."

"Oh yeah, you don't just walk into people's houses."

"He was looking for Arlington House," said Sluke. "The door was probably ajar anyway, thanks to Jess and Bess not closing it properly, so he thought he'd come in and have a kip."

"Hmm, sounds fishy to me," said Snotty.

"You're getting really paranoical, you are. There's nothing to worry about, I've told you. He was harmless anyway, scared rigid of a little rabbit."

"Okay then, let's get back to bed," said Snotty.

"I wanna drink first," said Sluke, going to the fridge and getting out two cans of Coke. "One for me, and one for the real hero," he said, opening one can and pouring

36

some out for the rabbit. "He's the one who caught the tramp. You should be grateful to him. Lucky he was here. Cheers."

2

Snotty and the New Social Worker

I

It was Saturday morning in Camden Town. The streets were full of stalls and crowds and tourists. Outside the Midland Bank cashpoint, Snotty and Sluke waited patiently in the queue. Well, Snotty appeared to be waiting fairly patiently. Sluke on the other hand was shifting from one foot to another, rolling up his trouser leg, scratching his head and moaning quietly to himself.

Snotty told Sluke to stand still, not to draw attention to himself, though he himself was becoming mildly agitated. There were three tramps leaning against a railing near the cash point, drinking from beer cans, and arguing with each other. Snotty thought he recognized one of them. Perhaps they were going to mug him, once he'd got his money out.

Across the other side of the road, Bessie and Jessie were keeping watch. They were supposed to warn Snotty should a policeman be in sight. Not that Snotty was doing anything illegal. He had his mother's cash card, with her permission, and had been given instructions to use it, but they all feared that a policeman might not believe this, suspecting that a twelve year old with a cash card had possibly stolen it. Snotty knew he could prove he was doing nothing wrong, but in proving it, he would expose the fact that he was living alone and might be taken into care.

At last they got to the top of the queue. Snotty inserted his card and turned to Sluke. "Come on then, quick, give us the numbers."

Sluke had been put in charge of memorizing Snotty's mother's PIN number. He was, after all, supposed to be the mathematical brainbox of class 1Z, St Andrew's Road School. Snotty was usually near the bottom in Maths, and in English, and in History, and in Geography, in fact in most things. But then he was deliberately keeping a low profile, school wise. Why show off and do well, which of course he could, if he really wanted to, so he said. Hadn't he once got C++ in Art? (Whatever that means.)

Sluke was now pulling up his right sleeve, examining several splodgy marks on his arm. One splodge looked vaguely like a cannon, as seen on the Arsenal emblem, the team which Sluke supported. Sluke liked to pretend it was a tattoo, a real tattoo, showing he was a really hard man but, as it had been done with a felt pen during an RE lesson, it had faded and smudged within half an hour. Another splodgy mark might well have been the remains of a rude drawing of a group called Take This or Take Heart, even Sluke had forgotten its name as it was now so long ago. He'd only done it to annoy Bess and Jess.

"Must be on this arm," said Sluke, pulling up his other sleeve. "Ah, here's some numbers. But who's this geezer Gladstone? Was he that Arsenal centre back who turned out to be real rubbish?"

39

Behind them in the queue, several people were becoming irritable, wanting to know who or what was causing the delay.

"Oh I remember," said Sluke. "It was that History test. I was gonna cheat, only she never gave us that question. Now that was a cheat, if you ask me . . ."

"Stop messing around," said Snotty. "Where the hell's the number? Everyone's looking at us."

"Calm down," said Sluke. "I've told you before not to get paranoical."

"What's that say there?" said Snotty, pointing to some letters near Sluke's elbow.

"NIP?" said Sluke looking puzzled. "I'm not nipping myself. It'll hurt . . ."

As Sluke was examining his arm, trying to work out the hieroglyphics, a bossy woman with an umbrella pushed Snotty aside. She took his card out of the machine and gave it to him.

"Out of the way, boy," she said. "I've stood for enough of this nonsense. How old are you, anyway, child?"

Snotty muttered something at her under his breath, then took his card and went round the corner, pulling Sluke with him.

"That was all your fault, you idiot," said Snotty.

Sluke was still looking at his arm, hoping to make sense of the writing. He then started bending almost double, practically lying on the ground, waving his arm in the air.

"You get some funny folk around these days," said one of the tramps.

"I'm not staying here," said another. "That one's got fleas."

"Ah, I've found it," said Sluke. "I was reading it

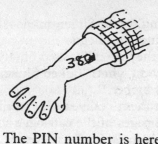

upside down. The PIN number is here, just above my elbow . . ."

Snotty and Sluke waited till the bossy woman had gone, then they joined the queue again. This time they got the money out with no difficulty.

2

"It says here you can send flowers by fax," said Snotty, reading from a mail order brochure. "Amazing."

"Yeah, amazing," said Sluke, not looking up. He too was sitting reading a catalogue.

"But how do they do it?" asked Snotty.

"How do they do what?" asked Sluke.

"Send flowers by fax."

"They squash them really, really small," said Bessie, turning over the pages of the catalogue she was reading. "Then squeeze them down the telephone wire, and send them to whoever you want to send them to."

"Just small bunches, mind," said Jessie, flicking through her catalogue.

They were all sitting in Snotty's bedroom, helping Snotty to decide on what vital new equipment was needed for the house. After Snotty had got the money out of the bank, and bought some food and drinks, they had all gone with him to Dixon's to buy another television set. Snotty had been finding it awfully difficult managing on three, whenever his three friends wanted to watch a different channel. Alas, none of the TV shops in Camden Town would accept Snotty's mother's Visa, or one of her cheques, or his insistence that he had her permission. One shop even called their security department, so Snotty hastily departed.

Instead, they had picked up some mail order catalogues and brochures, deciding that was the best and safest way to order a few new essentials. All they had to do was fill in his mother's Visa number. No questions would be asked.

"Yeah, it is amazing what they can do these days," said Snotty. "Here's another advert – champagne by fax. That must be dodgy. It's a wonder the bottles don't break, coming through the wires and that . . ."

Three pillows flew through the air. Followed by three persons, namely Sluke, Bessie and Jessie. "You dum-

dum, Snotty," they all yelled. "You'd believe any old rubbish."

After they had jumped on him, hitting him with the pillows, rolling him on the floor, they explained to him, very slowly, how a fax worked. They then returned to a quiet contemplation of their catalogues.

"How about this," said Sluke, who was reading a catalogue which specialized in Home Innovations. "A barking dog alarm."

"You what?" asked Snotty.

"It's a thing you hang on the inside of your front door. When it's moved, even a titchy bit, you hear the sound of this horrible dog barking. A bargain at £19.99, if you ask me. It would scare off any tramp, or Mrs Cheatham."

"Who's scared?" said Snotty. "I'm not."

They all went back to reading.

"This is what your life is lacking," said Bessie, reading a sports catalogue. "A heated Spurs shirt, all sizes. It's got a miniature heating element inside the collar. It means you'll never get cold when you're playing in the street in the winter."

"I don't get cold," said Snotty. "I move too quickly."

"Now this is what you do need for school," said Jessie, reading about Education Accessories. "Your own French tutor."

"Male or female?" asked Snotty.

"Neither," said Jessie. "It's a sort of little keyboard with a micro chip which has been programmed with 100,000 French words. Only £59.99. You could keep it under your desk and in seconds translate anything Miss asks you . . ."

"I'm brilliant at French already, thank you very much," said Snotty. "I mean mercy bow cup."

"How about this Revolutionary Portable Exercise bike," said Sluke, putting on his best reading voice, "which turns into a sonic molechaser, ideal for repelling moles harmlessly, and is also good for saving space in your wardrobe as its ingenious interior allows you to pack away vast amounts, especially recommended for airline travellers, comes in 600 denier polyester or PVC vinyl, the choice is yours, Snotty . . ."

"Look, just shurrup reading out the stupid things," said Snotty.

"I'd like a CD Rom thingy," said Sluke. "Then I'd find out what CD Rom means."

"How about a camcorder," said Jessie. "It would be

really useful for filming our football games, then we can play them back. Look, you can get an editing machine which does slow motion play backs."

"Great idea," said Snotty. "We'll get one."

"I think this new mobile phone is what you really need," said Bessie, reading a section on Sports Toys for the Young Executive. "It looks like a pencil case, but is actually a mobile phone. Oh, it only has three numbers, but you can programme them how you like. And you can get it in Spurs colours."

"Now that is stupid," said Sluke.

"Fill in the order for one of those," said Snotty. "See if they do footballs as well. We could do with a new one."

But none of the catalogues did anything as simple as a football. They all seemed to specialize in gimmicks.

"Hey, look," said Jessie, bringing the catalogue to him, pointing out that there was a special hot line, whereby you could ring up, give the order and your Visa number, and items would be dispatched at once.

"That's much better," said Snotty.

"You can also order by fax," said Jessie. "I really think you should get one, Snotty. You can send written messages instantly."

"Much easier for you," said Sluke. "You don't have to talk, so nobody hears your childlike voice. You could send a fax to school pretending to be from your mother, and nobody would ever know."

"Hey, that's great," said Snotty.

So they ordered one of those as well, using the hot line. It was delivered that very day and thanks to Jessie and Bessie, who were very good at reading instructions, they got it fixed up very quickly and showed Snotty how to leave his phone in the fax mode.

On Monday afternoon, when Snotty got in from school, he was surprised to find his first fax waiting for him. He hadn't quite realized that it could receive as well as send out messages.

The fax was addressed to him, by name, Nottingham Bumstead, not to his mother.

It was from Camden Social Services, from the desk of Mrs Pratt, team leader. She had made a visit to Snotty's house, some weeks previously, to check he was OK, having had it reported that he was living alone, probably by Mrs Cheatham being suspicious, or perhaps by Miss Eager, his teacher.

During Mrs Pratt's visit, a real telephone call had

come through from Snotty's mother, somewhere in Africa, while Mrs Pratt was actually sitting there, which was very fortunate for Snotty. Mrs Pratt had therefore gone away happy, or so it had appeared, believing that Snotty was in no great danger.

This new message showed Snotty that she was not totally happy. It was marked urgent.

There had been one previous letter marked Camden Social Services, addressed to his mother, which he had ignored. There might even have been more, but Snotty had switched door numbers with Mrs Cheatham's house, just to confuse any chance callers at his house, or people spying on him.

But this message had come straight into his house, uninvited. It informed him that there would be a visit from Camden Social Services at 4.30 on Wednesday.

"Oh no," moaned Snotty. "Why did I buy a stupid fax machine. I should have got the heated Spurs shirt instead, or that stupid dog alarm . . ."

4

On Wednesday at 3.25, just before the bell rang, Miss Eager called Snotty out and made him stand in a corner. He'd done nothing wrong, in fact he'd done nothing all day, trying hard to be even more non-existent than usual. Perhaps that was his mistake, so he began to think as he leaned against the wall, his arms crossed, an enormous scowl on his face. It might have been better if he had tried to contribute something to the class, opened his eyes now and again, or his mouth, put his hand up about six inches and looked as if he was on the point of answering one of her potty questions, or thinking about answering it, or if he had even just given the impression of having listened to one of her potty questions.

Sluke was making faces behind Miss's back, trying to make Snotty laugh and get him into more trouble.

The bell rang and Snotty made a dash for it, but Miss Eager grabbed him by the arm.

"Mr Ponsonby wants to see you. At once."

"Oh God, miss," moaned Snotty. "I've gorra be home early tonight."

"Don't take the Lord's name in vain, Nottingham," she said.

"Yeah but today it's really urgent, see," said Snotty. "I can't be late. Me Mum said."

Snotty added the last three words without thinking, using the sort of excuse he had used all his life whenever he didn't want to do something, or share something, especially share something, like sweets, drinks or his football.

"Oh she's home is she?" said Miss Eager, just a trifle too brightly.

"Who said she was away?" said Snotty, his eyes narrowing. He thought he'd kept that a secret.

"Oh I was told she was away," said Miss Eager. "In India, is it? Somewhere very exciting anyway, but a long way away."

"You're wrong," said Snotty. "Sussed again."

"Please don't use that expression," said Miss Eager. "Well, I'm glad to hear she's back, if she is back. Now off you go and see Mr Ponsonby."

In the corridor, Sluke, Bessie and Jessie were waiting for Snotty, ready to run home with him as fast as possible and start tidying up.

"Another trap," said Snotty. "It's happened again. There's a constipation against me."

"You mean conspiracy," said Jessie.

"I've gorra go and see stupid old Ponsonby. Here Jess. You take the keys and start clearing up. I won't be long."

Jessie and Bessie rushed off while Sluke went with Snotty to the Science Department to see Mr Ponsonby, Head of Science. It was in another wing, in some prefab huts, and they got lost trying to find it. Sluke waited outside. When Snotty reappeared, they both ran as fast as they could to Snotty's house.

"So what did he want?" asked Sluke as they ran.

"That stupid rabbit. He says I didn't look after it properly. What a cheek! It's had a nervous breakdown, or something. Gone deaf as well, or had a heart attack. I dunno."

"After all that ice-cream we gave it," said Sluke. "I could have eaten more."

"And he says someone's been mucking around with its tag."

"Tag?"

"You know, on its stupid ear," said Snotty. "I saw you pulling it when you were trying to nick its ice-cream, you greedy pig."

"What a lie," said Sluke.

They ran on, both puffing, with not enough breath to talk any more, but Sluke was thinking hard. The tag on the rabbit's ear had struck him as being a bit strange. It had seemed so big, and he'd thought it was making a slight ticking noise. He hadn't mentioned this to Snotty, not wanting to start him off again being paranoid and all that and imagining more conspiracies.

5

Bessie and Jessie had done a great job in a short time, managing to drag up a two-seater couch and a little table from the basement and to set them up on the first floor, moving some of the space invaders and video games to one side. They had also found the kettle and two cups and saucers and one old tea bag, rather dusty, but unused.

"Cakes!" exclaimed Jessie. "We haven't got any cakes."

"I'm not hungry," said Snotty.

"I mean for Mrs Pratt," said Jessie. "She guzzled them all last time she came. Give me some money, Snotty, and I'll run to the shop."

"And what about milk?" said Bessie. "We'll need milk for the tea."

"I think there's some left over," said Snotty, leading the way downstairs to the football pitch.

"Left over from what?" said Jessie. "The last war?"

Snotty opened the first fridge, with a struggle. The door had got a bit jammed, thanks to ten thousand goals being scored in the last few weeks. It was full – but only with Coke. They opened the other fridge. It too was full – with ice-cream. Snotty moved a few tubs while Jessie and Bessie stood well away.

"If there's any milk in there, it won't half pong," said Jessie.

Snotty opened the freezer compartment, took out a plastic bag marked Livver, done in Snotty's best hand writing, hence the spelling.

"Ugh," said Sluke. "I hope we're not eating that."

Snotty went to the sink and ran the envelope under the hot tap. When it began to melt, he opened the envelope and gave Jessie a ten pound note, still half frozen. He kept all his spare money, frozen in the fridge, convinced that no burglar would ever think of looking there.

"Right, get some cakes and milk at the shop, Jess," said Snotty. "As fast as you can. It's nearly half past four. She'll be here in a minute."

Jessie, the fastest runner in their form, dashed off, leaving Snotty and the others to finish trying to make the house appear as normal as possible.

"What about the football pitch?" said Bessie. "It looks sort of, well, like a football pitch."

"I could get some paint and cover up the goals," said Sluke. "And the scores."

Snotty stood looking round at the walls of the downstairs room, reliving past triumphs. Every surface was covered with scores. Even the fridges. "Hmm, don't think we'll have time for a paint job," he said.

"Where did you put the curtains that were in this room?" asked Bessie. "I could sort of drape them artistically and try to hide the jagged bits. Everyone knows your mother is artistic, Snotty . . ."

The downstairs room had been two separate rooms, many years ago, but Snotty's mother had made them open plan, so you could walk from one to another. Snotty, in order to make a proper football match, had made the plan rather, well, opener. Sluke, being in theory the stronger, as he was tall for his age, had done most of the manual work, but not very well. There were several jagged edges, gaping holes, nasty cracks, hanging bits of plaster. That was one of the reasons why their football was now a bit worn.

"No, we haven't got time to worry about this room," said Snotty. "We'll just have to make sure we keep her out of here. Are you listening? We'll take the old bat straight up the stairs, and fill her up with tea and cakes. You know what a fat pig she is . . ."

The front doorbell rang, very loudly, just as Snotty was being very, very rude.

"I bet she heard you," said Sluke. "You shouldn't have said that."

"It might be Jessie," said Bessie.

"Well see who it is then," said Snotty. He never liked to reveal he was at home till he knew who it was, so Bessie went to the window and peeped out.

"It's neither," said Bessie.

"You mean neether," said Sluke. "I say neether. You say neither."

"Look just shurrup, Sluke," said Snotty. "This is serious."

"I mean it's not Mrs Pratt or Jessie," said Bessie. "Looks like some kid."

52

"Then we won't answer it," said Sluke.

The doorbell went again and again, then there was the sound of someone banging on the door by hand.

Sluke went down the hall and tried to peer through the letter box.

"It is some kid," said Sluke. "Least I think it is. In scruffy jeans and trainers and a football shirt by the look of it. Got a fox on the front. Now what team has a fox on the front? Can't see any name. Or his face."

"He'll soon go away," said Jessie.

"Oh no I won't," said the voice as the letter box was opened from the other side. "I've come for a game."

"Get lost," replied Sluke, "whoever you are."

"It's not that Sixth Former, is it," whispered Snotty, "the one who's always on at me about having a party? Don't let him in."

"I still can't see his face," hissed Sluke.

"Hurry up," shouted the voice. "I've come to play football."

"We haven't got a pitch," said Snotty.

"Oh yes you have," said the voice. "I know you have."

"And we haven't got a ball," said Sluke. "It's bust."

"No probs," said the voice. "I've bought my own. Mitre, three quarter size, real leather, really brilliant ball. Listen."

They could hear the ball being bounced on the front step outside. Sluke and Snotty looked at each other. They had forgotten to buy a new one. All the same, they still suspected it was the Sixth Former.

"You've got the wrong house," shouted Sluke. "Try next door."

"Mrs Cheatham hasn't got her own football pitch,"

said the voice. "She's not lucky like you, Snotty. And she's only got one fridge."

They all looked at each other. How could this unknown person know so much about Snotty's house, when he had gone to such trouble to confuse people with its number and to keep his life, and his lifestyle, a secret?

"So come on, let me in, will you?" said the voice. "You're not scared I'll score too many goals, are you?"

"Look, just push off, whoever you are," said Sluke. "You're not wanted here."

"But I am," said the voice. "I've got an appointment."

Through the letter box a hand appeared, clutching an identity card, holding it upside down. Bessie lay down on the doormat and read out "Camden Social Services". On it was a photo of a young man named Fred Forster, his hair in a pony tail, looking about eighteen.

"I'm in Mrs Pratt's team. She can't make it. Unfortunately. So she's sent me. Fortunately. Come on. Get your butts in gear, you guys and dolls. Me and Jessie, or is it Bessie, will play Snotty and Sluke and I'll give you a ten goal start, OK?"

They looked at each other, then slowly opened the front door.

6

"Oh this is excellent, really excellent," said Fred, admiring the football pitch, measuring the angles with his eye, noticing the ancient scores on the walls and checking the two fridges. "Do these count as part of the pitch?"

"Yeah, in off the fridge is a goal," said Snotty, glaring slightly, expecting Fred to say it was a stupid rule.

54

"Oh excellent," said Fred. "So who's got the most assists? The Italian or the German?"

Snotty and Sluke looked at each other, puzzled. Fred

was going round the walls, examining the scores. "Oh you don't seem to keep a record."

"How do you mean?" asked Sluke.

"Well, it would be interesting to see if more goals were scored off the Zanussi at the Kop end of the pitch, which is what I presume you call this end, because it gets the most crowds, or off the Bosch at the clock end. You could collect stats and do graphs and have a Fridge World Cup . . ."

Sluke, who was a great collector of facts and figures about football, was most impressed by this idea. Snotty gave a quick smile at the idea of a world cup between fridges.

"It was always my ambition when I was your age to have my own football pitch," said Fred. "I had my own pencil set and protractor, but that was about all. Didn't do me no good. Never found out what a protractor was for . . ."

"How old are you anyway?" asked Bessie.

Snotty and Sluke had already taken a liking to this young man, to his clothes, his hair, his language, his knowledge of football and his air of boyish enthusiasm, but Bessie was being more wary.

"Too old," said Fred.

"What happened to your hair?"

"That's a bit rude, Bessie," said Snotty.

Bessie glared at Snotty, furious that Snotty, of all people, should be telling her off for being rude.

"You had a ponytail in your photo," said Bessie. "Now you've got a skinhead."

"Number three cut, actually," said Fred. "Camden Market's Best Cut. That photo is really ancient, done when I was a student, centuries ago."

"How long have you been a social worker?" asked

56

Bessie, still determined to check him out.

"All my life," said Fred. "Social workers are born, not made, just like footballers. Right, you and me, Bess, we'll kick towards the Kop end."

Jessie arrived back, after they had been playing for about ten minutes, carrying the cakes and the milk. She looked amazed to see someone new playing football with them.

"Where's Mrs Pratt?" she asked.

"She's injured," said Fred.

"What?" asked Jessie.

"I'm subbing for Mrs Pratt," said Fred, racing down the wing. "She's in the treatment room, but the physio says she should be fit for the World Cup Fridge Final . . ."

Fred put the ball through Sluke's legs, dribbled round Snotty, did a clever one-two against the rear wall, back heeled the ball against the fridge and then headed in the rebound to make the score 10–10. So far, Sluke and Snotty had not managed to score one goal.

Fred ran the length of the pitch giving a victory salute. "U-ni-ted! U-ni-ted!"

Fred then announced it was half-time, they'd all have a rest. Snotty did not protest. Usually he dictated when half-time would be, if a goal was in or out and anything else that had to be decided, often after a lot of argument. The others didn't always like Snotty being so bossy, but it was his house, his pitch. Fred had somehow taken over control of the game, but in an easy, friendly way, without provoking any arguments.

Sluke got Cokes out of the fridge, and handed them round, but Fred said he would drink the milk. Sluke was about to start on the cakes, but Fred stopped him.

"Not during a match, Slukey-pukey," said Fred.

57

"Winning team will have one cake each, OK?"

Everyone nodded.

"This second half is gonna be pretty important," continued Fred, "so you better be ref, Bessie, OK?"

It made it a better match, having a proper ref. When it was finished, with Fred's team winning, they had another rest.

"Time for another game, Fred?" asked Snotty.

"Sure, why not?" said Fred. "I'll just go to the lav. Upstairs, innit? Then when I get back, I'll be ref. In the game after that, Snotty will be ref, then Sluke, then Jessie, OK? Everyone will have a game with a different partner, and everyone will have a go as ref. Right, how many games will that make? You work it out, Sluke, you're the maths genius, ain'tcha?"

Sluke got a clipboard, some paper and a pen, and began working out a list of teams and fixtures and refs,

which took him some time, not being a total genius, so they didn't notice that Fred was quite a long time at the lavatory.

On his return, Fred took the clipboard from Sluke and used it while he was ref, shouting out comments and making notes, as if he was a professional coach.

"Snotty, you're showing signs of nervousness with your left foot. I think you'll need a bit more extra surveillance training or there could be tendencies to problems. Sluke, just because you've got the Italian on your side, I don't want you playing *catenaccio*. Jessie, you know there's no offside, so get up there and poach. Bessie, you'll have to practise with that fridge a bit more. You're being too respectful. I want people in my team who are not intimidated by the reputation of the opposition, even if they are household names in Germany . . ."

When it was Sluke's turn to be referee, he suddenly had a great idea. He rushed upstairs to the games floor and brought down the camcorder, one of the three new items Snotty had bought on the hot line. It took him some time to get the hang of it. He shot a lot of blank walls and bare floors, not realizing it was switched on, but eventually he worked out the focus and the zoom lens and all the other functions.

They played for two hours altogether, before Fred said he would have to go.

"You can come to McDonald's with us," said Snotty.

"Er, no thanks," said Fred.

"I'll pay," said Snotty.

"You've got enough money, have you?" asked Fred.

So far, Fred had asked no questions, made no personal remarks throughout his whole visit, not like Mrs Pratt who had tried to cross-examine Snotty on everything.

"Yeah, loads of money," began Snotty, "my mum left

me her . . ." Then he realized he was giving secrets away. "Er, I mean my mum gives me, I mean it doesn't cost much, for a hamburger and chips . . ."

"No, don't worry, I've got to get home," said Fred, smiling. "I've got write-ups to do."

"What's that?" asked Jessie.

For a moment, Fred looked slightly worried, then he smiled, tearing his notes from the clipboard.

"Write-ups are just reports, that's all, on your progress."

"On our football skills?" asked Bessie.

"Precisely," said Fred. "Did I not tell you I am chief scout for the England Under–14 Football Team? Well, I'd better be going. Ciao."

"Come and have another game some time," said Sluke. It wasn't his place to offer such invitations, but Snotty nodded his head in agreement.

Bessie and Jessie had enjoyed the match very much, pleased there had been no argument for once, and that everything had been done fairly and equally. It had been good to have a new player, to vary the teams and the tactics. They had particularly enjoyed being on Fred's side. But they were still not totally convinced that Fred was really on their side, helping to protect Snotty not catch him out.

"That was really good," said Fred. "Excellent. Well brill. Thanks a bunch."

As he went down the hall, he started shouting and clapping "U-nigh-ted! U-nigh ted!"

"You don't follow Man U, do you?" said Bessie, hopefully. That was the team she supported, though she had never been to Manchester.

"No way," said Fred.

"Newcastle United?" asked Jessie.

60

"On your bike," said Fred, pointing to the fox on the front of his blue football shirt, and then to some tiny letters in the corner – CUFC.

"Not Chelsea?" said Snotty. He could go off Fred completely, if Fred turned out to be a Chelsea fan.

"Nope," said Fred.

"Glasgow Rangers?" asked Sluke. "They play in blue. Or try to."

"You're all wrong," said Fred. "I thought you were true football fans."

Fred opened the front door and went out, thanking everyone once again for the match. They could hear him going down the street, still clapping. "Carlisle U-nit-ted."

7

They didn't eat at McDonald's after all, deciding to get take-aways and come straight home. Sluke had thought of a good idea for their evening entertainment, a bit of

61

special viewing in front of their main TV, the seventy-six centimetre one, before it was time for them all to go home.

It took Sluke some time to work out the instructions for setting up the video and the TV so that he could play back the football game which he had filmed. They all jeered and yelled when at first all that came on the screen was shots of the blank wall and the bare floors.

"Where is Carlisle anyway?" asked Sluke.

"North somewhere," said Snotty. "Or perhaps Wales. Could be Scotland. Titchy place anyway. Must be his home town. Why else would he follow them?"

Snotty and Sluke always felt slightly superior, following big teams, though they were at least their local teams.

"I like people who follow little teams," said Sluke, condescendingly. He was fiddling with the fast forward button, trying to get to the match itself. "Better than following big teams, when you haven't even been to watch them."

"Carlisle were in the First Division once," said Jessie, ignoring Sluke's dig at her for following Man Utd. "A long time ago."

"Shows loyalty," said Snotty. "That's good. I hate people who change their teams, just cos someone's doing well. That new kid in our class, he changes his team every week, depending on who's top of the league."

"Yeah, I don't like that," said Sluke. "If you follow a team, you should follow them for life. Or longer."

"Hey, what's that?" said Jessie, jumping up, pointing to the screen. The bare walls and bare floors had given way to some writing.

"Tune it in properly," said Bessie. "Let's see if we can read it."

Sluke pressed pause and managed to freeze the screen.

62

While trying to get the hang of the camcorder, and film the football match, Sluke had instead zoomed in on the clipboard containing Fred's notes, the ones he had taken with him.

Fred's handwriting was very good so they could make out what he had written. It began with a detailed description of each room, including the bathroom with the hole in the floor, notes which Fred must have made when he went off to the lavatory.

Then there were individual notes on each of them, particularly on Snotty, but not on his football skills, though some of the words were similar to the ones Fred had used.

"Nottingham shows several nervous signs at being left on his own, indication of some behavioural problems and paranoid tendencies, and will require further surveillance . . ."

"Oh no," moaned Snotty. "I've been caught again . . ."

3

Snotty and the Raid

I

"Mum, there's a funny noise," murmured Snotty, half asleep, hoping his mother would cope, as she always did. Then he went back to sleep.

The noise returned, this time much stronger, wakening him up properly. He groaned, realizing his mother wasn't at home.

For the first few moments most mornings, he usually did wake up thinking everything was normal. Then came a feeling of slight panic, wondering how he would cope. Then he remembered that he had been coping, very well. Then he counted his blessings, going through them, room by room, item by item, mail catalogue excitement by mail catalogue excitement.

He managed to go through his excitements so well, so thoroughly, so lovingly, that he fell asleep again. Only to be wakened once more.

"Oh not again. I can't bear any more stupid noises. It can't be that stupid rabbit. So what is it? Must be old Mrs Cheatham. Or her stupid lodgers. What are they doing in there?"

The noise had been a tick-tick-tick sort of noise at first. Now it had turned into a fatter, splishier, splashier noise. He looked above his head and saw there was water dripping down in the corner. Drip, drip, drip. He groaned and turned over. He had noticed a sort of brown patch on his ceiling a few days ago but ignored it, thinking it was just age, or caused by Sluke practising overhead kicks, or perhaps from that time when they'd had an ice-cream fight.

"Oh no. The roof must be letting rain in. How am I gonna get it mended. Oh no!"

He closed his eyes again. "And it's Thursday. That's all I need."

Thursday was swimming, which Snotty hated. "I could just stay here, and swim on my own, the way that water's coming in."

He got up, found a bucket and put it under the leak, then went down to make himself some breakfast. Ice-cream, followed by ice-cream.

As he ate his ice-cream, he thought about the leaking roof. He didn't even know how to get up there. If only his mother was at home, she would know what was causing it, how to get it mended, which builders to call. There used to be a list of workmen's numbers in the kitchen, on a board on the wall, but it had been covered with football scores. She had an Indian builder she used a lot, now what was his name?

"They all think I'm so lucky, having a house on my own, but they never think of things going wrong, oh no. They just say 'Lucky Snotty'. Never realize all the responsibilities. Oh no."

He got his Spurs bag, put in his swimming things, but before going off to school he went next door and knocked on Mrs Cheatham's. He had vowed never to ask her for help, as she was so nosy and bossy, but this was an emergency.

It was raining hard, so he stood on her top step, trying to shelter. He rang the bell and waited, putting his school tie straight, pulling up his socks, rubbing each trainer on the back of his trouser leg to try and make them a bit cleaner. Perhaps he should buy new trainers, instead of new gadgets to play with. And perhaps he should buy some new socks. He'd been wearing the same ones for weeks. His mother did have a washing machine, down in the basement, and Snotty had been told how to use it, but he had never listened. Now it was impossible to get at, thanks to all the furniture which had been dumped in the basement. "Not my fault, actually."

Snotty opened Mrs Cheatham's letter box and peeped through. "Hello, Mrs Cheatham. Are you in?"

He listened. There did seem to be some sort of scuffling inside, but it might just have been her cat.

"Hello-ee."

Snotty's mother always said 'Hello-ee' or 'Coo-ee,' when she went to see Mrs Cheatham, mimicking Mrs Cheatham herself.

"Hello-ee," he repeated. "It's me-ee. Snott-ee."

He smiled at the sound of his own stupid voice.

"Oh hurry up, you old bat," said Snotty.

He could hear footsteps inside. If Mrs Cheatham was at home, she would have answered the door by now. It must be her lodgers. He hadn't seen the latest ones. If they were in, they must be hiding.

Snotty opened his Spurs bag and got out a felt pen and tore a page out of his English work book and started writing a note.

Dear Mrs Cheatem
Urjent. Onlie I
need Mr
Hashish

He had put the note through the letter box before he realized he had not signed it.

"She'll know it's me. Who else has got such brilliant handwriting?"

Then he went off to school.

2

Swimming was last lesson at Kentish Town Baths. Snotty hated getting undressed, going in the water, getting out of the water and getting dressed again. Most of all he hated the showers. There were always one or two bigger lads flicking towels at him, messing around, mocking him. Even Sluke wasn't much support when they went swimming, keeping in with the bigger lads, leaving Snotty on his own.

Snotty found himself getting dressed beside Zot, the new posh kid. He was just as small and weedy as Snotty, but unlike Snotty, he was a brilliant swimmer. Almost, but not quite, as good as Bessie and Jessie, but then they had been swimming almost from birth and were in some club and were always swimming in competitions and galas.

"Jolly good swim," said Zot.

Snotty at first pretended not to hear, looking for his socks and underpants which he feared some joker had hidden.

"That was a jolly good swim," repeated Zot.

"You said," grunted Snotty.

Zot still had leftover bits of his prep school accent, which of course he couldn't help, and they would soon be knocked out of him but, all the same, Snotty didn't want to be seen associating with a posho, even if he had

3' 6"

turned out to be such a good swimmer.

Someone had pinched some of Snotty's clothes. He looked around, under the bench, on the floor, then noticed that Sluke was wandering around with two pairs of underpants on his head, trying to be witty, to amuse the bigger lads. As he passed, Snotty grabbed one pair and gave Sluke a sly punch. Under the bench, he found his missing sock.

"It's my best thing, swimming," said Zot.

"Huh, what's good about swimming?" grunted Snotty, putting on his clothes.

"Well, it's very good exercise," said Zot. "This is my second swim today. Terribly healthy."

"You what?" said Snotty. "You been to this dump already? I wouldn't come here if I was paid. It's a health hazard, if you ask me."

"We have a pool at home, actually," said Zot, lowering his voice slightly. "And I have my own swimming instructor."

"Well, I've got my own indoor football pitch," said Snotty, blurting it out before he could stop himself. "And sometimes this England coach comes and takes us for training . . ."

"Oh, you are lucky," said Zot. "That's what I really want. When my pa comes back from Africa, he says he'll have one built for me. So he says. Do they cost much, Nottingham?"

Snotty hated being called Nottingham. It just showed how new this new kid was, calling him by that name.

"I dunno," said Snotty, shoving his wet towel and costume in his Spurs bag, regretting having boasted about his football pitch.

"Hurry up, you boys," shouted Mr Prodd, the PE master. "Last one dressed will feel my boot up their backside."

Teachers are of course not supposed to hit pupils these days, but Prodd was always grabbing people by the ear or the arm when they got out of line. Not Snotty. He took great care to break no rules, or at least not get caught, but Sluke had often been pushed around by Mr Prodd, just for being Sluke.

"Good bit of swimming there," said Mr Prodd, coming over to Zot, all slimey smiles. "There's a gala at the end of this term, and I'm sure you'll be in the team, so I was just wondering if your father would present the prizes. I've got all his records . . ."

"What a creep," thought Snotty, moving away. He checked his locker for any leftover clothes, as instructed by his mother, and hurried down the corridor.

Outside it was still raining. He stood waiting for Bessie

70

and Jessie to come out of the girls' changing rooms, having promised to take them to McDonald's. He was always starving after swimming, even though he did very little actual swimming, spending most of his time cowering and shivering. He wasn't going to wait for Sluke though, after what he'd done, mucking around with his clothes.

Beside the barrier, outside the swimming baths, was a Jaguar, its engine purring, a uniformed chauffeur at the wheel. Snotty was swinging his Spurs bag and scowling. The chauffeur was watching Snotty, warily, as if he was the sort of kid who might just let his scruffy bag scrape someone's posh motor.

"Like a lift home, Nottingham?" said Zot, coming out of the swimming pool entrance, followed by Bessie and Jessie.

"Huh," said Snotty. "Not going home."

"Well, we can drop you off wherever you are going, can't we Kevin?" said Zot.

"No problem," said Kevin the chauffeur, with little enthusiasm.

"No thanks," said Snotty. "I prefer to walk."

"We'd prefer a ride in a Jaguar to McDonald's, wouldn't we Jess?" said Bessie, admiring the car.

"Hey, that's a jolly good idea," said Zot, all smiles. "I'd like to come with you."

"There's no parking," said Snotty, rather rudely, turning away, followed by Bessie and Jessie.

In Kentish Town High Road, Bessie and Jessie were still going on about how awful Snotty had been to Zot, and how they would have liked to have gone in his lovely car.

"Why don't you get one, Snotty," said Jessie, "on your mother's Visa?"

"Ha ha," said Snotty.

"He's a good swimmer, isn't he?" said Bessie.

"Yeah, I hope he's in the team," said Jessie.

"Pity about his accent," said Bessie.

"He can't help that," said Jessie.

"I think he's nice," said Bessie. "Don't you, Snotty?"

"No, he's a boring show-off . . ."

The girls exchanged smiles as they all went into McDonald's. Waiting for them, just inside the front door, was Sluke. He'd come out of a side door of the swimming pool to avoid Mr Prodd and taken a short cut through a lane. Immediately he put his arm round Snotty's shoulder, showing he was his best and dearest friend.

"I thought you did well at the baths today, Snotty old son. Very fast."

"Fast?" asked Jessie.

"Yeah, I don't think I've seen Snotty get dressed as fast in his whole life. Pity about the swimming . . ."

"Get lost," said Snotty.

3

They queued up in four different queues, just to see who got served first. This was a game Snotty always played. The winner got an extra hamburger.

Sluke appeared to have chosen the quickest queue, and was soon very near the front, waving and jeering across at Snotty's queue, till a Sixth Former behind Sluke pushed him out of the way. It was then Snotty's turn to wave and jeer. Snotty was the first to reach the top of a queue, which was just as well as he had all the money, so the other three left their queue and waited for him.

They all got Big Macs, and double french fries, and chocolate milk shakes and apple tart. Just a little snack to keep them going till their evening meal at home.

"Oh no, look who's at that table," said Snotty. "Let's go upstairs."

He had spotted Fred, the new social worker, who was sitting at a table with a group of other people, all of them women.

"I don't trust him," said Snotty as he led the way upstairs.

It was fairly crowded, but they got a table beside two old men who were sitting reading newspapers.

"I bet Fred's with the rest of Mrs Pratt's team," said Snotty starting on his hamburger. "Did you see them? They all looked like social workers to me."

"You mean because they had specs," said Jessie.

"Exactly," said Snotty.

"That's just stereotyping," said Jessie.

"You can't type with a stereo," said Snotty. "A stereo is for playing music on."

"They could be police," said Jessie, ignoring Snotty's silly remark. "The cop shop is just round the corner."

"Women police?" said Snotty.

"What's wrong with that?" said Bessie. "The head of Kentish Town Police is a woman. I read it in the *Ham and High*."

"Perhaps Fred is in the police," said Snotty. "That would make sense. Making those notes on me."

"Well, I think Fred's a good bloke," said Sluke. "I dunno why his notes worried you. He was only doing his job."

"Yeah, but he didn't tell us he was making notes," said Snotty. "Very sneaky. He pretended it was football stuff he was writing."

"No, he didn't," said Bessie. "You just presumed it was."

"I think it's good, anyway, that he should be keeping an eye on you," said Jessie.

"What do you mean?" said Snotty, glaring at her. "I don't want anybody keeping an eye on me, thank you very much. I can manage perfectly on my own."

"So you think," said Bessie.

"What if something goes wrong with the house?" asked Jessie.

"The house is fine, no problems," said Snotty, having forgotten about the leaking roof.

"I bet Fred would help you, if you did have problems," said Jessie. "That's his job."

"Rubbish," said Snotty. "All social workers want to do is put you in care. I've seen a film about them on telly. That's what they like doing best. So I don't want anyone to find out about my mum being away. Is that clear?"

He lowered his voice and looked round, just in case anyone was listening. One of the men nearby put down his newspaper and Snotty immediately recognized him, but couldn't quite remember his name.

"Don't stare," hissed Snotty, "but that old bloke behind Sluke . . . I said don't look, Sluke. Where have I seen him before?"

"Search me," said Jessie. "I don't actually have a list of all the people you have seen in your life."

"Be good if in your brain you had a rewind system," said Bessie. "So you could flick through it and check on anything that's ever been seen by your eyes, even if you didn't register it at the time."

"Be better if you could fast forward," said Jessie. "See ahead to all the things you are going to see in the future."

"That could be good," said Sluke. "Be great to know Spurs were going to be relegated, even before the season had begun . . ."

"Look shurrup you lot," whispered Snotty. "OK, Sluke, look at him now, while he's reading his paper."

Sluke turned round, his mouth open, looking dopey, then his mouth closed shut, biting his lower lip, when he too recognized the man sitting just behind him.

"It's him," hissed Sluke. "The tramp. The one what was in your basement . . ."

The man had had a shave, looked cleaner and better dressed, but Sluke was right.

Snotty tried to hide, as if somehow he was guilty of something.

"What tramp? What are you talking about?" said Jessie.

"Shussh," said Snotty.

The tramp turned to the front page of his paper and then leaned over to his companion and started reading out one of the stories.

Snotty quickly finished off his food, trying not to catch the man's eye, telling the others to hurry as well.

As he left the restaurant, he could hear the tramp still reading out some court case – in an Irish accent.

4

There was water coming down the stairs when they got back to Snotty's house. The bucket had filled up and overflowed onto the floor, through the next floor, and down the staircase.

"I always knew you were lucky, Snotty," said Sluke. "Your very own indoor swimming pool."

"Oh God, what am I going to do?" said Snotty, looking horrified.

"I hate those old fashioned pools where you just swim

76

up and down, like boring old Kentish Town," continued Sluke. "I much prefer those modern leisure pools, the ones with shoots and slides, tunnels you go down, black runs and red runs and artificial waves and all that stuff. They're dead exciting. They're excellent. I've been to one in Portugal on holiday, and there's supposed to be a good one in South London somewhere . . ."

"Oh belt up, Sluke," said Snotty, giving him a hard push so that he slid along the hall and ended up lying in a small pool of water.

"I'm just trying to cheer you up," said Sluke.

"I want help, not cheering up," said Sluke. "Go and see if Mrs Cheatham's in and if she's got the builder's phone number. I left her a note asking her."

Bessie and Jessie bounded up the stairs. They found the overflowing bucket and emptied it, then got some old towels and sheets and started mopping up the wet floors and staircase.

"Where's your Yellow Pages?" shouted Jessie to Snotty who was wandering round the house, moaning at the mess.

"You can't dry floors with paper," said Snotty. "I'll look for more towels . . ."

"I mean the book, the trade directory, dum-dum," said Jessie.

"Oh yeah," said Snotty. "Never thought of that."

He led the way into his mother's little office and found the Yellow Pages and started flicking through the pages.

Sluke returned, shouting up the stairs that he couldn't get Mrs Cheatham to answer the door, though he was sure there was someone inside.

"Radios, radiators," said Snotty, reading out aloud.

"Hey, what're you doing?" said Sluke, coming into the room. "I thought there was a panic on, and here's you reading some baby book. Lots of pictures, Snotty. Big print. Do you want any help with the long words?"

"Refur-bish-ment," read Snotty, struggling with the pronunciation.

"Hmm, that is long," said Sluke. "But we don't want feeding, do we, not after all those hamburgers?"

"Residential Care," continued Snotty. "Hmm. I'll probably end up there soon enough. Riding Schools, hey I didn't know they had Riding Schools in Camden Town. Roller Shutters? Jessie, what's a Roller Shutter. Is it a sort of fair ground ride, like on Hampstead Heath . . .?"

"Give me the book," said Jessie, taking the Yellow Pages from Snotty's hands. "Roofing Materials, hmm, we might need that. Roofing Services. This is it. Now

"OK, the school welfare inspector was behind it, checking up on me. They're after me. They just don't want me living here, on my own. They want to put me away."

"You can come and live with us for a while, if you like," said Bessie. "Our mum won't mind."

"It would save you worrying about the roof," said Jessie.

"No, I've got to stay here," said Snotty. "Look after the house. That's what my mum told me. She'll be back soon, anyway."

"Yes, but when's soon?" asked Sluke.

Snotty didn't reply, but lay on the floor, looking at the wall. The others made faces at each other, half feeling he was being stupid, imagining things, and half feeling sorry for him.

"You should look upon the Social Services as being on your side," said Jessie. "You've got it all wrong. They're not out to get you. Just making sure you're OK. That's their job."

"Yeah, but what about the police?" said Snotty. "Why are they following me as well?"

"The police?" asked Sluke.

"That tramp," said Snotty. "I bet he's a cop, an undercover cop."

"Don't be daft," said Sluke. "Just cos we've seen him again, smartened up this time, doesn't mean a thing. They have baths and stuff at Arlington House. I've often seen those blokes outside Camden Town tube, scruffy one day and then quite smart the next."

"So why has he changed his accent?" asked Snotty. "Answer me that."

"You what?" asked Sluke.

"I thought you hadn't noticed. When we caught him

81

in the basement, he had a Scottish accent. Today he sounded Irish."

"You don't know the difference, Snotty," said Sluke. "You can't do accents anyway."

"They can sound very similar," said Bessie.

"I know the difference," said Snotty. "And I know it was part of his cover, because he's following me."

"Why?" asked Jessie.

"To put me in prison," said Snotty, turning over and looking at the other wall. Perhaps he had mistaken the accent, but he wasn't going to admit that possibility. He was still convinced something was going on. The others looked at each other, raising their eyebrows, giving little sighs.

"Look, you're getting really carried away," said Jessie, very slowly. "OK, so you might be right that Fred was making secret notes about you, but that's his job. It's really stupid to think the police are interested in you. You've done nothing wrong. You've now got delusions of what is it, Bessie, that phrase?"

"Glandular fever?" suggested Bessie.

"Yeah. I've got that as well," said Snotty, "living in this damp house. And with you lot, cos you're all drips."

Snotty got up, smiling at his own feeble joke, and found the battered football.

"Come on, we'll play one-a-side," he said. "Me against Bessie. First to ten goals."

They started playing again, with Snotty this time appearing a bit happier. Bessie let him win, which made him more cheerful. Then it was Snotty against Jessie with Bessie keeping the score while Sluke watched out of the window, waiting for the roofing men.

"There's an old van trying to park across the road," said Sluke. "That could be them."

"What does it say?" asked Bessie.

"I don't know. I haven't spoken to it, yet," said Sluke. "I don't talk to strange vans. They take you away, if you do that. Or if you get like Snotty, imagining rabbits are filming you . . .."

"I mean what does it say on the side of the van?" said Bessie.

"There's no name on the side," said Sluke. "Hmm, looks a right old wreck. Perhaps they're dumping it. Your street is really going down, Snotty. There's an old banger further along as well. What a mess. Worse than our estate, and I thought that was bad. Hey, there's also an old van outside Mrs Cheatham's. That wasn't there when I was knocking on her door. That's funny . . .."

"Pity you're not," said Bessie, writing the scores on the wall.

"Here's another van arriving," continued Sluke. "It's now right outside your door, Snotty. They could be builders, but they're just sitting inside, waiting. One of them's looking at an *A-Z* and another's speaking on a car phone."

"Everyone has those these days," said Bessie.

"I think all the vans must be roofing blokes," said Sluke. "It's all your fault, Jessie. You shouldn't have sent the fax as well as phoning them. Every dodgy builder in North London is arriving to do your roof, Snotty."

"Good," grunted Snotty, still playing.

"But they're all waiting for something," said Sluke. "I wonder what?"

"Emergency plumbers usually have flashing lights," said Jessie, coming off the pitch, having been beaten by Snotty, and going to the fridge to get herself a drink. "Can you see one like that, Sluke?"

"No, don't think so, but I can hear some sort of noise further down the street . . ."

"Right, come on, Sluke," said Snotty. "I've hammered everyone so far, now it's your turn to get stuffed . . ."

Outside, there was the sound of a police siren blaring and then the squeal of brakes as a police car slewed to a sudden halt, skidding across the pavement and finishing at the bottom of the steps leading up to Snotty's front door. Doors flew open at the back of the three vans and men started running across the road, all heading for Snotty's house. The two biggest, burliest men went straight for the front door, forcing it open. Some of the other men had bulging pockets and might have been carrying guns.

"All right," shouted a voice from the front hall, "this is a police raid. Nobody move. Everyone stay exactly where you are . . ."

84

The two biggest, burliest policemen burst into the football pitch room and stood in the doorway, watching Snotty, Sluke, Jessie and Bessie. Then a smaller man entered, clearly the leader of the raid, and walked slowly round the room. The rest of the men could be heard rushing up the stairs.

"My friends have got to go home now," said Snotty.

"Just stay where you are, sonny," said the leader. "That goes for all of you."

"I know you've come for me," said Snotty, "but they've done nothing wrong, so if you don't mind, their mums will be waiting for them . . ."

"Nobody's going anywhere at the moment," said the leader.

One of the bigger men was examining the walls round the doorway, peering at results from the hundreds of games which Snotty and his friends had played.

"This looks suspicious," he said. "A lot of scoring has been going on."

"That's what it's for," said Snotty. "And I do most of the scoring. It is my pitch."

The two heavies looked at each other, and then at Bessie and Jessie, wondering how kids so young could be running a place like this.

From upstairs came the voices of the other police searching the house, going from room to room. From time to time they could be heard exclaiming, shouting things to each other, remarking on items they had discovered.

The door opened and the tramp appeared, or at least the man who had led them to believe he was a tramp.

"It's all very weird," he said to the leader. "Looks like a lot of stolen goods, unless the young gentlemen here collect computer and video games, or they're about to open a music shop, but we've found nothing else, so far . . ."

"None of it is stolen," said Snotty. "My mum bought it all. I mean it's all been bought with my mum's money. I've got the receipts to prove it . . ."

"Where is your mother, sonny?" asked the leader.

"Out," said Snotty, "but she'll be back soon."

"Then we'll wait," said the leader. "Carry on searching."

The tramp went back upstairs while the leader prowled round the room. He opened one of the fridges and looked inside. It was filled with Coke cans.

"Check all these," he said to one of the heavies.

"Hey, don't touch those," said Sluke. "They're counted. Two each per game per person, so there's just enough to keep us going till the weekend."

The heavy took two of the cans and put them in a black plastic sack. The leader was now looking in the other fridge.

"What's all this then?" he said.

"Ice-cream," said Snotty. "And you can't have any."

"And this?" asked the leader, pulling out an envelope from the freezer compartment.

"You can read," said Snotty. "It's liver."

"I can read," said the leader, "but someone can't spell."

He looked at it for a long time, turning it over and smelling it, then he put it back in the freezer and closed the door.

"Nothing to report, sir," said the tramp, returning. "We've checked everywhere."

"Hmm," said the leader, thinking.

"What do we do now, sir?" said the tramp.

"We'll just have to wait till Mrs Cheatham returns, won't we? He says she'll be back soon. Well, we can wait . . ."

He studied Snotty's face, looking for telltale signs, but Snotty was of course well versed in giving nothing away, or looking stupid, whichever seemed most desirable at the time.

"Mrs Cheatham doesn't live here," said Snotty, rather confused, wondering if he was about to fall into another trap.

"So you live here on your own, do you?" said the leader. "A kid of your age. A likely story. The Social Services wouldn't allow it for a start, or the School Inspectors."

Snotty didn't know how to reply to this. Having gone to such trouble to pretend he wasn't on his own, now he was being asked to do the opposite.

"How old are you anyway?" asked the leader.

"Nearly twelve," said Snotty. "Eleven years, nine months and three days."

"Hmm," said the leader, pulling out some notes. "And your mother, Rosie Cheatham, is aged sixty. I suppose it could be possible, just . . ."

"She's not my mother, I've told you. Mrs Cheatham lives next door at forty-four."

"Isn't this forty-four?" said the leader, beginning suddenly to look angry, scowling at the tramp. "If you've got the wrong house . . ."

"This is forty-two," said Snotty. "The door number sort of fell off in a storm, and so did Mrs Cheatham's, not my fault. People are always mixing us up . . ."

The leader took a mobile phone from his pocket and rang a number. "Has anyone come out of this house? What? Never mind which flipping number. The house we've just raided. You have been watching. OK. Or next door? Oh God. Either side. Has anyone come out, either side? Good. Then keep watching."

He put his mobile away and turned to the tramp. "It's probably too late. You've made enough noise to waken the whole street, but we'll check anyway."

Then he turned to Snotty. "Which side is forty-four,

where this Cheatham woman lives?"

"That side," said Snotty. "I don't think she's in, but somebody is. Her lodgers, I think."

"We'll go through the roof," said the leader. "Get up there at once. But do it quietly. And don't do any damage."

The tramp led his men up the stairs again, out of the trap door and onto Snotty's roof. Then they forced open Mrs Cheatham's trap door in her roof. There was silence for a while, then they reappeared at Snotty's front door.

"Nothing there, sir," said the tramp. "They've scarpered. But it was the right house, sir. I've found this note, sir, asking for Hashish . . ."

"Hmm," said the leader, turning to Snotty, all smiles this time. "Sorry about that. These mistakes do happen. Apologize to your mother. We'll of course make good any damage. We'll get someone round right away to put new hinges on the front door, and anything else we've disturbed . . ."

"What about the roof?" asked Snotty. "I hope you haven't damaged it."

"We did notice quite a few slates had come loose," said the tramp, "but I don't think that was our fault."

"Well get up there and put them all straight," barked the leader. Then he turned to Snotty, Sluke, Jessie and Bessie.

"And I'd be obliged if you didn't talk to anyone about our, er, little visit. We think we know who the lodgers were next door, and we'll catch them next time. This is my private number, if you ever see any of them again, perhaps you could ring me."

As the leader and all his policemen were leaving Snotty's front door, a yellow van arrived, rather beat-up and battered. On the side of it were the words 'Roofing Helpline.' The driver, on seeing so many policemen, turned his van round and drove quickly out of Snotty's street.

"We don't need any roofers now," said Snotty. "The job's been done, and for free."

4

Snotty the Hostage

It was celebration time at Marine Ices, Snotty's favourite restaurant in Camden Town, London, England,
Great Britain, Europe, the World. Snotty had booked a
table in advance, the best one, knowing that it was
always full on Saturday lunch times. Sluke, Bessie and
Jessie were being allowed to go through the menu,
having anything they liked, which was pretty normal,
really. Snotty always let them do that, if he had been to
the bank and topped up with enough money. Quite a
bit of it had already been spent, with a few new toys
and excitements beside him in his Spurs bag, but he had
enough for them all to really enjoy themselves.

They were celebrating several minor triumphs, such
as getting the roof done, toasting each other in a mixture
of lemonade, Coke and orange juice, with a dollop of
pistachio ice-cream on top, Snotty's own creation, which
a new Italian waiter, who didn't speak much English,
had kindly made up for them. Then they celebrated the
thought of minor triumphs to come, such as watching
Mrs Cheatham's face when she discovered that her last

lodgers, now gone, were drug dealers.

"You must say 'alleged drug dealers'," said Jessie. "Nobody is guilty till they have been convicted."

"Isn't it 'nobody is convicted till they are guilty'?" said Bessie.

"You two ain't gonna be all clever clogs today are you?" said Sluke.

"Now, now," said Snotty, beaming at his friends. "This is a happy day. I don't want anyone falling out. Cheers."

"Cheers," said the others, raising their glasses and slurping, and in Sluke's case also burping, rather loudly.

Round about them, several parents with much younger children looked rather disgusted by the sight and sounds of what Snotty's party was drinking, and were telling their own children that no, they could not have the same.

"Right, what're your main courses?" said Snotty, leaning back, looking expansive, going a bit too far, till his chair began to fall backwards, but he was caught just in time by the Italian waiter.

"Cheers. *Forza Italiano*," said Snotty, in his fluent Italian, picked up from the sports pages. He did think about saying spaghetti bolognaise, but he'd read somewhere that that was not Italian, as spoken by Italians, like hamburgers is not German. Or something. He was in a very good mood, for Snotty, his blank face departed, his scowl lifted, happy thoughts filling his mind.

There were several moments of peace and quiet at Snotty's table while they each went through the menu. Snotty's lips moved as he read, because that was the way he read. It was part of the anticipation, to hear the foody noises in his head.

Snotty was also celebrating the fact that he had not

been guilty of paranoia, or so he had explained to the others, several times. It had turned out that people *had* been watching him and his house. He had not imagined it. The others had been wrong to accuse him of that. But, in the end, they were not watching him for the reason he had suspected, so everything had turned out all right.

He hadn't, after all, been going a bit potty, with living on his own in the house, which was what they were starting to suggest. And he himself was beginning to half suspect. So that was all right as well.

On the other hand, he didn't really want to live on his own for ever. That could make him go a bit potty. But why was he thinking these things? This was a happy day. Hadn't he just said that?

"Right, I'm having a pizza," said Snotty.

"But you always have that," said Jessie. "Why don't you try one of the specials on the board? You can read Italian, can't you?"

"They're just jokes," said Snotty.

"Don't be stupid," said Sluke. "How can dishes on a menu be jokes?"

"I know they are," said Snotty. "Waiter, there's a fly in my soup. That's an English joke. But they have their own Italian jokes."

"What are you on about?" said Sluke. "I think you are going potty."

"Waiter, can I speak to the manager, please."

The manager came over and Snotty asked him to explain the special on the board which that day said 'Ravioli Gazza Della Sport'. It was a joke name, the manager agreed, referring to a footballer and a newspaper, but it tasted very nice, very special.

"Thank you my man," said Snotty. "Grazie."

"I thought he was called Dante, not Grazie," said Bessie.

"Look, I have been coming here for ever," said Snotty. "I do know about this place."

They then started an argument, all in good temper, about who had eaten at Marine Ices the longest. Sluke said he first came centuries ago, when oh, he must have been seven or eight, but under cross-examination, he admitted he had never been inside before, sitting down and having a meal, till Snotty had started treating him. Until then, he had only ever queued up outside and bought an ice-cream at the window, but he maintained that still counted.

"No, it doesn't count," said Jessie. "Snotty was talking about eating here."

"You eat ice-cream," said Sluke.

"You don't," said Jessie. "You just shove it in your gob or your ear or up your nose, that's you Sluke."

Jessie then gave an impersonation of Sluke eating, using all her arms and legs, licking bits off the table, and off the floor, which naturally upset Sluke, who then tried to think of how to get his own back.

"This is you swimming," said Sluke, using all his arms and legs, but up in the air, flapping wildly. "You think you're so good, but you're a rotten swimmer, you are."

"This is you keeping in with the big kids," began Jessie, going down on her knees.

"Look you two," said Snotty, still beaming. "I don't want any argufying. This is a happy day. I've told you."

It was unusual for Snotty to be the peacemaker, calming everyone down. Usually, people had to do that to him.

"By eating," said Bessie, returning to the subject

under discussion, "Snotty meant sitting down eating – didn't you, Snot – so in that case . . ."

"Don't call me Snot," said Snotty, for a moment looking slightly less calm. "I'm not Snot."

"I thought it was cos you always had a snotty nose," said Sluke. "When of course you were much younger . . ."

The parents at the next table looked over, wondering if they should move their precious darlings now to another quieter, nicer table.

"It's derived from Nottingham," said Jessie. "That's what you always say, don't you Snotty?"

"No, no, that's not the origin," said Bessie. "It's cos, as a little boy, you were always saying 'S'not fair.' So the name stuck. That was what your mum once told me."

At the reference to Snotty's mum, they all went quiet. There had been an unspoken agreement between them not to talk about his mother, in case Snotty got upset.

"S'not fair," said Snotty, then stopped and smiled, realizing what he'd said.

All the others laughed as well.

"Anyway," said Jessie, getting back to the subject. "Me and Bessie have had meals here, inside, proper meals, since we were six. That's when we were first taken, so there, we're the winners. Taran taran . . ."

"You're both sussed," said Snotty. "I had my first meal here when I was six days old."

"Liar," said Sluke. "Pants on fire. How could you?"

"Well, after my mum had me in UCS," began Snotty.

"That's another lie," said Sluke. "You couldn't be born in a school."

"Okay then, UCH, I made a mistake, University College Hospital, do you want me to spell it out, Sluke?"

97

"Carry on," said Sluke.

"Not if you're going to interrupt," said Snotty. "Anyway, my mum stopped here on the way home from having me, see. So she put me here, on this seat, in my wicker basket thingy . . ."

"How do you know it was this seat?" asked Sluke.

"Shurrup, Sluke," said Jessie. "I've never heard this story before. Go on Snotty, please."

"Well," continued Snotty, "she's in Marine Ices and, after eating something, she goes off home and leaves me behind. She wasn't used to having a baby, you see, and had just forgotten I existed."

"Oh poor Snotty," said Jessie and Bessie, putting their arms round him. Even Sluke wanted to hug him, but couldn't quite manage to do it.

"So things haven't really changed, have they Snotty?" said Sluke sadly.

"What do you mean?" asked Snotty, suspecting he was being got at.

"Oh nothing," said Sluke. "Poor old you."

"So what happened?" asked Jessie.

"She came back, didn't she," said Snotty. "She was only away five minutes. Then she fed me, cos I was crying."

"What did you eat, Snotty?" asked Sluke.

"Oh, grow up," said Jessie. "What do you think he had?"

"Milk shakes of course," said Snotty.

They all laughed. When they'd finished their huge meal, they left the restaurant together, arms round each other.

2

They walked through Camden Town market on their way back to Snotty's house, looking at various stalls and shops, watching the crowds, listening to the shouts of the street vendors, enjoying the different sorts of music and smelling various food smells from all over the world.

"Don't say it, Sluke," said Jessie and Bessie together. "You can't be hungry already."

"I just feel like trying some Thai food," said Sluke. "I really do think it would help with my Geography homework."

"Don't talk about homework," said Jessie. "This is a happy day, remember."

They stopped at a junk stall and Snotty decided to buy an old Spurs mug, which had Gazza's face on the side of it.

"Shows you how old it is," said Sluke.

"Pity he wasn't playing this afternoon," said Snotty.

"They'll get stuffed anyway," said Jessie and Bessie. Spurs were playing away at Manchester United that afternoon, so naturally they were hoping for a Spurs defeat.

"Don't talk like that," said Snotty. "This is still a happy day."

"We can't stay long this afternoon," said Jessie, as they entered Snotty's street. "We've got to help our dad in the garden."

"Yeah, and I really hate gardening," said Bessie.

"And I can't be too late," said Sluke. "I've got to go shopping with my mum, worse luck."

"Well, it is a happy day for me," said Snotty. "Pity about you lot. Nobody bosses me around, or makes me do things I don't want to do."

Snotty looked up his street and in the distance he could see somebody standing on his doorstep, or it might have been Mrs Cheatham's doorstep. It was still too far away to see exactly.

"Oh no, what's happening now?" said Snotty. "I think somebody's waiting for me."

"Don't start that again," said Sluke.

As they got nearer, Snotty could see that there were in fact three people waiting on his doorstep. One of them was Mrs Cheatham, looking very angry. Another was Fred, the social worker, in a suit this time. The third was Miss Eager, from school.

There was also a battered van outside his front door, which might or might not have been another roofer, wanting to be paid for having been called out, or an undercover police car, waiting for something or someone.

Snotty turned round and started hurrying back the way he had come.

"What are you doing, Snotty?" said Jessie. "There's nothing to get worried about. This is a happy day. Remember?"

"I've forgotten. I've got to go somewhere," said Snotty, breaking into a run.

A Jaguar, which had been slowly coming down the street the other way, did a U-turn and drew to a halt beside Snotty. The chauffeur opened the front passenger door and beckoned to Snotty.

"Come on, have a ride," he said, smiling.

Snotty recognized the car. He wasn't quite sure about the driver, though his uniform looked familiar, but he quickly jumped into the front passenger seat.

The driver, still smiling, leaned over and put a blue and white towel towards Snotty's face. For some reason, Snotty thought it must be a Spurs towel he was being offered, a football souvenir, something else to add to his collection. In his Spurs bag, which he was still holding, he had several Spurs souvenirs.

Snotty felt very happy indeed. Happy that things had turned out so well, and happy to be getting away from the people waiting for him on his doorstep.

So happy, he began to feel dizzy and dozy, as if he was falling asleep. Then he passed out.

He lay slumped in his seat, unconscious, while the Jaguar accelerated out of Snotty's street and disappeared into North London at high speed.

3

Snotty woke up slowly. He had been dreaming about scoring the winning goal for Spurs and the whole crowd had been cheering. In the distance, he still seemed to hear the cheers in his head as he looked round the little dark room, trying to work out where he was, what had happened.

Gradually, his eyes got used to the half darkness and he realized it wasn't night time, as he first thought. A pair of thick curtains were pulled across the only window, keeping out most of the light, but he could detect a few chinks. It was day time, though he didn't know which day, or what time of day.

He felt a bit dizzy and sick. Too much lunch at Marine Ices? No, it must be that towel that had been put round his face. That's what had sent him to sleep. But why had anyone done that, then dumped him here, in this little room?

His eyes moved round the room, followed slowly by

his brain, trying to identify shapes. He was lying on an old-fashioned iron bedside but the rest of the room appeared totally empty of furniture. On the floor beside his bed he could make out his Spurs bag, lying half open. Somebody had looked through it. The Gazza mug had been broken in half.

He leaned over to see if his other Spurs things had been damaged, but found he could only move a few feet. His right leg, which was sockless, was secured by a chain to the leg of the iron bedside.

"Oh, you're awake are you, Zotty," said a man with close cropped hair coming into the room.

Snotty stared at him, not quite hearing what he'd said, wondering where he'd come from, trying to decide if he was the man in the Jaguar, now with his cap off.

"What?" said Snotty.

"Wanna cup of tea?"

"Don't like tea," said Snotty.

"Well, suit yourself," said the man. "I suppose you're more used to drinking champagne and eating caviar at home."

"Don't like champagne," said Snotty.

"Too much too young, I shouldn't wonder," said the man.

"Only had it once," said Snotty. "My mum gave me a glass to celebrate something or other . . ."

"Marrying your dad, probably."

"I haven't got a dad."

"Good one, Zot," said the man. "Well, your dad won't have a son unless he knows what's good for him – know what I mean?'

"No, actually," said Snotty.

"Oh actually, is it actually," said the man, mimicking Snotty's accent, an accent Snotty never knew he had.

"All that money spent on your private school hasn't been wasted, has it?"

"I don't go to no private school," said Snotty.

"I know that," said the man. "Not now, but you did. Really stupid, if you ask me, taking you away from that school, just for his principles. Or public relations, more like. If I had his money, all my kids would go to Eton. In fact I might do that when he pays up. What do you think, Zot? Will he pay up quick or what?"

"I don't know what you're talking about," said Snotty. "And my name isn't Zot."

"Good one," said the man. From the floor, on the other side of the bed, he picked up a sock and shoved it under Snotty's face. It was the sock Snotty had been wearing.

"So," said Snotty, "it's my sock. Smells a bit, probably, but so what. That happens with trainers. Not my fault . . ."

"Read your own name," said the man, pointing to a little label, neatly sewn inside the sock 'Zot Bee'."

"That's not me," said Snotty. "And it's not my sock."

"Well, you were wearing it."

"I must have put it on by mistake, when we went swimming at school. I've probably got Zot's underpants on as well."

"Spare us," said the man, turning away. "Right, if

you don't want a cup of tea, that's it for the moment. Personally, if I was you, I'd drink a cup of tea now, while you've got the fingers to hold the cup, know what I mean . . ."

"What?" asked Snotty.

"Your dad will get the message in an hour. The minute he gets back from Africa. Every day he doesn't pay up the million quid, we'll send him one of your fingers."

The man left the room. Snotty suddenly felt very sick. He lay back on the bed, closed his eyes, and fell into a half sleep.

4

Snotty woke up. He could hear cheering again, real cheering, the deep roar of cheering which rises up and reverberates when a goal is scored. It was coming not from his head but through the darkened window from a short distance away. Its rhythms sounded so familiar. Or was he imagining it, still living in his dream?

He lay still and listened carefully. The noise died down, then it returned, little flurries of it, sporadic clapping, the occasional booing, some whistling then, yes, he could clearly hear supporters chanting in unison. Out there, somewhere, a real football match was going on.

"Can't be White Hart Lane," he thought to himself. "The lads are away today, at Man U."

He waited for the next burst of excitement, the next round of chanting, ready to repeat in his head every syllable, every word.

"Goo-ners. Goo-ners" went the cry. It didn't quite make sense. Then after an enormous round of clapping, he finally made out three staccato sounds "Ar-sen-al, Ar-sen-al".

"Oh no, it's Arsenal. Bad enough being kidnapped in mistake for Buzz!'s stupid kid. I've also ended up somewhere near Highbury. Oh no. Forced to listen to stupid Arsenal fans. Ohhh. Talk about torture. Ughh. And I thought this was going to be happy day. Oh no . . ."

Snotty's moans and groans brought the man back in. He stood at the door, looking in.

"You OK?"

"No, not with that noise."

"Great noise. The lads are winning."

"I hate Arsenal," said Snotty.

"You're not a Spurs fan are you," said the man. "They're getting stuffed 3–0. Ha ha ha."

He closed the door again, laughing. In the next room, a radio was turned up, which was giving the Spurs-Man Utd match commentary. There was the sound of a window being opened and the crowd noise suddenly increased.

"Oh no," groaned Snotty. "He must be watching the Arsenal game, as well as listening to the radio. That means we must be very near Highbury, near enough to see something. It also means it can't be five o'clock yet, as both matches are still going on."

With his free foot, Snotty managed to reach the nearest wall. Summoning up all his strength, such as it was, he gave a strong push – and the bed glided across the floor towards the window. Through a crack in the blinds, he could make out the Arsenal clock in the far distance. He could also see the top of the stand, some of the executive boxes, but not the pitch itself. It was enough to enable him to pinpoint roughly where he must be. He had been to Highbury three times in his life, but only of course for Arsenal-Spurs matches. He wouldn't go there for Arsenal games, being a true lily white supporter.

With another push of his leg, he propelled the bed back to roughly where it had been, but not quite. This time, he was right over his Spurs bag. He bent down, looking for his Spurs scarf. He took it out and started waving it, a bit shakily, a bit pathetically, but he was determined to show loyalty to his team.

"Even under desperate circumstances, let no one say that Snotty Bumstead deserted the lads. Tott-ing-ham!"

That was his own joke, pronouncing it the way Ossie used to, in that Ossie's going to Wembley song.

"Heh, I've got an idea . . ." he said to himself.

From his Spurs bag he dug out an old and battered Spurs felt pen. As carefully as he could, he crossed out the word Tottenham on his scarf and started to write HELP I'M A HOSTAGE. Alas, the pen ran out after the world HELP.

"Typical, these cheap, stupid pens . . ." Snotty grumbled. All the same, he pushed his bed back to the window, scrambled behind the curtains and held up his scarf. Just for a few seconds though, as he was scared the man would come back.

"I bet nobody will see it, behind this stupid window. They're all watching the stupid match."

Snotty came away from the window and pushed his bed back to its usual position.

There was a huge roar. Arsenal had scored again. In his fury, he let his scarf drop from his hand. As he leaned down to get it, he noticed his Spurs pencil box.

"If it was a real pencil case, I could write a note and drop it out of the window. 'Please rescue – I am held hostage at Arsenal.' But of course it's only a joke pencil box, that stupid novelty thing I bought from that stupid mail order catalogue . . . Oh . . ."

Snotty waited for the next really big roar, which he knew would come if and when Arsenal scored again.

"I never in my whole life thought I would be waiting and praying for Arsenal to score."

There it was, an absolutely massive cheering and roaring and then chanting and clapping. Snotty quickly opened the pencil case and dialled the number A. It only had three buttons, A, B and C, and A was the only phone number he had programmed, mainly because it was the only number he knew automatically, without having to think. In other words, his own home number.

"Hi, it's Zoe Bumstead here. Many apologies. I'm sorry I can't make it to the phone at the moment! If you want Nottingham, he should be in from school soon. If you have any messages, speak after the silly old bleep. Byee . . ."

It was his mother's voice, her recorded voice, the one she had left on the answerphone when she had first gone off. He and Sluke had doctored it slightly from time to time, knocking a few words out, putting some in, just to make it sound different and pretend to people that she was still at home. Which of course she wasn't. It was still only her recorded voice.

"Ar-sen-al! Ar-sen-al!"

Snotty could hear the man in the other room, joining in the cheering. He quickly closed the pencil box telephone and shoved it into his Spurs bag.

"Arsenal are now three goals up," said the man, bursting into the room.

"How's Spurs doing?" asked Snotty.

"They've got a goal back," he said. "Dead jammy. From a penalty. You can give a little clap now, while you've still got hands. Ha ha ha."

Then he closed the door again and left Snotty on his own.

5

There was silence outside, the sort of dull, eerie, echoing silence which comes when a huge noisy crowd has departed and only the memories remain. The match was over. Everyóne had gone home.

In the background, creeping under the door, came the

faint marching beat of that familiar tune which introduces *Sports Report*. Snotty pushed his bed as near to the door as possible and by straining his neck and ears was able to make out the voice of James Alexander Gordon reading the classified football results. He could tell by the rise and fall of his voice when the home side had won, or the away side had won, or whether it was a draw, but he couldn't quite hear the names of each team.

"Doesn't matter anyway," thought Snotty, falling back on his bed. "Who cares about football results! I've got more important things to worry about. What *am* I gonna do? Buzz! won't pay the million pounds, cos he'll know stupid old Zot hasn't been kidnapped. He'll think it's just a joke, a hoax. He'll just tear up the ransom note and not even tell anyone. But the kidnappers will still think I'm Zot! Oh no. They'll still be waiting for their money, so they'll start, oh no . . ."

Snotty punched his bed in fury, and tried to kick the walls, but with only one foot free, his kicks were pretty feeble. So he lay still, going over what might happen.

"I suppose Jessie and Bessie will eventually realize I've been taken. They're not stupid. But they probably went straight home, as they said they had to. They won't know what happened. They'll think I just went for a joy ride in Zot's Jaguar. Oh no. It will be Monday at school before they start missing me. Tuesday by the time they tell anyone. And I'll be missing two fingers by then . . .

"When they do realize, who'll pay the money to rescue me? Nobody. They can't. There's only ten pounds left in the fridge. Oh no . . ."

Snotty got out his mobile phone again from his Spurs bag and stared at it.

"If only I had programmed in some more numbers.

Or if only it was a proper phone, not a stupid executive boring toy phone. I could ring that policeman, except I've forgotten his number. Or 999. Or anyone, anywhere . . ."

Then he had an idea. If he waited till the end of his mother's old recorded message, he could leave his own message, a new one, telling the world what had happened.

"But who will hear it? And when? I'll have to rely on Sluke getting into the house, or someone, and I've still got the key. And then rely on someone playing back the messages, some time, some how. I could be a gonner by then. But it's a chance . . ."

Snotty picked up the pencil case phone and dialled A.

"Hi, it's Zoe speaking . . ."

"Oh shurrup, you stupid woman," began Snotty.

"Snotty! That's not the way to speak to your mother . . ."

Snotty listened in amazement. It was his mother's real voice, really speaking, but he couldn't quite hear it as there was a lot of shouting and noise in the background. Was it Sluke, mucking around, rearranging the old message? No, Sluke wouldn't have got in yet, not without a key.

The football results had finished. Snotty could hear the radio being switched off in the next room, so he quickly put the phone back in the bag in case the man reappeared, crowing about the Arsenal result. There was silence for a bit, then the sound of the television started drifting under the door.

Snotty got the phone out of the bag and carefully pressed button A again.

"Snotty!" shrieked his mother.

"Shhh," whispered Snotty. "Listen carefully. I'm in

113

a room near Arsenal stadium . . ."

"What?" said his mother. "You're at a football match. Oh that's good, Snotty. I wondered where you were. What? Sorry, I can't hear very well. No, not you Snotty. I've just opened some champagne to celebrate my return home and Mrs Cheatham is on her second glass and so is Miss Eager and someone called Fred, oh shush, everyone . . . that's better. Now what were you saying, Snotty, darling . . . ?"

Snotty began again, slowly, but urgently. His mother, who was always quick on the uptake, soon realized it was not a joke.

"I've been kidnapped, by mistake," said Snotty. "They think I'm Zot, you know, that pop star's son . . ."

"Of course I know him," said his mother. "I've just come back from Africa with Buzz! That's the secret project we've been on. Saving the World. The biggest charity film ever made. I wasn't able to tell you . . ."

"You've got to get me out," said Snotty. "Even if they realize it's a mistake, they'll still do something terrible . . ."

"How near Arsenal are you?" asked his mother.

Snotty explained his position, as best he could.

"Right, the clock end, I know that. Fred, hand me that *A-Z*. What floor do you think you're on? Just esti-

mate. The curtains are drawn, did you say? What colour? What does this man look like? His hair, how old?"

Snotty could tell that his mother was making notes and also giving instructions to Fred to go into Mrs Cheatham's and ring the police at once.

"I was brought here in Buzz!'s Jaguar," said Snotty.

"I know it," said his mother. "And I know the number."

"They must have pinched it," said Snotty, "because it wasn't his usual chauffeur."

"How are you managing to phone me?" asked his mother. "Is there one in your room? How do you know they're not listening on the other line . . ."

Snotty explained it was a new sort of phone, a joke executive toy, very expensive, but it did work.

"I bought it with your money, actually, Mum, so that was lucky, with your Visa card, actually, you don't mind do you? Sluke said it wasn't worth all that money . . ."

"Of course I don't mind," said his mother. "I don't mind anything, but you better hang up. Keep it hidden and don't use it again, in case they hear. And don't do anything to upset them. We'll have you out of there very quickly . . ."

"When?"

"Soon," said his mother, hanging up.

6

Snotty's house was full of people. All evening there had been a wild welcome home party going on – not just for his mother, but for Snotty the hostage, now turned into Snotty the hero.

It had only taken an hour for the police to locate the flat where Snotty had been hidden, thanks to Snotty's excellent description. And it had taken them only minutes to overpower the man who had been guarding Snotty. The Jaguar, parked in an underground car park, had been a vital clue.

His mother was giving out champagne in the football pitch room, but not to Mrs Cheatham. She had already had too much. The police were also there, giving out statements and being interviewed by some reporters and television people whom Snotty's mother had kindly allowed into the house.

"Good job you opened up this floor, Snotty," said his mother. "Makes it so much bigger when you have a big

party. We couldn't have got so many people in, without your good work."

"Er, have you been upstairs yet, Mum?"

"Not yet, darling, but I'm looking forward to it. Bessie and Jessie and Sluke have been telling me it's excellent."

Buzz! was also at the party, and had promised to sing a few of his lovely, caring songs later. So was his son Zot. All he wanted to do was have a game of football with Snotty, using both ends and both fridges, but so far there were too many people and not enough space. While they waited, Sluke, Bessie and Jessie explained all the rules to him, and went through a few of the more notable matches and past triumphs, taking him through the scores on the walls.

Fred was also there. He too would have liked a game, but he had to listen to Mrs Pratt, his team leader. She was boasting to three reporters about how well she had kept an eye on young Nottingham and, yes, she would give an interview to the television, as long as it was a networked programme.

Miss Eager was telling another reporter that Snotty was really a very good pupil, no trouble in class. She had always tried her best to be kind and considerate to him, knowing all the time that his mother had had to go away for a while, on an exciting film project. Oh yes, she knew, but had kept it awfully quiet. Sworn to secrecy, and all that.

The reporters then started interviewing Buzz! about the film itself. He told them it would be seen by millions all over the globe, and would save millions of poor people, millions of sad animals, millions of lonely fish and millions of homeless trees. He then praised the great work of Zoe Bumstead for organizing and researching it all. She had done so well that she had been promoted from researcher to executive producer.

"That means I won't need to go off on long trips ever again," so she told Snotty later. "Well, not secret ones."

"That's good," said Snotty.

"But if I have to, you can always come with me in future. That'll be nice, won't it, Snotty?"

"Yeah, great," said Snotty. "Could even be excellent. As long as it doesn't mean being away when Spurs are at home. That could be difficult . . ."